It Happened One Midnight

Books by Saranna DeWylde

It Happened One Midnight

Men Are Frogs

Fairy Godmothers, Inc.

The 10 Days Series

How to Lose a Demon in 10 Days

How to Marry an Angel in 10 Days

How to Seduce a Warlock in 10 Days

IT HAPPENED ONE MIDNIGHT

Saranna DeWylde

ZEBRA BOOKS
Kensington Publishing Corp.
www.kensingtonbooks.com

ZEBRA BOOKS are published by

Kensington Publishing Corp.
119 West 40th Street
New York, NY 10018

First Zebra Trade Printing: January 2022

ISBN: 978-1-4201-5316-3

ISBN: 978-1-4201-5319-4 (ebook)

10 9 8 7 6 5 4 3 2 1

Printed in the United States of America

Dedicated to BabyBat2

Your sweet potato curry kept me fortified long into the night with my fingers dancing on the keys. This book wouldn't be here without you. There are a lot of books that couldn't have been born without you. I love you more than words can ever express.

I would be remiss if I didn't add my thanks to Ms. Gibson. I still think of you every time I type "really."

Prologue

Petunia Blossom had almost reached Peak Fairy Godmother.

She and her sisters, Bluebonnet and Jonquil, were so close to the pinnacle of greatness.

In the last year, they'd recruited a new fairy godmother in training for the academy, they'd helped break a curse (Petty chose to ignore the fact the curse was her fault to start with; she was counting it as a win), and they were working their magic right under the noses of mortals.

Further, they'd managed to not only save their sweet little town of Ever After, filling up all the stores of magic with love, but they were exporting it to the fairy realm and to the rest of the world.

Petunia was quite pleased.

The only thing missing was their granddaughter Juniper's Happily Ever After.

She sighed over her morning tea and toast in their cottage kitchen.

Jonquil stopped what she was doing with the black lace and blood-red hydrangeas she'd been fiddling with, attempting to create a bouquet that would suit the Dracula-themed wedding. Nothing seemed to be quite right.

"I recognize that sigh, dearest. Tell us what kind of plot you're hatching?" Jonquil encouraged.

"Me?" Petty feigned innocence.

Bluebonnet snorted. "Obviously, you. Shall I start some ice cream sodas?"

Petunia grinned. "Yes. I think you should."

"As long as it's not Gwen and Roderick again. You know they asked us to leave them alone," Jonquil warned.

Petty waved her off. "No. Fie on them at the moment, anyway. How dare they resist our good intentions?" She laughed. "I do understand, and I'm giving them their space. I'd be upset if someone continued to try to push me to someone I wasn't ready for."

Bluebonnet dropped the glasses she held, and they shattered on the ground. "Did you just say you were wrong?"

"Let's not get hysterical," Petty said. "Of course not. I wasn't wrong. We planted the seeds. They just have to take root and are slumbering through the long winter. Just wait. They will work out on their own."

Bluebonnet used her wand to clean up the mess and reconstitute the glasses. "Mm-hm." She fixed Petty with a sharp glance. "Your stance wouldn't have anything to do with the fact that Ransom and Lucky are taking them along to Brazil, does it?"

Petty looked around, her eyes wide. "Whatever would I do in Brazil?"

"Aha! Caught you. I didn't accuse you of going to Brazil." Bluebonnet crossed her arms over her chest.

Jonquil nodded sagely. "She's got you there."

Petty rolled her eyes. "No, she doesn't. I would assume that to meddle with them in Brazil, I would need to be *present in Brazil*."

"Oh, please. You're a fairy godmother. You can meddle from anywhere."

Petunia shrugged. "Whatcha gonna do?"

"Not bother those kids. Until it's time," Jonquil said. "That's what you're going to do."

"I'm not. But sometimes things happen. Call it fate," Petunia said.

"I'll call it Petunia," Jonquil said with a snort.

"I swear, I'm not going to do anything. I promised. But, if, say, their accommodations might have *accidentally* overbooked, and they have to share a room . . . a very small room on a very hot night . . ."

"We all know that's your favorite trope." Bluebonnet began making the ice cream sodas to fortify them with the sugar they needed to plot Happily Ever Afters.

"It works! But actually, I really promise I haven't done anything. But a godmother can hope." She grinned. "No, it's time to switch hats."

"But, I've not gotten a new hat in so long." Jonquil patted her hair.

"Not like that, dear. We need to work on a project closer to home. Not a godmother hat, but a grandmother hat," Petunia explained.

"I'm still not following. What's wrong with godmother hats? I mean, we could get some pointy cones of wisdom to wear for the Dracula wedding, but I think they wanted to go with the obsidian and ruby tiaras for the bridesmaids. Plus, we don't want to offend any witch guests in attendance," Jonquil said.

"Sister. Darling. Light of my Happily Ever After," Bluebonnet began. "She means Juniper."

"Oh!" Jonquil pressed her palm to her forehead. "I swear, it's like the sprites have run off with the last two brain cells I had to rub together."

"You need sugar. You'll feel better in a moment," Bluebonnet promised.

"Speaking of that, we should definitely take a vacation in November. We deserve it. I was just thinking this morning that we have accomplished so much. We haven't ventured out of

Ever After for anything but work in a long time. Now that we have magic to spare, we should go to Jamaica or something."

"Oh, I agree. We can use our portal passes, so we'll still have time for the Christmas weddings," Bluebonnet said.

"I need you to know, sisters, that I absolutely cannot be assed to put on my youthful body. I am quite comfortable in this one, and I will be on the beach as I am," Jonquil stated.

"Thank the powers, me too." Bluebonnet brought them their ice cream sodas. Today, they were butterscotch with chocolate chips.

"As if. I want to rest, not be bothered by some man in a Speedo."

They all paused, obviously considering.

"I mean, maybe. It's been a long time. My clock tower has bats in it," Petunia confessed. "Bats. I mean, they're very nice but . . ."

"Girl, you and me both," Bluebonnet said.

"Spiders and webs, I say." Jonquil nodded. "I was torn, for a moment, between thinking I needed to get out there, so I know what our charges are dealing with and deciding that this is not going to be a working vacation."

"Too right. How about this. We should go to Miami, spend a weekend in our younger bodies, then go to Key West with other old folks. Maybe do some diving, swim with the turtles. Read some Dee J. Holmes and Jasmine Silvera. Drink things out of coconuts," Petunia offered.

"I like this plan. Can we stop on the gulf side of Florida, too? I want to go to Captiva," Bluebonnet said.

Jonquil snorted long and deep. She sounded like a truffling pig. "You just want to go to Captiva to get some of that ghost pirate booty. That's what you're about."

The three of them stopped, sighed, and were all obviously considering the merits of ghost pirate "booty."

"Oh, hell yes, I do." Bluebonnet leaned her cheek into the bowl of her hand. "I don't know about you two, but Captain

Drake Gregorian in those breeches is just the cure for what ails me."

Petunia thought about calling her one-time friend Jack Frost, but then dismissed it entirely. What would he do in Florida besides be miserable? Anyway, this wasn't about them. It was about Juniper.

Petty cleared her throat. "Sisters. Back to the task at hand."

"Which is?" Jonquil prompted.

"Um . . . where was I?" Petty asked.

"Hats," Bluebonnet said.

"Oh! Right. Hats. Not godmother hats, but grandmother hats. Juniper, of course!"

"She's coming to visit, isn't she?" Bluebonnet asked.

"Yes, I was going to suggest we call her, because I have a plan," Petty said.

"You always have a plan," Jonquil replied.

"Well, yes. Do you remember when we used to go visit April and Juniper? The little boy next door who would come over and play?" Petty asked.

"Little Tomas! He was adorable." Bluebonnet waved her wand, and an image of Tomas shimmered in the air. "He's not so little anymore. Why, he's a man." Bluebonnet sounded as if the fact were a scandal instead of a natural progression. Little boys grew into men. It was just how things worked.

"Neither is our Juniper. She's a woman grown, and it's time to give her a story like the ones she writes about. Tomas has always been her one. I can see the threads. Only, they've been running parallel for so long, they need a . . . shall we call it, inciting event to knock them together. Then, when they untangle, they'll discover their threads entwined not in a tangle but a forever plait."

"That's very poetic, Petunia. Juniper must get her writing skills from you," Jonquil said.

"She gets your pragmatism," Petty said. "And Bluebonnet's sweetness."

"Wait, how is she our granddaughter again?" Jonquil asked. "I'm sorry, I forget these things."

"There are three of us, so I understand why you're confused," Bluebonnet said. "And it was so very long ago. Do you remember that time in the Cotswolds when we foiled Rumpled Butt Skin?"

"That guy! I hate that guy," Jonquil moaned. "I'd blocked it all out."

"I remember it fondly. Because I hate that guy. And I'll never say his actual name out loud. Ever." Petty crossed her arms over her chest. "Anyway, that baby he tried to take, we protected her when we gave her some of our essences, essentially claiming her for fairy. So anyway, Juniper is a descendent of that baby."

"Don't tell her I forgot," Jonquil whispered. "I feel terrible."

"Circumstances being what they are, it's totally acceptable. It's not like you said you didn't love her, or wouldn't help her. You'd just managed the impossible and scrubbed Rumpled Foreskin from your mind. I wish I could. I admire your resourcefulness," Petty commended.

"I shall forever call him Rumpled Foreskin. That's my favorite yet," Bluebonnet mused.

"So. Juniper?" Petty prompted.

"Yes, yes." Bluebonnet waved her wand, and the hologram of Tomas disappeared. "Your plan?"

"Well, you know how she hates it when we matchmake, but . . . do you remember when she and Tomas were little, they decided if they weren't married by thirty, or some ridiculous number . . . thirty-four, yes, that's it. If they weren't married, they were going to marry each other?"

"You're not going to expect her to keep that promise, are you?" Jonquil asked.

"Not exactly, but I think we can use it to our benefit. We'll get her to bring him with her, and then we'll work our magic!" Petty grinned and took a gulp of her ice cream soda. "And nature will work hers."

Jonquil gasped. "I can't believe I forgot this!"

"What now?" Bluebonnet asked.

"The Dracula bride! Betina! She told me she was reading Juniper's Dark Underworld series when she met Jackson. When I told her that she was our granddaughter, she asked if she could get signed copies of *Phoenix* for her bridesmaids' gifts."

Petunia grinned. The fates had clearly spoken. "This gives us the excuse we need to call her."

"Quite, quite," Bluebonnet said, and downed the rest of the butterscotch soda.

Petty pulled out her cell phone and dialed Juniper's number. When she answered, she put the phone on speaker so that Jonquil and Bluebonnet could hear her.

"Sweet pea! You're on speaker!" Petty said.

"Hello, Grandmothers." Juniper's voice was cheery. "Hold on a minute, will you?" In the background, she whispered, "No, no. Not that one. Oh my God, what is that? *No*. Why is it yellow? Stop playing. I'm about to get hangry." Back into the phone, she said, "Sorry, I'm helping Tomas pick out a suit for his firm's fundraiser, and he promised me lunch. What are you troublemakers doing today?"

"We won't keep you long, dear. We just wanted to double-check you're still going to be able to make it for the Samhain celebration and the fireflies?" Petunia asked.

"And to ask a tiny favor," Jonquil interjected.

"A favor? Of course! Anything!"

"Anything?" Bluebonnet questioned.

"Anything except let you fix me up. That's not the favor, is it?" Juniper grumbled.

"No, no. The bride in one of the weddings we're planning has asked if she could get signed copies of *Phoenix* for her bridesmaids' gifts," Jonquil said.

"Oh my God. Seriously? This is the best thing that's ever happened to me. Of course. This just made my year," Juniper cried.

"Betina's wedding will be on Samhain, so if you're here . . . ," Petty prompted.

"Of course I'll be there, and bring books. I wonder if she'll let me post this on social media? This is too cool," Juniper said.

"So, how is Tomas?" Petty ventured.

"He's doing very well. And no, before you ask, he's not seeing anyone. Nor does he want to see anyone," Juniper said.

"Of course he's not seeing anyone. Otherwise, how is he going to marry you?" Petty said.

"Oh stop, Gramma Petty."

"Do you two still have that deal? About getting married?" Bluebonnet asked, being helpful since Juniper told Petty to stop.

"Of course," Juniper said, obviously teasing. "But that's just when we get old."

"Thirty-four isn't old. I think that's a good age," Jonquil offered.

"You should bring him to Ever After. We need to start planning. You're going to be thirty-four next year, and we want to make sure you have the kind of wedding you want."

"Gramma Bon-Bon—"

"You are taken, right? I mean, if you weren't"—Jonquil looked around the room at her sisters before continuing—"we'd just have to try to set you up with someone wonderful. You need inspiration to write your books."

"I have plenty of inspiration. And if you could never say that again, that would be wonderful. Do you know how many men have tried that line on me?" She groaned. "They find out what I do and then get all smarmy and actually the opposite of every romance novel hero ever and say, 'I uh, could offer you some inspiration for those dirty scenes.' As if the whole point of the book is just the sex and not the part where love conquers all. Fucking savages."

Petunia nodded in understanding even though Juniper couldn't see the action of support. "And they are obviously undeserving of you, your talents, your heart, or your bed."

"Gramma Petty! Don't talk about my bed," Juniper cried.

"Well, why not? It's a normal, natural, beautiful thing and—"

"Oh God, that's worse. Just stop. Please. I'll do anything."

"Even bring your fi— Tomas?"

"He is not my fiancé," she said.

"Oh, definitely bring your fiancé, we'd love to see him," Bluebonnet chirped.

"Tomas and Juniper, finally sitting in a tree . . ." Jonquil sing-songed obnoxiously.

"Tomas is my best friend," Juniper tried to argue.

"Of course he is, lovie. It's really the thing when you marry your best friend. It's the sleepover that never stops!" Bluebonnet said.

"We haven't seen him since you were both little. Oh, Juniper. I'm so happy for you," Petunia said, trying her best not to giggle.

"Grandmothers. I—" she began in a stern voice. "Wait, you absolutely can't try to set me up with anyone if I bring a fiancé."

"We would never do that," Bluebonnet said. "It goes against the fai—"

Jonquil slapped a hand over Bluebonnet's mouth.

"Against the code," Bluebonnet finished.

"What code?" Juniper asked.

"Never you mind that," Petunia said. "You go ahead and get back to picking out your clothes for the benefit. A fiancée's work is never done. But be sure to bring something for the masque. It's going to be amazing."

"You'll both love it," Bluebonnet said.

"I need to make sure Tomas can get the time off," Juniper said weakly.

She needs to talk him into it, Petunia mouthed silently.

I'm texting with Estella right now. She'll guilt him into it, if she has to, Jonquil mouthed back.

Bluebonnet cackled loudly. "I'm sure he will."

"Okay, gotta go. We have a lot to do for this wedding. Did we tell you it's going to be at Castle Blackheart, along with the masque?" Petunia said.

"Castle Blackheart? Where's that?" Juniper asked.

"Lots of changes since you've been to Ever After. You'll see," Bluebonnet promised her.

"Hanging up now. Love you, love to Tomas. See you soon," Petty said.

"Byeeeeee," Jonquil said, and dragged the word out to the last possible second.

"Love you both!" Bluebonnet added.

Petunia clicked the button to end the call and looked around at her sisters with a very satisfied look on her face.

"I think it's wise we get April and Estella in on this scheme. Never underestimate the power of a mother who wants to see her children happy," Petty said.

"Yes, good one, Jonquil," Bluebonnet agreed.

Jonquil studied them. "Do you ever think maybe we shouldn't push so hard? Juniper seems very happy with her life the way it is."

"Here we go," Bluebonnet said. "I know this is your role in the group, but it's tiresome."

"You need more sugar," Petty suggested.

"You always think I need more sugar," Jonquil drawled.

"You always do," Petunia said.

"That's a fair point, I suppose." Jonquil nodded.

"Listen," Bluebonnet began. "She is happy, and that's wonderful, but the right person complements that happiness.

And she wants someone. I know she does. She's told me she'd like to fall in love, and we're going to make it happen."

"I suppose." Jonquil cocked her head. "I just want to make sure we're doing what's best."

"I know," Petunia said. "We have this talk before every mission. Did you know that?"

"It's my job to keep us grounded. To make sure we're on the right path," Jonquil replied.

"Yes, and we appreciate you," Bluebonnet said. "But we're jumping right in the thick of it with Juniper. It's time."

"I can't wait to watch her realize she loves him," Petunia said with a sigh.

"I can't wait to watch him realize that love is for him, too." Bluebonnet's sigh joined her sister's.

"I can't wait for that vacation." Jonquil went back to fiddling with the bloodred hydrangeas and the black lace for the bouquet. "This thing is giving me fits."

"Remember: pirate booty," Bluebonnet encouraged.

"*You* remember pirate booty. *I* want no such thing," Petunia said.

Jonquil arched a brow. "The maid doth protest too much."

"Mind your business. We have Happily Ever Afters to engineer before we can even think about vacation."

"We should get new business cards. Happily Ever After Engineer," Bluebonnet said.

"Oh, I like it," Jonquil agreed.

"We are so late. Zuri is going to kill us. We're supposed to talk scheduling with her this morning," Bluebonnet said.

"Already on it. I texted her and told her to take the day off. With our compliments. I think she and Phillip are going to take a long weekend." Petty winked.

"Did you see the fireworks from the castle last night? Their love lit up the sky with actual rockets," Bluebonnet said.

"I know." Jonquil grinned widely. "We do good work."

Petty knew in her heart and in her bones that what Jonquil said was true.

Though, she couldn't shake the feeling that they were on the verge of something more than simply Peak Fairy Godmother. Petty wasn't sure what it was, but she didn't like it.

Not in the least.

Chapter 1

After ending the call with her grandmothers, Juniper sank back into the overstuffed leather couch that sat just outside the changing room of the Elegant Gentleman and looked up at her best friend, Tomas Rivera.

Engaged. Grammas Petty, Bon-Bon, and Jonquil were obsessed, and somehow, they'd maneuvered her into a fine pickle.

She cocked her head to the side and tried to imagine being engaged, married, or—hell—even dating her longtime pal. They'd been friends for so long, Juniper had forgotten which one of them was the bad influence.

Him, probably.

No, her.

Eh, she'd have to say it was a tie. When misadventures were on the menu, both of them ordered more than either of them could chew.

But they had some really great stories. Her favorite one started with, "One time, in Vienna . . ." when they'd gone backpacking the summer before college. She smiled, remembering how she'd been so afraid that trip had been their last hurrah. How their friendship would change. How they'd inevitably grow apart.

Only they hadn't. Their friendship had only gotten stronger. Better.

"Does that smile mean you like this one?"

He grinned back at her and showed off one of the suits he was seriously considering for the Hernandez and Williams annual fundraiser for the homeless shelter. This year, they were hoping to add a traveling medical van to their services. Tomas and Juniper were excited to help make that happen.

Tomas had exceptional taste, and the suit looked damn good. It fit him well straight off the rack. He was lucky like that. The cut was exceptional, but the style wasn't quite right. The affair was a hassle to dress for because it wasn't a formal event, but business attire didn't quite fit the bill, either.

"Of course, it looks amazing," she began.

"But, you don't like it for the fundraiser?" He nodded. "Me either. It's not quite right."

"Exactly what I was thinking."

"That's why I bring you along." He started to shrug out of the jacket.

She laughed. "You bring me along because you love me."

"That too." The corner of his mouth quirked up into a grin. "So what was up with the grandmothers? Were they trying to set you up again? I swear, those ladies have a one-track mind."

She pursed her lips and considered. Juniper wondered what sort of bribe would work to get him to play along. "They've decided we're engaged."

Tomas laughed. "*Dios mio*, why would they think that?"

"I'm not sure how we got there, honestly. I think it has to do with that promise we made when we were kids." She nodded. "Yes. I think so."

"The one where we promised to get married to each other at thirty-four?" He was still laughing.

"Yeah. I mean, it *is* next year. Gramma Petty said if we're going to do it, we need to start planning." She shrugged.

He stopped laughing, a serious look on his face. "She's right. I mean, I don't see any other prospects in sight for either one of us. Might as well."

"Oh, stop." She rolled her eyes. "As if."

"As if, what?" He looked over his shoulder to the mirror. "Yeah, still hot. Even though we're about to be the ancient and decrepit age of thirty-four."

She flashed a grin in return. "Why did we think that was so old, again?"

"Kids, eh?" He shrugged. "But let me guess? The grandmothers took it seriously? Or they pretended to."

"They did."

"And you let them."

She cringed. "I did. You don't understand the pressure."

"Uh, have you met my mother?" He arched a perfectly sculpted black brow.

"Oh. Yes. Right." She coughed. "But I would totally understand if you told her we were engaged. I'd even play along to get her off your back."

He snorted. "You'd make me pay for it, though. I'd have to bring you tamales every Friday for the rest of my life."

"You already do that. So make it Wednesday and Friday."

"Fair." He nodded.

"So you'll do it?"

"What? You're serious?" He draped the jacket over his arm.

"They won't stop trying to set me up unless you come with me to visit them for Samhain." At his blank look, she added, "Halloween?"

"And pretend to be engaged?" If his brow crawled up any higher, it was going to disappear into his hairline.

"It can be a long engagement."

"It can't be forever. This is bound to blow up in our faces." He shook his head.

She bit her lip. "I know, but . . ." Juniper knew it was time to pull out the big guns. She always knew how to get her way with Tomas. She widened her brown eyes and knew she looked much like a cocker spaniel. He could never say no to the eyes. Especially when she blinked slowly and pouted, just a little.

"Woman. Stop it."

She continued to stare and let her mouth turn down at the corners just a bit.

"I am a hardened divorce attorney. Those eyes aren't going to . . ." He sighed. "Fine, but I have conditions."

Juniper rewarded him with her best smile.

"Big faker."

"No, I really would've been that sad if you said no."

"You're not getting my cooperation for free."

"I can't make tamales, so I don't know what you want from me." She pursed her lips, confident that she would, in fact, get his cooperation for free.

"First, when we break up, it has to be mutual. I love us both too much."

A cackle burst from her. "You're so right. I definitely do not want to be on the wrong side of Mama Estella. And you don't want to be on the wrong side of my mother, or my grandmothers. Gramma Petty got that nickname for a reason." She nodded slowly. "Oh, definitely. It has to be amicable."

He nodded, his face serious. "I'm glad we're agreed. But you know, if we're not careful, both of our families will have us trotting down the aisle like a couple of breeding show ponies."

She wrinkled her nose. "Eww. Why would you say it that way? That's disgusting."

"I know!" His tone indicated he obviously thought there was nothing worse.

Juniper knew Tomas was anti-commitment, but she didn't realize he was that bitter. "Do you really feel that way about marriage?"

"I . . ." He looked around to make sure they were alone. "I'm a divorce attorney."

"I know. Obviously. I held your hand through law school and helped you study. I brought you Thai food after you passed the bar. This is not a surprise."

"Then my feelings on marriage shouldn't be a surprise."

She rolled her eyes. "Oh, come on. Pessimism is boring."

He reached out and tucked a piece of hair behind her ear. "That's what I love about you. No matter what, you still believe. You believe enough for both of us."

"Speaking of, I just got my author copies of *Thunderbird*!" She rummaged in her bag and pulled out her newest release.

He reached for it, but she held it back.

"I don't know, Tomas. If you don't believe, you might not be worthy of a copy. It is a romance novel, after all."

"You already made me wait. I will not bring tamales Friday if you don't give me that book right now."

Juniper held it up. "*This* book? This *romance novel*, with love, and of all the horrible things, a Happily Ever After? Is this the book you want, Big Bad Divorce Attorney?"

He narrowed his eyes. "I read spy novels, too. That doesn't mean I'm going to go out and hunt for *Red October*."

Juniper loved that he read her books. He'd been reading her stories since she first put her fingers on a keyboard and banged out an awful, teen-angst ridden agony aunt "romance" where everyone died at the end. And then became vampires. And then got staked. And came back as ghosts. And then they were reincarnated. And then . . . Yes, it was a wreck, but she'd been hooked.

So had he.

"Oh fine, I suppose." She let him take the book from her hands.

He opened to the front page where the dedication remained mostly the same from book to book.

For Tomas, who believed.

Juniper had thought he'd be used to it by now, after seventeen books. Only his reaction never changed. His face beamed with pride and he pulled her up into a tight hug.

"I still can't get over seeing my name there. I'm so proud of you." He kissed both of her cheeks and then slid the book carefully into his briefcase. "I can't wait to find out what happens to Cordelia and Daniel." He cast a glance back at her face. "You know you were wrong for how you left it at the end of *Sphinx*."

She cackled and couldn't help thinking she sounded a bit like Gramma Petty.

"Ha!" he exclaimed. "I knew it. You just like to torture us."

"Honestly, I love that you're so invested. It means you love them as much as I do. I can't describe how that feels."

"You're still not getting out of owing me a favor for this fake fiancé nonsense."

"As if I would. But really, you should be grateful. They're not above trying to set you up with someone, too."

He held up his index finger. "Ah, but you see, they're not my grandmothers. I don't have to go visit them."

"Do you really think they'd let that stop them? They'd just call your mother. Then where would you be?"

"Damn."

"Uh-huh." She pursed her lips. "But I'm feeling generous, so what do you want?"

"You have to be my date to the fundraiser—"

She opened her mouth to protest, but he cut her off.

"And you have to wear a dress."

"Fine, I'll wear a dress, but I'm not doing heels."

He narrowed his eyes. "That was surprisingly easy. What aren't you telling me?"

"There's a masquerade ball in Ever After on Samhain and we have to go."

"Ever After? Oh for . . . I forgot your grandmothers lived in that weird little town. How sober do I have to be?"

She considered. "Eighty-twenty?"

"I'm not going to make it." He gave an overdramatic sigh.

"Have you been watching those soaps with Mama Estella again?"

A guilty look flashed across his face. "She had them on when I was fixing her sink."

Juniper laughed. "How dare you start a new show without me."

"Mama will be happy to catch you up, I'm sure."

"Listen, maybe when we get to Ever After, you shouldn't tell people details about your job. It might be kind of a downer," she teased.

"You think?" he snorted. "Far be it from me to bring the real world to fairy-tale land."

"You know how I feel about that description." She crossed her arms over her chest.

"I . . ." He gestured helplessly.

"Either sum it up in your own words, or I'm going to make you listen to my dissertation on assholes and fairy tales."

"Fine." He rolled his eyes. "I don't know why I do these things for you. You're absolutely ridiculous."

"I am. And you love me anyway. So. Let's have it."

"I will not refer to things I find unbelievable as fairy tales," he grumbled.

"Why not?"

"Fairy tales are stories about perseverance and hope."

"And?" she prompted.

"And only assholes shit on other people's hope. I'm not an asshole."

"See? That wasn't too painful."

"It was a little painful, but definitely not as bad as listening to you recite your talking points for an hour and a half."

"That only happened once." She bit her lip. "I was . . . miffed."

"Miffed?" He shook his head. "I still think you'd have been a great lawyer."

"I think there's only room for one legal beagle in this relationship."

"A beagle? That's what you think of me? I'm a Malinois. Smart, efficient, highly trained, and a force to be reckoned with."

She snorted. "Legal Malinois doesn't really have the same mouthfeel, my friend. Mangy Malinois, maybe?"

"That's it. No tamales for you."

"Let's not be hasty." She leaned forward to grab his hand.

"No, that's a bridge too far. And you burned it down. I'm done with you," he teased.

"You're a brilliant barrister. I've got it! My next novel! *The Bloody Brilliant Barrister*, featuring handsome Latino heartthrob Tomas Rivera. Killer of Hearts, and Bringer of Delicious Tamales."

He nodded as he considered. "I suppose that's a little better. Keep going."

"No, that's all you get."

"Come on. I did the thing you like. It's your turn. A man needs to be told he's handsome as often as a woman needs to be told she's beautiful. Make with the compliments. The one about my jaw." He motioned for her to start.

"You're insufferable. I never should've started this. Try to make my friend feel better after a nasty breakup and this is the thanks I get." From her tone, it was obvious she didn't mean a word of it. She was happy to remind Tomas at any time of all of his good qualities.

"But you love me."

"I suppose."

"And my jaw."

She snorted. "Fine. You have a jaw like a rotten jack-o-lantern—no, that's not the one?"

Juniper could tell by the expression on his face that he wasn't amused. She rubbed her hands together and cracked her knuckles. "Okay, I'll give you a good one. You *did* indulge me with the fairy-tale thing."

She studied his face for a long moment and for the first time since college, she considered how she'd describe him if he were a character in one of her books. When they were in school, he'd had a definite edge to his jaw that was sharp, defined, and at one time, she'd said it had an edge like an anvil. It still did. That hadn't changed. Only, back then, there'd still been a softness to his face, a remnant of the boy he'd been.

He was one hundred percent man now. With all the hard edges that brought with it, although she wasn't going to tell him that.

Juniper continued to stare at him, and for the first time, it really hit her that he could be one of the guys she wrote about.

Not for her, of course; they were just friends.

Except he had every single quality she'd write into a hero.

He was hot as sin, kind, generous, thoughtful, honest. He did things to make her happy without caring how it might look to other people. Reciting her policy on fairy tales was ridiculous, but he did it because she wanted him to.

He was pretending to be her fiancé to make her grandmothers happy. For all the walls he'd erected to keep himself safe, he had a huge heart.

Juniper was overwhelmed by emotion.

How would she put that on the page?

"Tomas Rivera was a beautiful man"—she held up her hand when his belly laugh would've interrupted her—"his jaw was made of iron, and his cheekbones were like sharp blades. The softness of his long lashes against those stern angles seemed like an incongruity, but they framed his most powerful weapon of all. Eyes that could see through any shield, down through flesh and bone to the very marrow. Eyes that could pull you down into the darkness and make you forget you're afraid of drowning."

Tomas stopped laughing. He looked like he'd been slapped. "Whoa, really?"

"You asked for it. You got it."

"I suppose that'll have to keep me stocked for a while," he said in a dazed tone.

"You *suppose*? Bitch, that was fantastic."

He laughed again. "Yeah, it was. I wasn't dropping shade on your lovely gift. It was just . . ." He shrugged. "It was really good."

Maybe she had taken it a little too far. She'd gotten caught up in the moment, and while she did feel those things, Juniper realized they might've sounded more intense and implied a deeper meaning she hadn't intended.

Then she shook the thought off. They'd been friends for too long to worry about every little word they said to each other. Her brain was being slightly stupid because she'd just realized that he was more than *her* Tomas.

She knew that, logically, but it had just been driven home with a hammer that he was a man. Not just male, because obviously. *But a man.* The kind of man she wrote about. It had changed her perspective for a moment. She wasn't sure she liked seeing him with new eyes. Juniper knew he was a good man, but she didn't have those feelings for him, and she didn't want to have them. Things were perfect as they were.

"Of course it was really good." She lifted her chin. "I'm a professional."

"Are you now?"

"We do not have time for that. We still have to find your suit, and if you don't take me to lunch soon, this is not going to end well."

"Okay, I have one more option. I saved the best for last. I think this is the one."

"You should've tried that one first."

"I still had to try this one." He motioned to the suit he wore. "I'm going to buy it. A man can never have too many suits."

She nodded in agreement.

"Oh, and while you wait, there are cola gummies in your bag." He winked at her.

Juniper tore into the bag and stuffed a couple in her mouth while he went back inside the dressing room to change.

Now that her stomach wasn't trying to eat her from the inside out, she felt much better.

When he came out again, she knew why he'd been saving it for last. It was absolutely perfect. The material was obviously silk, but the color was almost an iridescent ocean blue. The contrast against the warm color of his skin and his jet-black hair was striking.

Her eyes were drawn to the jaw that she'd been asked to describe, down to the way the suit jacket framed his shoulders. She tore her gaze away. She needed to turn off romance-novel brain. Now was definitely not the time.

"Wow. Yes. That one. That one for every event you go to for the next five years."

"You think it'll work for the masquerade?"

"Well, I suppose, if you decide to go as a hot lawyer?"

"I'm always a hot lawyer. I should probably shake it up."

"But you're definitely buying that one, right?"

"Obviously. With the purple pocket square?" He held it up.

"Obviously."

"Good. Bow tie, I think."

She nodded.

"Since we're pretending to be a couple, I think your dress should match my pocket square. We'll be *that* couple. You know the one." He smirked. "Oh, on second thought, this fake fiancé thing is going to be fun."

Juniper was absolutely convinced that hijinks were about to ensue.

But not before lunch. She refused to get into trouble on an empty stomach.

Chapter 2

Tomas Rivera was supposed to be prepping for a meeting with a client, but instead, he was looking at the picture of his best friend that sat on his desk.

Most people thought she was his wife or his girlfriend because of the prominent placement of her picture. They always seemed strangely sad and disappointed when he corrected them. He couldn't figure out why, when his clients were going through what was an oftentimes ugly divorce, they wanted *him* to be married. It didn't make any sense. Although, he supposed misery loved company.

A cold flash of guilt washed down his spine.

If Juniper could hear his thoughts, she'd be exceptionally hurt and disappointed.

Her smiling face looking at him on his desk reminded him to have hope. To be kind. It reminded him that some kinds of love were real. Romantic love was practically a fetish, and he hated how it was so idolized. If people were more reasonable about their expectations and understood that what people thought was all-consuming passionate love was simply a biological imperative, a hormonal trick, everyone would be better off. But the love for friends and family? Now, that was something he knew to be true. It had been proven to him time and time again.

He knew Juniper would do anything for him.

And apparently, he'd do anything for her.

Even pretend to be engaged.

He picked up her picture and smoothed his thumb over the edge of her likeness. Tomas supposed if he ever did actually get married, it would be Juniper. He couldn't imagine life without her, and it was always there at the back of his mind. That someday, he would lose her. He wouldn't be the most important man in her life any longer.

She'd meet someone.

She'd fall hard.

And she wouldn't be his Juniper any longer. Not like she was now.

He remembered when they first met. They'd been six. His mother had brought him to the park to play in the sandbox. Only, there hadn't been any sand. Just mud. A girl with dark pigtails had plopped down in the mud next to him, and they'd not been able to build anything so grand as a castle, so they called their mud mess a fort and that moment had been the beginning. They'd been inseparable.

Tomas clearly remembered the first time they'd made the promise to get married at thirty-four if they didn't marry anyone else.

The first time had been at his tenth birthday party. One of his cousins had been teasing him because his best friend was a girl. Carlos said that Tomas might as well marry her. Juniper had told him with all the conviction in her little heart that she *was* going to marry Tomas. They'd do it when they were thirty-four because that's when she'd have all of her big teeth and a white dress.

The second time had been when he was sixteen. She'd broken up with her first serious boyfriend. She said she would never trust another boy with her heart. Except for Tomas. He'd reminded her that her relationship was doomed to fail anyway because she had to marry him when she had her grown-up teeth and a white dress.

The third time had been a bit more complicated. He'd been

twenty-six, and it had been at Carlos's wedding. They'd been doing shots and dancing all night. The event had been full of good food, laughter, family . . . As the evening had wound down, they were both drunk and lying in the grass by the country club pool, holding hands and looking up at the spinning stars.

The stars had definitely been spinning.

Like a damn disco ball.

Carlos had yelled that Tomas should kiss her.

Tomas still remembered the hazy formation of what would've been the worst decision of his life. He'd propped himself up on his elbow and looked down at her, lying there in her breezy summer dress, hair spread in the grass, her lips pink and inviting, and he'd thought, *Yeah, I should*.

He'd started to lean down toward her face.

She'd wrapped her arms around his shoulders and she'd said, "Look at you, getting ideas just because I've got my big-girl teeth and white dress. We're not thirty-four yet."

He'd realized then what a terrible mistake it would've been. Tomas would've ruined the one thing, apart from his mother and her side of the family, that was steady in his life.

So instead, he'd kissed her forehead, and tried not to notice how good it felt to have her in his arms. Or the sultry look in her eyes. Or, *Dios mio*, when her hand had come up to cup his cheek. It had taken him months to stop thinking about that moment. How much his body wanted something more, and how it had almost tricked his mind into believing in a mirage.

The memory of it had come slamming back into him in wave after wave as she'd described him as if he'd been a character in one of her books.

He definitely had to push that to the far reaches of his mind.

He didn't know what they'd thought was so magical or important about thirty-four. He decided that maybe when they called this sham of an engagement off, he could tell their respective families that they'd raised the marriage age to eighty.

Romantic love never lasted. As evidenced by the fact that the marriage of his cousin whose wedding had almost inspired the worst mistake of his life had ended in divorce this last year.

He'd meant it when he said that he admired her for being able to look at the world around her, see the way people treated each other, and still believe. Still have hope.

His Juniper was magic that way.

A knock sounded on his door, interrupting his thoughts.

"Mr. Rivera? Your two o'clock is here," his assistant, Jocelyn, said.

He scrubbed a hand over his face. He hadn't reviewed the file. "Give me five and then send them in, please."

"Mr. Williams would like to see you in his office when you're done."

"So noted. Thank you," he said.

"Coffee? Water? Tranquilizer?" she said in a faux-sweet voice.

"Oh, damn. It's that guy, isn't it? The one with the anxiety-induced eczema and he wants to sue his wife for emotional damage."

Jocelyn nodded. "She's threatening a countersuit for destruction of property. It's in the file."

"What?"

He flipped open the file and saw just exactly what the husband had destroyed.

For the insane amount of money listed, he'd thought it had to be a car, a closet full of designer bags, or maybe even a beach house.

No.

It was a one-of-a-kind, pure silver, hand-crafted dildo designed by a famed New Zealand silversmith and jeweler. It had a name. It was called simply Heaven.

Heaven had a list price of half a million dollars.

Half.

A.

Million.

Dollars.

When his wife had refused to have sex with him, he'd taken her prized toy, a propane torch, and a YouTube video on how to smelt silver at home, and he'd . . .

"Jesus actually wept," Tomas muttered.

The Dildo Killer entered his office and sat down in the plush, overstuffed chair in front of Tomas's desk. Jocelyn brought them both glasses of water, and he took a sip to steady himself.

"Mr. Squires," he began.

"Jim, please."

"Jim, would you like to tell me what happened since the last time I saw you?"

"You don't understand," Jim said.

Tomas nodded slowly. "Yes, that's why you're going to explain it to me."

"We talked about reconciling. It didn't go well."

Tomas waited for him to continue.

"We started fighting. I told her I still loved her; she said she still loved me."

"So what was the problem?"

"She said she didn't want to have sex with me anymore. Rachel said she'd spent so many nights in heaven by herself, that it wasn't worth the effort."

Ouch. Not worth the effort?

"And you said?"

"If she wasn't such a frigid bitch, it wouldn't be an effort." He sighed. "Then she said if I knew how to use my tongue for something besides being a *whiny* bitch, she wouldn't be a *frigid* bitch."

"So this caused you to destroy Heaven?"

"Don't call it that."

"I think a dildo with a price tag of half a million dollars might deserve to be called by its name? No?"

"I was just so mad." Jim shook his head and began scratching at a patch on his arm. "That woman drives me crazy. Look at this!" He waved his arm in front of Tomas's face. "This is her fault."

"Do you remember why you married your wife?"

"Of course I do." Jim was quiet for a long moment. "She was my best friend. We grew up together."

Tomas couldn't help but think of Juniper. They'd grown up together. They were best friends. Tomas knew that he'd been right not to cross that line, because this was the most likely destination.

Well, not destroying a half-a-million-dollar dildo, but a place where everything was broken.

"And now you want to take her to court to get her to pay you because you have a rash."

"She's taking me to court for—"

"For destroying her property." He decided then that Jim wasn't simply annoying, he was possibly dangerous. Tomas had handled many divorces over the years, and destruction of property was often an indicator of physical violence.

He did not want to represent him.

"I thought you were my lawyer. Did she get to you? Are you fucking her?" Jim had puffed up, and he reminded Tomas of a blowfish.

Tomas stared at him until he deflated.

"I am your lawyer, and I'm trying to help you. You're going to have to take the loss on the dildo." Those were not words he'd ever expected to utter aloud, but here he was.

"My brother said I could say it was mine, and then I'll only have to pay her for half of it."

Tomas sighed. "Is that really where you want to go with this?"

"Maybe."

At one time, the man in front of him had claimed to love the woman he was now ready to fight to the death with over a dildo. She had claimed to love him, too. They'd invested in the tradition, coming together with their families, speaking their vows in front of all of their loved ones, and this was what it had come to. Dildos, propane torches, threats, and lawsuits.

"Why don't you think about what you want to do and give me a call in a couple of days," he suggested. In that time, he'd be working out a strategy to drop the man.

"You think I should just pay it, don't you?"

He leaned back in his chair. "I do. How would you feel if someone treated your mother or your sister the way you're treating Rachel?" Tomas quickly realized the man in front of him would think they deserved it. So he tried another tactic. "What if she treated you this way? What if she'd taken a blowtorch to your Bentley?"

Jim's mouth dangled open, but then he promptly shut it.

"Do you think she would do that?" He pulled up his phone and began swiping and slapping at the screen. "I'll kill her."

"Phrasing, Jim."

"You know what I mean. But do you think she would? Take a blowtorch to my Bentley, I mean?"

"I don't know your wife. You do. What would she do?"

His face went pale. "She's very competitive."

"If you only pay her for half the dildo, she should only be responsible for half your car." Tomas shrugged. "If you want to use the law to your advantage, be aware that she can use any trick you do. How far down the rabbit hole do you want to go?"

What he really wanted was to get the man out of his office. Jim started scratching at his arm again, and flakes of his skin wafted from him to settle on the brown arm of the chair.

"You're supposed to be smarter than her lawyers. I heard you're a shark. That's why I wanted you."

Tomas didn't want to be a shark. Not for other sharks, anyway. He remembered how hard his mother worked when his dad abandoned them. She worked two jobs, went to college full-time, and still managed to be a warm, present, and attentive mother. All the while, his father had been jet-setting across Europe with all the money he'd hidden in the Caymans without a care in the world.

Tomas had become a divorce attorney to see that men and women fulfilled the promises they made. He was a champion of the hard-luck cases and he preferred to represent single parents whose spouse had tried to dick them over.

Tomas didn't want to be the one doing the dicking over.

"I don't think you're the right attorney for me."

Relief washed over him. Tomas didn't think so, either. "Fair enough."

"What, you're not going to fight to keep me as a client?" Jim seemed incredulous.

"Our office took this case as a favor to your brother, but you're not the sort of client who is aligned with our philosophies. Best of luck," Tomas said, and went to the door to hold it open for him.

Now, he was going to have to tell his boss that he'd lost the client. That he'd not bothered to refer him to someone else in their office.

Truth be told, he was prepared to deal with any fallout, but he didn't expect too much. Hernandez and Williams had a certain reputation.

"I'll have your job for this," Jim growled.

Tomas highly doubted that. He was going to be too busy fighting in court over a dildo and a Bentley.

He comforted himself with the thought that if he did lose his job, it was for the right reasons. After Jim was gone, he took a deep, cleansing breath and squared his shoulders and walked toward Warren Williams's office.

The door had been left open, and Warren was studying some files on his desk, his brow furrowed.

"Come in, come in." He motioned to the chair in front of his desk. "Tell me how the meeting with Jim Squires went."

"He fired us."

Warren raised a brow. "Oh? Any particular reason why?"

"Mostly because I wanted him to."

Warren's face was unreadable. "You going to explain this?"

"He's not someone who fits with our goals as a firm. He's not who we want to be associated with us in the community." Tomas felt good about his decision.

Warren still had no outward reaction. "His family could have cut a sizable check for the med van."

"We'll find funding elsewhere."

Warren's face broke into a wide smile. "That is exactly the answer I was hoping you'd give us."

Tomas suddenly realized that this had all been some kind of test. Just like when they'd hired him. "This was a test?" He shook his head.

"We're doing very well, and we're looking to support that expansion by adding another partner," Warren replied.

Tomas tamped down any excitement he felt because he knew this came with a caveat. He knew what Warren wanted from him. He wanted to see him moving toward a serious relationship. What their clients would call "stability." Which he found to be incredibly ironic.

While technically what the partners wanted from him wasn't legal and could possibly fall within the parameters of discrimination, it was something that happened behind the scenes all the time.

"But," Tomas prompted.

"But, John and I want to see you at least maintaining a relationship." Warren eyed him. "I'd like to introduce you to my niece." He held up his hand before Tomas could object. "She's beautiful, but, of course, I'm biased; she's career-driven and talented. You have a lot of the same goals. She'll be at the fundraiser."

Tomas was suddenly grateful for the grandmothers' meddling. "I'm actually bringing a date."

"Is it that gorgeous best friend of yours, Juniper?"

"It is."

"Have you finally seen what all the rest of us know?" He smirked. "That you two are absolutely perfect for each other?"

Tomas forced a laugh. "Yeah."

"How did this happen? More important, *when* did this happen?" Warren was obviously skeptical.

"Today, actually. I know that sounds like I'm just avoiding the issue, but I swear, I'm not. She was helping me pick out my suit for the fundraiser and . . ." And what? Her meddling grandmothers decided the two of them were getting married and now they're along for the ride? "And we got caught up in a moment, and we've decided to just go with it."

He wasn't technically lying.

Technically.

Warren eyed him hard, as if trying to ferret out any holes in his story. Just like a good lawyer would do. "So when is the first date?"

"Our first actual date will be the benefit." Tomas figured that he might as well reap the benefits from their little charade. "We've been friends for a long time, though. Since we were kids. Best friends."

He refused to think about Jim and what he'd said about he and Rachel having been best friends, too. That would never happen to Tomas and Juniper because they weren't going to cross that line for a mirage of Happily Ever After.

"We had a pact that if we were both single by our mid-thirties, we were just going to do it and we are."

"Wait, you're engaged?"

"Stable enough for you?"

"I have to admit, this sounds a little too convenient, Tomas." Warren steepled his fingers.

"Believe me when I say that there is nothing at all convenient about this. But I can't imagine spending my life with anyone else."

"*That* I believe. We'll talk after you set a date for the wedding."

Tomas realized then that there was zero way he'd convince Warren to offer him the partnership before he was shackled tight. He was going to have to give further thought to leaving the firm and going out on his own. Tomas refused to be denied something he'd earned simply because he didn't want to get married. One thing had nothing to do with the other.

Except, he realized that he meant what he said. He couldn't imagine marrying anyone, but he didn't want to spend any of the time he'd been given with anyone but Juniper.

He took a deep breath. It would be so easy for this to get away from them.

Her grandmothers imagined themselves to be champion meddlers, called themselves everyone's godmothers. They were incredibly good at matchmaking, and getting people to do exactly what they wanted.

If he and Juniper weren't careful, they'd end up trotting down that primrose path to unholy matrimony thinking it was their own idea.

Then, he'd lose everything.

Chapter 3

It was no wonder that Juniper or Tomas hadn't had a serious relationship with anyone other than each other in the last several years.

Instead of going out to meet people, or being social, they spent the weekend either at his apartment, her house, or together with their moms. Last weekend, they'd taken their mothers to the pumpkin patch, even though it was early in the season, and they'd loaded up on treats from the farm store. From apples to cider to homemade jams and jellies to cheeses made on the neighboring farm, and they'd spent the evening playing board games.

It occurred to Juniper that she liked their routine. She wasn't interested in blind dates, or the club scene, or hitting the bar. She especially wasn't interested in any online dating. She'd rather gouge out her eyeballs with a melon baller. Or snort a line of angry fire ants.

She'd tried online dating a few times, and it was the worst thing she could imagine doing to herself. Every single man she'd met had been the definition of awful.

Ninety percent of men she'd matched with thought that because she wrote romance novels, she was immediately down to sext. Nothing had been a bigger turnoff. She'd started telling them that writing was her job and if they wanted her words, they could pay for them. Ten bucks a text.

Tomas reminded her that there were good men in the

world. That someday, she'd find someone who loved her like he did, and more. Someone who cared about her mind, and her heart, as well as doing things with her body. He couldn't be the only good man, after all. Or could he?

She'd started to doubt she could have all three. She wondered if maybe she just had to let Tomas take care of her heart and mind, and bus in an escort for the rest. All in all, it didn't seem like an awful prospect. Escorts wouldn't say anything to her they weren't paid to say.

Unlike the one guy who had told her that if she didn't like the way she was treated, she should stop writing those books because real men weren't like that, and everything did, in fact, have to do with their penises.

She'd told him if he liked waving his around so much, he should eat a whole bag of them, smashed, to bring out the best flavor. Then she'd blocked him and deleted her profile.

After that, there was that guy she'd dated who'd worked at the law firm with Tomas. He'd be at the benefit. Jace hadn't been a bad guy—it just hadn't ended well. She'd gotten food poisoning after sushi and . . . Her stomach flipped at the memory, and Juniper paused to steady herself.

She wasn't going to think about the Sushi Debacle. No one needed to remember that. Especially not her.

Juniper needed her stomach in game-day shape because Tomas was bringing his tamales.

Her excitement for these tamales never got old. She never turned them down. There was never a week where she said, "Tamale Friday? I just can't."

She always could.

Always.

There was nothing like them in the whole wide world. If she was honest, just in the quiet of her own mind, she liked his better than Mama Estella's. Of course, she'd never so much as breathe a syllable of that out loud.

He'd even taught her how to make them herself, but there

was something more magical about them when he made them.

Her job was dessert. She'd made chocolate-dipped strawberries to celebrate finishing her last book, so she'd made a double batch, and she had a bottle of champagne she'd yet to crack. She'd set them out on the coffee table. The only light was from small string lights that cast a soothing glow.

It occurred to her that if someone were to see this scene from the outside that it might look like something it wasn't. It had all the earmarks of *romance*.

Maybe this had been her problem all along. Maybe neither of them could find anyone because they had all the trappings of a relationship, except the trap. Or, at least, she knew that's what Tomas would say.

The trap, and the sex.

But that would be gross, right? RIGHT? He was Tomas. He wasn't actually a guy. He was just her best friend.

She allowed herself, for one single second, to remember what he'd looked like in that suit when she'd permitted her brain to perceive him as something more.

Instead of his jaw, his cheekbones, or his shoulders, or any of the things she usually described about her heroes at first glance, she thought about his hands. How strong they were. The things they'd done for her. The things they could do for her. *To* her.

She didn't describe the hero's hands until the heroine did because that meant things were about to get *hot*.

A strange arrow of lust shot through her, and she decided that no, this was not a healthy train of thought.

Unbidden, she remembered that moment several years ago in the grass under the stars at his cousin's wedding, when she'd been so very sure Tomas was going to kiss her.

And kiss her he had, but on her forehead.

She wondered what would've happened if he had really kissed her. Juniper decided that their lives probably wouldn't be much different. They might've tried to have a relationship, but ultimately, because he didn't believe in marriage, they would've broken up.

Because Juniper knew what she wanted, and she refused to settle for anything less than everything.

She didn't care if her wedding was big or small, if it was simply reciting vows in front of a justice of the peace on an average Wednesday morning. But she knew she wanted to be married to the person she fell in love with.

So even if an attraction bloomed between them and it could take their solid foundation of friendship, respect, and trust to the next level, he wasn't her person because he didn't want the same things she did.

Juniper was in the business of love, and she knew that people were not DIY projects. She knew she had to accept him completely as he was and not expect or want him to change.

Logically, she knew this. Emotionally, she knew this.

But something was wrong with her, because now that she'd opened that door, her body didn't care about what the other parts of her had to say.

Images of that night, that memory, began to play themselves over and over in her head. Except the memories had morphed into something else. Into scenes of white-hot desire.

She smacked herself lightly, double-timing, to be sure she made solid contact with each cheek.

"Get a grip, J." She shook her head. "Lost your damn mind. What's wrong with you?" she whispered aloud to herself.

This was normal, she was sure. Her body had assumed that because she wasn't in contact with other men, that she must be stranded on a desert island with Tomas, therefore, he was it. He was all that was left, and it was time to propagate the species.

The second the thought had formed, she had two reactions.

One was to feel utterly guilty for dismissing one of the best men she knew as a last resort.

The other was a quick reenactment in her head of what it would look like to be stranded on a desert island with him. So, of course, she was immediately thinking about how often they'd be naked.

Forced proximity was her favorite trope to write about.

Stranded in snowstorms, fighting for their lives against the powers of hell, hiding from the bad guys, and, of course, there was always *only one bed*. Or they were forced to travel on a single conveyance, where they had to be pressed up against one another.

Juniper knew exactly what she needed to do.

She needed to start another book and pour absolutely all of this into the characters and let it play out on the page. Maybe when she and Tomas were eighty, rocking on the porch together and sipping iced tea, she'd tell him about the strange twist her thoughts had taken one time.

For some reason, that made her eyes tear up.

She definitely did not have the time or the headspace to deconstruct that.

A knock sounded on the door, and for a moment, Juniper panicked. She looked down at herself and realized she looked like she'd just crawled out from under a rock.

It wasn't as bad as Deadline Juniper. Deadline Juniper was a complete trash muppet who didn't brush her hair, sometimes forgot to brush her teeth, and wore coffee-stained T-shirts and was the least sexy human being to ever dredge herself up from a keyboard.

She was clean, her hair had been brushed and stuffed up into a loose bun, and her toenails were even painted. Although, she wasn't one of those cute girls who could do the messy bun and looked relaxed chic. She looked like she'd gotten a squirrel to pose on her head but it was about to run at any moment.

But she supposed that was a talent.

Why the hell did she care what she looked like? This was Tomas. Just Tomas.

He'd actually seen Deadline Juniper in the stinky flesh. He'd even hugged her.

This was fine. She was fine.

Well, no, she wasn't. She needed to fix her head or she was going to make a huge mistake. Juniper wasn't worried she'd ruin their friendship, because nothing could do that. It was one of those things that would be forever.

But it could be complicated for a while, and why would she ever set herself up for failure and heartbreak? On purpose?

Juniper also knew that if she let herself put Tomas into that role, that no one else would ever come close, and as much as she loved him, she had other dreams for her life. Other experiences she wanted that he didn't. She realized that maybe she'd already done that. She hadn't been dating or even seriously thinking about dating in a long time. Her dreams weren't going to happen if she didn't take steps to put them in motion.

Some stray maggot of a thought wiggled in the back of her brain, but she didn't want to think about it. She couldn't. All she'd find there were revelations she wasn't ready to deal with.

"Juniper?" he called through the door. "My hands are full of tamales. You gonna let me in?"

She realized she'd been standing there like an idiot. "Only because you have tamales," she said as she opened the door.

The smell of the tamales wafted up to greet her, and she peeked beneath the foil. "Yes, precious. Come to Mama!"

He closed the door behind him with his foot and carried them into her kitchen, where she'd laid out plates and forks.

"Are those chocolate-covered strawberries I see on the coffee table?"

"Yep. I made a double batch."

"I'm going to need them. It's been a hell of a week," he said.

"What happened?"

Tomas plated the tamales. He gave Juniper three, but she motioned for him to continue until he put a fourth one on her plate.

"Work stuff. I've got a tentative offer for partner," he began.

He didn't sound as happy about that as he should have. He'd been gunning for partner for some time, and this should have been celebratory news. Instead, Tomas wore a scowl, and his jaw ticked.

"What's wrong? I thought this was what you wanted."

"It comes with strings. Strings they know damn well I don't want."

"Not that stability crap again." She rolled her eyes.

"Yeah, and I may have used our little ruse to get out of being set up with Warren's niece." He sighed. "But he was on to us. He said we'll talk once you and I set a date."

Juniper bit her lip. "Ugh." Then she recalled the earlier track of her thoughts. "Maybe you should meet his niece. Maybe she's wonderful. Maybe she's your person."

And maybe, if she saw Tomas dating someone, she'd stop stagnating and try dating again, too.

He shot her a dirty look. "That's the meanest thing you've ever said to me."

She laughed. "No, but seriously. Maybe she wants the things you want, too. Maybe she doesn't believe in the institution of marriage, either? Not every woman wants to get married."

"I'm sure she's wonderful, but I already told him we were engaged."

She narrowed her eyes. "*After* we break up, maybe you should let him introduce you."

"Trying to get out of our deal?" he teased.

Juniper put her hand on his arm. "Nah. I just want you to be happy."

"I am happy. Or I would be, if people would leave me alone."

"It's exhausting, isn't it? Everyone, and I mean everyone, is on our cases about when we're going to stuff ourselves into their ideas of what happiness looks like."

He put his hands on the counter and turned to look at her. "That's not something I expected to hear from you."

"Why not? Because I believe in Happily Ever After? It's not HEA if it's on someone else's terms. The whole point is to live your life, with your person, the way that's authentic to both of you. Other people's expectations don't play into that."

Tomas nodded slowly. "Okay, that's something I can get on board with. Why didn't you say it that way years ago?"

"Oh, I don't know. It's almost like that element is in *every single book I write*. But I mean, I can draw you a picture with the fat crayons." She shrugged.

He laughed but then paused to consider. "No, you're right. Now that I think about it."

Juniper rolled her eyes and took her plate. "So what are we watching tonight? It's your turn to pick."

"I was thinking a classic."

"Oh no."

"Oh yes."

She knew what he'd chosen, and she wasn't really complaining. She just liked to tease him. Honestly, her favorite pastime was teasing him.

There are other ways to tease him, that stupid, new voice in the back of her head told her.

Nope. She wasn't going to think about that. It didn't fit with what either of them wanted in the long term.

Doesn't it? that annoying voice asked.

No, she answered herself. Then said aloud, "Fine. I guess we can watch *The Ice Pirates*."

"Ha ha! Yes! Space herpes for the win."

She flopped on the couch with her tamales and tucked her feet under her. "Oh! I forgot the glasses for the champagne."

"Got it!"

He brought her a glass and opened the bottle. Then returned with his own food. She poured for both of them. Tomas grabbed the remote and cued up the digital copy of the movie in her dashboard. They watched it often enough.

"You know," she said as they settled in. "We're going to have to decide when to tell our mothers."

"I can't think about that right now."

"We could tell them it's a ruse to get the grandmothers to leave us alone."

"We could, but you know they'd tattle on us," Tomas said.

"You're right. They'd redouble their efforts."

They looked at each other, both wearing horrified expressions, and then they laughed.

"Maybe we should just do it. Everyone would leave us alone, and I don't think much would change," Tomas said.

Before she could think better of it, Juniper said, "We'd be married and still not getting laid."

He snorted. "That's nothing new. A client I had this week, since his wife refused to sleep with him, he took a blowtorch to her dildo."

Juniper almost choked on her champagne. "Oh my God, what?"

"It gets better. This thing was half a million dollars."

"I can't even wrap my mind around that. Holy hell, no wonder you're so tense. He sounds awful."

"He was. So I fired him."

She put down her plate. "Of course you did. Come here. I'll rub your shoulders."

"You just want me to fall asleep so you can turn off *Ice Pirates*."

Juniper grinned. "Yes, you've figured out my evil plan, but you'll let me because I've got magic hands."

He abandoned his plate and slid down onto the floor in front of her, where she began working on the knots in his shoulders.

She'd been doing this forever, and she wasn't going to turn off the movie. Instead, she'd make this his downtime, his safe place, and be the support he needed.

Of course, Juniper hadn't taken her rogue thoughts into account. She quickly realized the extreme error of her ways. She had her hands all over him and her brain wasn't playing nice.

She was suddenly intensely aware that he was seated between her thighs, her knees touching his shoulders. Juniper was newly cognizant of how *much* she liked touching him. Which was why, as soon as he was relaxed, she had to stop.

"Now, I'm going to owe you two," he murmured.

Oh no. No. No. She couldn't have that. His hands on her like this? Not until she'd exorcised this strange lust demon out of her body.

"You know I'll collect. Next book."

"No, no. Fair is fair. I like to give what I get."

I'll just bet you do.

Juniper's face heated. This was so stupid. Why wouldn't her brain and body cooperate?

"Don't worry about it. You take good care of me when I need it. Tonight, you need it."

"I do, don't I?" he agreed.

She continued to work her thumbs into the spot just at the edge of his shoulder blades that tended to knot up. Juniper kneaded his shoulders and back until she was able to lose herself in the rhythm and remembered that he was simply Tomas. Her best friend.

Just as a key slipped into the lock and the front door opened, Tomas said, "That's so good."

"Maybe we should come back later," her mother said as she stepped inside with Mama Estella.

"Mom! What are you doing?" she cried. "I gave you that key for emergencies."

"Sorry! We didn't mean to interrupt," her mom said.

"Yes, we did. How are you going to get engaged and not tell your mamas? Why did we have to hear it from your grandmothers?" Mama Estella demanded, hands on her hips.

Tomas got to his feet. "Mama, we hadn't decided how we wanted to tell you. We wanted to make it special."

"And we asked the grandmothers to wait. That wasn't for them to tell you." Juniper crossed her arms over her chest.

"Oh, don't be mad, *mija*." Estella held her arms open. "This is too wonderful."

Juniper found herself obeying and went to hug Mama Estella tight. Her mom was hugging Tomas, and then hugging Mama Estella, so she and Tomas hugged.

It was a veritable melee of hugs.

"We're so happy for you two. This is what we've always wanted for both of you," her mom said. "Since that first time you played together at the park."

"That's a little intense, Mom."

"A mother just knows what she knows," Estella defended.

"We brought you something." Her mom nudged Estella.

"We did!" She pulled out a small box from her oversize bag.

"Mama!" Tomas said. "You can't."

"I can, and I will. You will." Estella opened the box to reveal a ring with a princess cut emerald on a silver band inlaid with green chalcedony.

It was unique, and beautiful, unlike any other ring she'd ever seen.

"This was my wedding ring. It's been passed down through the women in our family for generations. It's said that it's magic. When the right man puts it on your finger, it will fit perfectly, signifying your heart's perfect fit." She shrugged. "Eh, it sounds better in Spanish. Like most things."

"I can't accept that," Juniper began.

"You can, and you will." Estella took her hand and held it out to Tomas.

Tomas shrugged and slipped the ring on her finger. It did, in fact, fit perfectly.

She rolled her eyes, sure the mamas had taken it to have it sized.

Estella beamed at her. "It never fit me when I was with Tomas's father. I should've known, but I didn't believe in those sorts of things when I was young."

"It's beautiful."

"Tomas!" Mama Estella snapped.

"What now?"

"Kiss your bride."

Juniper coughed and fanned her hand in front of her mouth. "We're fine. We just ate, actually. Bad breath. *So bad*."

"Don't ruin this for us, Juniper," her mother said. "Your marriage will endure bad breath. If that's the biggest of your problems, you'll have a happy life. He just gave you a family heirloom. His mother welcomed you into the family. This is how these things go. Now, kiss."

She and Tomas locked gazes. He shrugged. She shrugged. But they both stood there, not moving.

"It's a wonder the two made it this far," her mother said.

"Breeding show ponies," Tomas muttered.

She found that this time she agreed with him. "Mom. We're doing just fine on our own. I promise. We don't want to perform like trained monkeys."

Estella lifted her chin. "Kiss, and we'll go away."

Juniper needed this to be over.

She hoped against hope that when her lips touched his, she would immediately be reminded that she didn't think of Tomas that way. Kissing him would be . . . not gross, but it wouldn't light her on fire. Then, she could forget all this nonsense.

So it was Juniper who closed the distance between them. Juniper who wrapped her arms around him. Juniper who pulled him down and pressed her mouth to his.

And it was Juniper who, in that moment, realized things had gone horribly, terribly wrong.

His arms closed around her, pulling her tight against him, and his hand tangled in her hair, as she melted into the haze of desire that had overtaken her.

She was only vaguely aware that the mamas left without saying anything else, except for the muffled giggles and mutterings about young love.

Juniper knew she should stop. She should break the kiss, but she didn't want to. It was the most decadent sensation to be wrapped in him like this, to be the object of his desire.

He was the one who broke the kiss, but he didn't pull away. Tomas moved his lips to the arch of her neck and she pushed her hand through his hair and held him close to his work.

His erection pressed against her belly, and lust stabbed through her hard and fast. There was no denying it now, she wanted him.

Needed him.

And he wanted her.

"Oh God," she murmured.

Her voice seemed to be a cold wash of reality over them both.

The things she'd fantasized about had no place in their world. They both knew it.

He broke away from her, breathing heavily.

She wet her lips and realized she could still taste him, and wanted to again. "Not a big deal, right? We'll probably have to kiss again before this sham relationship is over. We should get comfortable with it."

"Comfortable with it," he repeated in a dazed tone. "Yeah."

"Yeah."

But they both stood there, not moving, not speaking for a long time.

"I, um, I'm sorry," he began.

"Don't you dare apologize."

"I shouldn't have gotten so carried away, Juniper."

"Oh, please. I'd be insulted if you hadn't."

He laughed, and that was when she knew this was going to be okay. "I suppose I'd have been insulted, too. We're both good at what we do. Of course we got carried away. Makes total sense."

"Totally," she agreed. "At least we don't have to figure out how to tell the mamas. And it got them to leave. I'd say it was effective in all ways."

He exhaled heavily and looked down at the floor. "I think I should go."

"Okay, but I hope you don't feel like you have to hide from me. When we stop telling each other things is when it's a problem."

"I'm not hiding from you. I promise. I think we both need to get our heads right."

That was for sure. "Fair enough."

She couldn't help but notice the ridge in his slacks was still very present.

And he noticed her noticing. "You see what I mean."

She laughed, and hated that it sounded more like a giggle. She was *not* flirt-giggling with Tomas. They were going to go straight back to normal territory where things like this didn't happen.

"I'm taking it as a win, personally. I look like I crawled out of a ditch, have tamale breath, and you still got teak." She squared her shoulders. "I feel kind of powerful."

"You should always feel that way."

The way he was looking at her made her think he wanted to kiss her again, and she wanted him to.

The moment between them hung gravid with possibility.

"We should probably talk this to death," he said. "Analyze everything. Talk about it until we never want to think about it again."

He took a step closer to her.

"Uh-huh."

"But my brain is not doing the thinking at the moment."

"Me either."

"*Dios mio*, that's not helping."

"We shouldn't do this, right? Not even as friends who are going through a dry spell."

"Wait, you have friends like that? Why didn't I know about this?"

She laughed. "It's a thing that happened in college. Evan? We were . . . friends."

"Hated that guy. Now, I really hate him."

They stared at each other for a long moment, once again in silence.

"We're not making any progress. I assume that going back to finish the movie isn't an option. So we either need to decide to wreck each other all night, or you need to leave."

"You decide. I picked the movie," he murmured.

"Not it. I kissed you first. Ball is back in your court."

He shoved his hands in his pockets, and she knew his decision before he spoke.

"Okay." He nodded slowly. "I'm sure it would be the best sex of our lives, but I love you too much to risk all the ways we'd hurt each other on the other side. We want different things."

Juniper couldn't help but think this felt like a breakup, even though it was nothing of the sort. Thankfully, that voice in the back of her head had decided to hold her tongue.

"You're right. So we don't have to talk this to death. We can try to forget it. I don't want to lose the physical intimacy we already have. I love that you hug me, that you kiss my forehead. That I can lean my head on your shoulder when I want to feel safe."

"I don't want to lose that, either, but I also don't want to feel guilty if I'm holding you and it feels too good. If I don't tell you, I feel like I'm lying to you."

"So we just need to try to navigate these waters as best we can and communicate."

"Like we've always done," he replied.

"So we're decided."

"You're not getting out of watching the rest of *Ice Pirates* next week. We're definitely decided on that."

"Yeah, that's really why we can't date, you know. You'd think it gave you special *Ice Pirates* privileges, and we can't have that."

He flashed her a grin, and a wink, and he was out the door.

Without his shoes.

And without hugging her.

She supposed this was the best outcome she could've hoped for. Juniper looked down at the beautiful ring on her finger and tried to pull it off, but it wasn't budging.

"Oh, not you, too."

It didn't mean anything at all that the ring wouldn't come off. It didn't mean that Tomas was her heart's perfect match.

It didn't mean that at all.

Chapter 4

Two weeks later, and the ring still wouldn't come off.

It wasn't too tight, or uncomfortable, but the darn thing wouldn't budge.

They hadn't had their weekly movie night—Tomas said because his caseload was too heavy. And while that had happened before, she couldn't help but wonder if it was because of what had happened between them after she'd kissed him.

He was still just as talkative on text as he always was, so she was trying to take him at his word and not overanalyze every single thing.

And otherwise, it seemed as if things had gotten back to mostly normal.

Except this ring.

Every time she looked at it she felt guilty for lying, and guilty because there was some part of her that wished it wasn't a lie.

She'd tried everything she could think of to get the ring to come off. She'd tried only drinking water for a whole day.

She'd tried oil.

She'd tried cold water.

She'd tried ice.

She'd tried soap and water.

Nothing was working.

She decided to try Gramma Jonquil. Petty and Bon-Bon

would both ask her why she wanted it to come off, but Jonquil was much more practical.

She dialed the number.

Jonquil answered after a few moments. "Juniper! I hope you're not calling to cancel? Betina will be so disappointed."

"Nothing of the sort, Gram. I have a problem I'm hoping you can help me with."

"Oh, let me get the girls."

"No, no. Just you."

She heard the sound of rustling fabric in the background and then dead silence. "Did someone do something to you? I'll roast them to a sizzling crisp the same as Petunia would!"

Juniper smiled. "No, it's not that serious. You're the practical one. So I thought you'd understand why I need help."

"Do go on, dearie."

"It's just . . . so, Tomas gave me his mother's wedding ring. Now it won't come off."

"Ah, I see. Pets and Bon-Bon would ask you why you'd want to take it off and would be absolutely zero help."

"Basically."

"I assume you've tried all the basics? Soapy water, cooking spray, coconut oil, ice . . ."

"No luck."

"Is there anything . . . I don't know . . . *special* about the ring?"

"Just that it's been in his mother's family for generations. I'm afraid I'm going to have to have it cut off."

"It's not that serious, child. I'm sure of it." Jonquil rustled around again before continuing. "Are there any legends around the ring? Good luck? Anything like that?"

"His mother said that it's supposed to fit perfectly when the perfect man puts it on your finger, or something."

"Have you tried asking Tomas to take it off?"

She hadn't, actually. "Why do you think that will help? It can't actually be magic."

"Did Estella say it was magic? Specifically?"

"She did."

"Hmm. Then I think it will definitely come off if Tomas helps. Try petroleum jelly, too."

For a moment, Juniper pictured herself walking into his office with a container of petroleum jelly and just what that would look like. She snorted.

"Honey pie, it might be good to have him help because you're nervous and stressed out. Also, if the ring incurs some damage, Estella can't blame you. It will be her son's fault."

"You're diabolical sometimes, Jonquil. I like how your mind works."

"Well, you should. Because you get it from me." Jonquil sounded very proud of this.

"Thanks. I'll see you next week. No, I won't forget the books."

"What else won't you forget?"

"To drive safely. Love you."

"Love you too. Give Tomas our love."

After she ended the call with Jonquil, she texted Tomas.

I know you're busy, but I neeeed you.

He replied instantly.

Come to the office. Bring coffee.

She smiled and grabbed her keys. Once she'd acquired a jar of Vaseline, one big enough it had to be some kind of gag gift, she stopped and picked up coffees and headed into the law offices across town.

No one stopped her as she headed through the door and straight to Tomas's office. She nodded at Jocelyn, who gave her a quick but harried smile and went back to typing on her keyboard.

When Juniper got into his office, she closed the door behind her, set down the paper bag, and pulled out the jar of Vaseline, setting it down on his desk.

He stopped what he was doing and looked at her.

He looked to the Vaseline.

Then back at her.

Tomas arched a brow pointedly.

"Not like that, perv. I can't get this ring off!" She shoved her hand toward his face. "I've tried everything."

"What makes you think I can help?"

"If we hurt the ring. I know your mother loves me, but she'd never forgive me."

"Correction. She'd forgive you, but she'd never forget. Or let anyone forget. You're right." He closed the file he'd been working on and came around from behind the desk. He took her hand, and he tugged on the ring, but nothing happened.

Tomas made a twisting motion to see if that would budge it, but nothing.

"Didn't I just say I'd tried everything?"

"Didn't you just say you thought I could help? I have to try."

She sighed. "Thanks for not asking me why I'd want to take it off."

"Well, since we're here, why do you? You're more likely to lose it if you take it off."

"I can't type with it on."

"That is definitely a problem. Shit."

They both looked at the tub of Vaseline. He sighed and picked it up, dipping his fingers into the jelly.

She wrinkled her nose. "Eww. God, eww."

"You're telling me. How much should I use?"

"I don't know. You probably use it more than . . ." She trailed off and cringed. "I don't know."

He snickered. "I mean, you're right."

"Oh God."

He spread the dollop over her finger and the ring, working the ring back and forth to try to get the Vaseline between the metal and her skin.

"That feels disgusting."

"I agree," he said. "Okay, you hold on to the desk, and I'm going to pull. Ready?"

She nodded.

He tugged and nothing happened. The ring was still firmly planted on her finger.

"Again," she said.

"If it hurts, tell me, and I'll stop."

He made a fist around her finger and pulled.

"Harder!" she ordered.

He tried again. "I'm pulling as hard as I can!"

"It's not hard enough. Harder!" she demanded.

"This isn't working. Let me get a towel."

He came back from his personal washroom with a towel in one hand, and he got another glob of Vaseline with his finger.

"I think it was too slick. I got it all on my hands."

He slathered the jelly on her finger and twisted the ring round and round. It was good and covered by the time he was done.

"Are we ready to try again?"

She grabbed hold of the desk with one hand and held the other with the offending ring out to him. He used the towel to get traction and began to pull.

"Twist and pull."

Tomas did as she asked and twisted it back and forth as he pulled. It felt as if they'd started to make some progress, and he pulled harder. He pulled so hard, the towel slipped and he careened backward, where he fell into a lamp that crashed to the floor.

"This, of course, means war," he muttered.

Tomas righted himself and made for her, but she jerked her hand away. "No, I want to keep my finger attached."

"I'm going to get that off if it kills me." He held out his hand. "Come here."

"No."

"Woman."

"Fine!" She knew she wasn't getting it off by herself.

"We need more lubricant." He put more petroleum jelly on her finger and went back to twisting and turning the ring to get some motion. "Can you feel it?"

She nodded excitedly.

"Okay, new plan. I pull, you pull. On three?"

She nodded.

"Three!"

They both pulled at the same time, but when the door opened, it startled them both and sent Tomas once again careening backward, but the inertia sent Juniper tumbling forward, too, and she landed precisely on top of him.

They both swore.

"Is everything okay in here?" Jocelyn bit her lip. "Sorry to interrupt, but we have clients in the front. *And they can hear you.*"

It took Juniper a moment to process exactly what that meant, but she realized what this must've sounded like to anyone who couldn't see what they were doing.

That feels disgusting.

If it hurts, tell me, and I'll stop.

Harder!

I'm pulling as hard as I can!

It's not hard enough. Harder!

Can you feel it?

Followed by the loud crashing sounds and . . . well, it was a recipe for . . . for something. She was absolutely mortified.

Juniper held up her hand to show Jocelyn the ring. "I can't get my ring off. He was helping."

"I see. I'll let him finish helping. I'll tell Mr. Williams." She closed the door behind her.

Juniper bit her lip. "Everyone thinks we were having sex. In your office."

Tomas laughed. "Well, I mean?"

"I can't leave. Not until everyone else is gone. I'm going to hide in your washroom until I can sneak out the back." Then horror dawned on her. "I can't come to the fundraiser. I don't know who was here and who wasn't. I mean, Mr. Williams was obviously here. I won't be able to look him in the face."

"I'll tell him what was happening. Jocelyn came in, and we were both fully clothed. It's nothing to be embarrassed about."

"And then, when we fell, she saw me hop on you like a jockey at the Kentucky Derby."

He cackled again. "This is too funny. Come on. After you forget to be embarrassed, you're going to laugh."

"Not today," she said as she tried to scramble off him.

And tried to stay unaware of how good it felt to have climbed him like a tree.

They'd decided they weren't doing this.

Although, she'd have to say, it seemed like fate had other ideas. She had a strange knowing in the pit of her stomach that told her no matter how hard they fought it, they'd opened a Pandora's box and they wouldn't escape unscathed.

"Maybe my boss will believe we're engaged now." He sat up. "I'm sorry, but I don't think that ring is coming off."

"Me either. Your mom is going to kill me when I have to get it cut off."

"Give it a few days, then we'll see about freeing you from its evil clutches, yeah? It might come off on its own. That is, unless it's hurting you." He used the towel to wipe the mess from his hand.

"It's not hurting me; it's just distracting me. I don't like wearing any jewelry when I write. I get very aware of anything on my body that's not supposed to be there."

He seemed to consider. "Anything?"

"Yeah."

"So you write naked? This has me rethinking all these writing retreats you go on."

She snorted. "No. You know what I mean."

"Yeah, I do," he conceded. "If it makes you feel any better, I think she was planning on giving the ring to you, anyway."

"Really?" Her heart did a strange little flip.

"You've always been a daughter to her the same way I've always been your mother's son."

"Aren't there laws against that?" she teased.

"Definitely," he replied. "Hey, sorry I've been so busy. I really have been just buried under this caseload."

"No biggie." She shrugged. "I seem to remember the last deadline I screwed myself on, where all I did was type and cry for a week straight, I ignored you pretty solidly."

"Yeah, you did. You still demanded tamales, too. I had to bring them in and put them in your kitchen. Silently," he said in an accusatory tone. "And then leave."

"I know." She grinned. "My readers are lucky I have you." When he didn't respond, she added, "Fine. *I'm* lucky I have you."

"There we go. A little appreciation." He squeezed her shoulder. "I meant to ask if you'd gotten a dress?"

"We'd both be shit out of luck if I hadn't since it's tomorrow."

"It's tomorrow? What's today?"

"Friday."

"I thought it was still Wednesday," he said in a panicked tone.

"It's all fine. I got the dress. It looks amazing. I'll meet you there at seven; we'll dazzle everyone and then go out for pizza."

"You should definitely eat something before. Are you sure you don't want to eat pizza early?" he asked with a knowing expression on his face.

"I do, but if I get anything on that dress . . . I'll eat light before I dress. I'll bring a change of clothes, and then we can go out?"

"Okay. What about the masquerade ball in Ever After? Do

you have any ideas about what we should dress as? Considering we leave Sunday."

"Well, I wanted to talk to you about that, but you've been busy. I got your costume for you."

"This is punishment for *Ice Pirates*, isn't it?"

She grinned. "Maybe. Could be. You'll never actually know."

"Out with it."

"We're going as the Phantom and Christine."

"Why do I have to be ugly?"

Juniper snorted. "Oh, please. The Phantom is hot. Plus, you can wear the suit from the benefit. I got the mask already. It'll be a classic, but with your own spin. Unless you want to wear your tux?"

"No, no. I think I like it."

"Add it to your packing list, so you don't forget."

"Right." He pulled out his phone and sent himself an email. "Thanks." After he was done, he said, "Since it seems I'm not getting anything else done today, you want to go eat?"

"I always want to go eat."

"Where do you want to go?"

"Oh no. We're not starting that. You issued the invitation. You pick. Those are the rules."

"Fine. Let's go to that Greek place on Third. The one with the crispy dolmas."

"Yes! But I need to wash my hands." They were still covered in Vaseline.

"There's another towel by the sink," he said as he went into the washroom and turned on the water for her so she didn't make a mess.

She cleaned up with the towel, washed her hands, and then used another towel to dry them. Then she inspected the ring again.

"That thing is good and stuck, my friend."

"At least it's pretty."

He grabbed his jacket. "And probably not cursed."

"You're not funny."

"No, really. My abuela was all about cursed objects. The car broke down? It was cursed. If I dropped my pencil, it was better to get another one. Because that one was cursed. The ring didn't fit my mother when my dad asked her to marry him? The *guy* was cursed." He laughed.

"Seriously?"

"Utterly. He drove her nuts. How have you not heard this story?"

"I don't know, but I think I'm definitely missing out."

"You are. She was one of my favorite people. I miss her all the time."

"I seem to remember she loved cardinals, didn't she?"

He nodded. "Yeah. She had cardinals all over her house. She said when cardinals appear, angels are near."

"That's a lovely thought." Juniper linked her arm through his. "I wonder if she'd think I'm cursed."

"Why would she think that?"

"All of my failed relationships have one thing in common. Me."

"They were also all shitheads."

"See? Cursed," she said as he led her out through the front of the office.

She tried not to look at anyone on their way out the door, but an older woman with white hair caught her eye and winked.

"Honey, from the sounds of it, if you're cursed, we should all be so lucky."

Juniper learned it was not actually possible to die of embarrassment. Unfortunately.

Chapter 5

Tomas didn't want to admit that things had changed between him and Juniper, but there was no denying it.

As he waited for her on the country club steps, he considered *how* things had changed. Before, when he wouldn't have thought twice about pulling her close, or pushing that lock of hair behind her ear, Tomas found that he restrained himself. He didn't want to accidentally spark that memory of what it felt like to kiss her.

The way she'd melted against him, but in a way that wasn't surrender. . . .

Too late.

What if they'd let their lust rule them?

Lust wasn't the right word for what had sparked between them. It was too common. Too simple. There was nothing common or simple about what he felt for Juniper.

But this was something they just couldn't have.

No, this was something *he* couldn't have.

The consequences weren't worth it. He knew Juniper too well to think she'd ever be happy with what he could offer her romantically.

Of course, reason abandoned him when he saw her get out of the cab.

He saw her legs first.

It was like some glamour shot of old Hollywood, the shapely curves of her legs sliding into view from the drape of lavender silk. Her ankles were encircled by the glittery straps of modern-day "glass" slippers, with dagger-sharp heels.

His first thought was to wonder what they'd look like propped up on his shoulders.

Tomas tried to shove that imagery out of his head, and lucky or maybe unlucky for him, the rest of her dress made it easy.

It was slit up the side, to show more of her gorgeous legs, but just when he thought it would be safer to move his gaze up to her face, he got sidetracked by the plunging neckline.

Finally, he tore his gaze away to meet her eyes, and that was the worst thing he could've done.

Because this carnal fantasy come to life was still Juniper.

It might've been easier if there had been some kind of guile in her eyes, some kind of tease, but she had the sweetest smile for him.

Her little awkward wave because she hated these things.

The box he held in his hand now seemed dumb. Inadequate. He'd gotten her a small blue hydrangea corsage. What had he thought this was, the prom?

He lurched forward to offer her his arm so she didn't kill herself in those shoes, but she was the one with all the grace.

"That for me?" She nodded with a wide smile toward the box in his hand.

He shrugged. "It's not elegant enough for that dress."

"I'll be the judge of that." Juniper took the box from his hand. "It's beautiful. What do you mean it's not elegant enough?" She held it back out to him. "Help me put it in my hair."

Tomas couldn't speak. So he simply took the bloom, removed the ribbon that would've been used to secure it around her wrist, and tucked it into the softly curled waves of black hair.

Their eyes met and she smiled softly, and didn't look away.

Tomas knew in that moment he was in deep, deep *caca*.

"Stop monopolizing your gorgeous fiancée, Tomas. Some of us are waiting none too patiently to see that ring," Helen Williams, Warren's wife, called from the entryway.

Juniper laughed and put her hand on the crook of his arm. Tomas took the cue to lead them up the stairs and into the crowd of people.

Helen led them to the partners' table in the grand ballroom and immediately clasped Juniper's hands.

"Your dress is glorious. Wherever did you find it?"

"Honestly?" Juniper smirked. "Thrift shopping." She turned her ankle out to show off her shoes. "These too."

The hell she'd found that thrift shopping.

"I know you didn't find this thrift shopping." Helen held up the hand with the ring and inspected it closely. "It's so unique. Tell me. Did you choose it together?"

"It's a family heirloom." Juniper's voice dropped to a conspiratorial whisper. "It's supposed to be magic."

"This is a story the rest of the ladies must hear. Come with me. I'll introduce you."

He watched as Juniper was led off to meet "the ladies."

Tomas decided the dress was worse from the back. It was cut so low he could see the dip of her waist.

He decided then they wouldn't be able to dance.

There was nowhere safe to put his hands.

Maybe he needed an exorcism.

A hand on his shoulder caused him to turn. John Hernandez, the other managing partner of the law firm, stood beside him.

"She's meeting the wives, Tomas."

He said this like he was narrating Pandora opening *The Box*. In any other instance, Tomas would think John was being overdramatic, but that was exactly what had happened. They'd opened a box that had been better left closed.

"She's met the wives before. It's fine. She's attended these events with me." He pretended like this wasn't quickly getting away from them like a turd rolling downhill.

"She hasn't met the wives like this."

Tomas exhaled heavily. "I know."

"Dani likes her a lot. She'd be disappointed if for some reason this didn't work out. And you know how much I hate to disappoint my wife."

"We all do," Tomas agreed.

He needed a stronger drink than the flutes of champagne that were being passed around the room to deal with this.

"I'm happy to hear that. I'm sure Warren has told you that we'll discuss everything after you and Juniper set a date."

Tomas didn't like being pressured or maneuvered, even when it was well-meaning. "It may be some time before we have that talk. Even though our engagement was spur-of-the-moment, we're taking our time and doing things our own way."

"Of course," John replied. "Wouldn't have it any other way, my friend."

But wouldn't he? He and Warren both had made getting married a caveat to making partner. That wasn't exactly letting him do things his own way.

He didn't know how to extract them both from this situation unscathed. Tomas was beginning to think that might be an impossible task.

When the orchestra began to play, John straightened his jacket. "That's my cue. Dani loves to waltz. I suggest you find Juniper before someone else sweeps her out onto the dance floor."

Only there was no chance of that.

The wives had seen to it.

They were a wave propelling her forward toward him, and no one dared stand in the way.

She wore a soft smile that seemed to be just for him, her cheeks flushed as she held out her hand.

Helen said something, possibly to the effect that they'd returned her safe and sound. He didn't really hear her.

He was filled with everything Juniper. Nothing else could penetrate his senses.

When he took her hand, she glided into his arms and they floated onto the dance floor. The hydrangea bloom in her hair smelled light and sweet, and the scent wrapped around them like a cloud.

The world came crashing in around him when his hand came to rest on the bare skin of her lower back. Suddenly, everything was too hot. Too much.

It was like he'd been flying and dropped out of the sky to land face-first on cement.

But they were still moving together, still somehow floating. It was an incongruity.

"How were the wives?" he said, needing to break the spell that had been cast over them.

"They were wonderful. Apparently, I'm going to be chairing a literacy initiative several of the patrons here have wanted to sponsor."

"Stuffing you into that premade wife box already, huh?"

"Actually, I'm excited about it. It's something that matters to me, and I can effect real change in the community." She leaned her head on his shoulder. "I hope the door is still open after we break up."

Right, he reminded himself. This wasn't real.

Only the way she felt in his arms definitely seemed real enough.

"You smell good," she murmured against his ear. "New cologne?"

"No. I was distracted when I left the house. This is just me."

She laughed. "Well, I like just you better."

"Oh? Are we going to get another romance-novel description?"

"If you like."

No, he already knew what dangers lay down this path. But his mouth refused to obey him. A lawyer's best weapon was his tongue, and his had turned on him.

"Do I smell like pine, an alpaca saddle, and alpha male?" He squinted. "What does beta male smell like?"

"Are you making fun of me?" she asked softly.

They joked about this all the time. He'd always thought it was good-natured. He loved her books. He loved how she wrote them. He loved why she wrote them. He didn't realize it might be a spot of contention for her.

"No, of course not."

"It kind of sounded like it. I know we tease each other about certain things. Sometimes I tell mean lawyer jokes and you tease me about purple prose but . . ."

Tomas couldn't bear the thought of hurting her. He hadn't wanted to admit how much he liked the way she saw him and what he really wanted was to hear more of it. His pride wasn't worth her distress.

"I didn't mean it that way. I'm sorry. Bridge too far, so noted." He pulled her a little closer so he could whisper in her ear. "I just wanted to hear it again."

"Hear what?"

"How you see me when you look at me through your writer's lens."

"If you just want your ego stroked, you know all you have to do is ask."

He wasn't going to let that thought evolve to its final form. Instead, he said, "I'm asking."

"Okay." She leaned her head on his shoulder again, but this time, her lips were almost touching his throat.

Strange waves of both familiarity and longing washed over him.

This thing that burned between them wasn't something

that was going away any time soon. In fact, he had a feeling that no matter how hard they fought this, eventually all roads led to surrender.

"It's not pine, it's sandalwood. The vanilla sandalwood soap you bought when we went to Brazil for Carnival after you graduated law school. You smell like . . . yes, that scent that's not dirty alpaca and sweat but indescribable and masculine." She paused.

"And what else? Midnight picnics and desire?" he ventured to tease.

"Midnight picnics smell like old fried chicken. If you smelled like that, I wouldn't be dancing with you."

"I like midnight picnics and fried chicken."

Her laughter was light and musical. "So that's the problem. That's why you're no good at relationships with women besides me."

"Obviously, I'm not good at relationshipping with you, either. I just insulted your life's work. And you took it in stride. So I must step in it fairly often." He said this with no rancor.

"Whatever." She snorted indelicately. "You apologized. You meant it. What am I supposed to do, stay mad?" Juniper pulled back to look up at him. "Oh, I've missed a very fine opportunity here."

"To extort me for more tamales?"

"Exactly."

Things had started to slowly slide back into comfortable territory. This was normal. This was his Juniper, not some fantasy goddess wrapped in lavender silk.

"Don't look now, but I think Jace is coming over."

"Not Food-Poisoning-Sushi Jace?" Jace was a new lawyer not too far out of law school that Juniper had had one absolutely awful date with after she met him at one of the office parties.

"Is there any other?"

"I didn't think so, but I don't know your life," he teased.

"If he asks to cut in, say no."

He stilled, his feet no longer moving. A grim kind of calm washed over him, replacing all the good things he'd been feeling. "Juniper, has he done something that your no wouldn't be enough?"

Tomas looked into her eyes, searching for the answer to his question, and mentally started planning all the ways he'd ruin the man. Financially. Professionally. Mentally. Physically.

"He just won't take the hint. I don't want to make things awkward for you at work."

"He'll take the hint," Tomas promised.

"Because we're engaged?"

"Because we're going to have a discussion about consent. You shouldn't have to be with another man for him to take the no."

"See? That's why there's a little bit of you in every hero I write."

He was stunned yet again. "What, really?"

"You're the only constant good man in my life. Of course you're in my books. I can't believe you haven't recognized bits of yourself."

"Does this mean I get to wear one of those shirts that reads *I Inspired Your Book Boyfriend*?"

"Totally. In fact, it's what you're getting for your birthday."

"Who knew I was missing out on all of these perks?"

"Really, what better endorsement is there?" She grinned up at him.

A voice interrupted them. "May I cut in? I'd like to give the bride my congratulations."

He looked over to see Jace, the subject of their earlier conversation. Tomas wasn't going to cause a scene unless he had to, and he didn't even want to pretend to be a jealous partner. The idea just rubbed him the wrong way. Perhaps because he'd seen what jealousy could do to men and women, and it was always ugly.

"This isn't a good time, my friend. My bride is telling me about her new book idea and I can't get enough."

"That's sweet," Jace said. "I can see that you're a good match. It was what I suspected all along."

Juniper bristled, but Tomas looked down at her adoringly. "Sometimes it happens that way. It's right in front of your face, and you don't even know it."

They began moving again, dancing, their bodies swaying together in their own special rhythm. It didn't matter that Jace was there trying to cut in. It didn't matter that the music had ended and the other couples had begun leaving the dance floor.

Nothing mattered until Helen's voice came from the stage, amplified by the microphone. "Our own Juniper and Tomas, practicing for their first dance as husband and wife."

He watched as awareness dawned on Juniper, and she blushed and waved to the other guests, who all clapped as he led her toward the exit.

"It's beautiful, isn't it?" Helen said as Warren joined her onstage and put his arm around her. "A firm of divorce attorneys and we still believe in love. All of us. Which is why we're here tonight. Love. Love of our fellow man. Our fundraising efforts have resulted in . . ."

He already knew what she was going to say. How much money they'd made. What they were going to do with the funds. Instead, he was still focused on Juniper.

"Did I tell you how amazing you look?"

"You should tell me again. It's my turn. You should tell me I smell good, too. I mean, it's the least you can do," she teased.

"No, no. I'm not the one who is gifted with those descriptions."

"Oh yes. Am I as beautiful as a filed motion?"

He cackled as he hooked his palm on her elbow and led her toward the door. "Stop. That's ridiculous."

"Hey, where are we going? Don't tell me we're sneaking away early. They'll notice we're missing."

"Yes, they will. And we can get away with it because we're newly engaged." He waggled his eyebrows in a suggestive motion.

She sighed. "Well, it can't be any worse than when we tried to get my ring off."

"Don't tell me you're not ready for pizza." In reality, he just needed to get her into some jeans and a frumpy sweatshirt. Her writing uniform.

"I'm always ready for pizza. And to take off these awful shoes. They're so uncomfortable."

"Wait, where are your pizza clothes?"

"Crap! I knew there was a reason I was supposed to drive instead of cabbing it, but I was looking forward to the good champagne."

"I guess no pizza for you."

"Don't play with me, Tomas. You know the lengths I'll go to for pizza."

"You're willing to risk the dress?"

"Of course. I can get another. Plus, I'm about to get hangry."

"I bet you forgot to nibble on something before you left the house, too." He gave the valet his ticket and waited for him to retrieve the car.

She sighed happily. "You know me so well."

"Gio's it is."

"Wait, weren't we going to get Greek?"

"We always say we're going to get Greek, and then we get pizza."

The car pulled up, and he accepted the key from the valet, tipped him, and waited for him to open the door for Juniper before he got in the car.

"You know what I want? Gyro pizza," she said.

"That's awful."

"Isn't it, though? With a tall, frosty glass of beer."

He drove the short distance to Gio's and tried not to notice how much this felt like a date. Tomas wondered if it would feel the same if she wasn't wearing that dress. He tried to put it out of his mind.

It was warm for October, they'd had what felt like a second summer, so the al fresco tables on the side patio of the restaurant were still open. Heating towers were scattered strategically around the tables just in case of a cold snap, and with one look at the twinkling white lights that hung overhead, Tomas knew Juniper would choose to sit there. It was too picturesque not to.

It wasn't long before they were eating, laughing, and talking just like any other night.

When she shivered, he took off his jacket and draped it over her shoulders. He was sure she was going to dump marinara all over it, but Tomas found he didn't actually care.

"Hey, look, all my food made it to my mouth. Tonight must be magic," she said.

"It's the jacket. It's magic."

"Oh! Speaking of magic, we should probably get home. Lots to do to get ready for the drive. Have you acquired appropriate snackage?"

"No. Have you?"

"No." She laughed.

"I better take you home then."

He paid the bill, and the short drive back to her place was uneventful. He'd half expected to see both of their mothers waiting for them, demanding to know how it went and if they'd set a date yet. He was relieved to see the hall was blissfully empty.

When they got to her unit, she put her key in the door but then turned around to face him. "I had a really good time with you tonight." Then she laughed. "I can still feel my freshman English teacher swatting my knuckles for using 'really.'" She bit her lip. "But it was. A really good time, I mean."

"We always have a really good time together. Even when I have to bribe you to come to work parties." He noticed the bloom in her hair had wilted, and he reached up to pluck it from the soft waves. "Looks like the night is over for her, too."

Juniper inhaled deeply, and he realized she was smelling her own hair. It made him smile.

"She made my hair smell so good."

"I'm glad you liked her."

"I liked a lot of things about tonight," she said, with an undertone in her voice he'd never heard before.

Then, Juniper looked up at him and closed her fingers around the stem of the wilted flower along with his. Everything about her had gone soft, almost out of focus. This was not a side of Juniper he'd seen before.

It was even more intoxicating.

"Do you want to come in?"

It wasn't a question she'd ever asked him before. She didn't have to. It was understood. Only, this was different. This wasn't "Come in, and let's hang out." This was a woman inviting a man into her home.

Into her bed.

Earlier in the evening, it had occurred to him eventually they were going to surrender to this thing, but he knew it couldn't be tonight.

But instead of telling her that, he said, "I've got an early morning. I have to clear some things off my desk before we go."

He'd broken the cardinal rule they'd set for themselves. To always communicate about what they were feeling, no matter how uncomfortable.

"Good night, then. Thanks for the pizza."

While she was all smiles, she didn't hug him like she usually did, and he knew it was for the best.

"I'll see you tomorrow."

He was already out to his car by the time he realized she was still wearing his jacket. Tomas couldn't risk going back for it. There was so much more at stake for them now than a simple suit jacket.

Chapter 6

She woke up on her couch wrapped in Tomas's jacket.

It still smelled of him.

Juniper curled tighter into the material. When she'd been telling him what he smelled like, she'd forgotten to tell him maybe the most important ingredient in the particular blend of scents that was uniquely him.

He smelled like home.

Or maybe it was best she'd kept that to herself?

What had she been thinking last night when she'd invited him in like that? She hadn't meant it to sound like the blatant invitation it was, but she hadn't wanted the night to end. It felt like a date, and if it had been anyone but Tomas, the date would've ended between her sheets.

Of course, if it had been anyone but Tomas, it wouldn't have been as much fun and she wouldn't have considered inviting him in.

Maybe this trip to Ever After wasn't such a good idea.

Maybe she should just go by herself and face the grandmothers. Put her foot down with the lovely old dears and tell them the truth. It would be a good way to get her head right. She knew these growing feelings for Tomas were just going to end in disappointment and heartbreak.

She couldn't and wouldn't try to change him.

But she couldn't settle for less than everything, either.

It was time for her to face the fact that maybe these feelings for Tomas weren't new. She'd been putting off acknowledging them because she didn't want to deal with them. Or the distance she'd have to put between herself and Tomas to make things right again. Denial was so much easier.

Her phone buzzed.

She'd bet dollars to doughnuts that it was one of the godmothers telling her she'd best be on the road soon. It was like they knew exactly what she was thinking.

Juniper picked up the phone and peeked at her notifications.

G'ma Petty: *Let us know when you're on the road.*

G'ma Bon-Bon: *Don't forget to bring that handsome man.*

G'ma Jonquil: *Bring Gummy Colas*

Mama E: *Are you on the road yet?*

Mom: *So what happened last night? How was the benefit?*

She smiled and started to put down her phone when it buzzed again.

Bestie: *Are they texting you already?*

Bestie: *Should I get cola and worms, or just cola?*

She texted Tomas back first. *Breakfast enchiladas?* She smiled, knowing damn well she wasn't getting breakfast enchiladas. *No? Fine. Cola and worms.*

Bestie: *Breakfast . . . No.*

Please? I'll be your best friend.

Bestie: *You're lucky I know you. Made them last night.*

Bestie: *But they'll be more like late-lunch enchiladas. I've got a ton of paperwork.*

She always asked for them on road trips but never actually expected to get them. She needed to do something nice for him.

You're actually the best. Can I help?

Bestie: *Nah. I just have to get it done.*

Want me to pack for you?

Bestie: *Did it last night. I'm ready to go. Although, I need to get this suit dry-cleaned after we get there. Can you find a place?*

On it!

Bestie: *See you soon. Oh, and will you text my mother?*

Yes. Done!

She replied to each of them in turn, promising she wouldn't forget the man, the gummies, and she'd be on the road in the afternoon. She also asked Bon-Bon about dry cleaning. Her dress would need cleaning, too, especially since she'd slept in it.

Juniper wrapped the jacket more tightly around her, unwilling to give it up.

"You're ridiculous. You're going to be in a car with him for hours, and you can smell him all you want. Maybe more than you want." She exhaled heavily, but her body made no move to obey her.

Juniper knew exactly what her problem was. She wanted to talk this out, but none of her outlets were available to her.

She definitely couldn't ask Mama Estella. She couldn't ask her own mother. She couldn't ask her godmothers. She'd lied to them all.

Juniper cringed. She wasn't a liar. But they'd pushed her into it. She cringed again. Juniper wasn't the kind of person to deflect responsibility for her own actions, either.

Maybe she needed to just come clean about everything to everyone? Including Tomas. They'd agreed that things had started to change, and if they needed to, they could talk about what they were feeling openly and honestly.

That was the mature, responsible response, and it was what needed to happen to keep their relationship strong and healthy.

Juniper knew that.

But she didn't think she was ready to face being mature and responsible just yet. Juniper could tell the godmothers and their mothers that they'd lied to give themselves a reprieve from their matchmaking tyranny, and she could face the repercussions of that. Not that she wouldn't feel badly when the godmothers and mamas were disappointed and hurt, although, she really should have thought that part through before she let the situation get away from her.

No, the thing she wasn't ready to process was that somewhere after that soul-shattering kiss, she'd realized that there was part of her that believed their childhood pact that they would be together. She'd unwittingly kept it in the back of her mind and why no man was ever good enough.

He wasn't her best friend. He wasn't Tomas.

When she was younger, when she'd wish upon a star to find someone to love, she always wished for someone like Tomas, but with sex.

Well, her wish had come true. She had Tomas. The chemistry between them had exploded like rocket fuel on launch day, and it still wasn't the kind of love she wanted.

Maybe she didn't really know what romantic love was. Had she idealized it so much through her writing, her dreaming, that she'd created a fantasy ideal that no man could ever live up to? Not even Tomas?

She laughed aloud.

Hell no, she hadn't.

Juniper shook herself out of her doubts and reminded herself who the hell she was. She was Juniper Blossom, Purveyor of True Love™ and Queen of Happily Ever Afters.

The grandmothers would be more upset with her that she'd doubted herself than about her lie.

Oh, how she missed them. It had been too long since she'd seen them. She wanted ice cream sodas for breakfast, pumpkin everything now that it was fall. There would be pumpkin coffee and tea, pumpkin cream cake, pumpkin bread, pumpkin pie, and pumpkin cookies. There'd be hot apple cider at night by a fire and Bluebonnet would fuss in the kitchen while Jonquil knitted, and Petty would have her nose in some kind of a book.

A tiny sliver of guilt stabbed her like a splinter. They just wanted her to be happy.

At least they weren't bothering her for great-grandbabies, although she supposed that would be next.

Yet, the idea wasn't awful. She could imagine bringing them to Ever After to see their three great-grandmothers and being able to pass on the incredible childhood experience she'd had. The place and her grandmothers embodied a kind of a childhood wonder and innocence. Of course, nostalgia could do that. But there was something special about Ever After.

One of the things her friends learned and were constantly talking about was never being able to really go home after flying the nest.

That even though they could physically be there, it was never the same.

Juniper couldn't say she understood what they were talking about. The grandmothers were the same as when she was a child. She was able to feel the same safety, the same sense of well-being she'd always had there. Maybe it was because the grandmothers never seemed to age. Or because the animals were so friendly and so used to people. Maybe it was also because the people there were so kind to every resident, including the animals.

Ever After had a strange weather pattern, too. It rarely rained, it was rarely hot, it only snowed for about a week around Christmas, and there were never tornadoes. The Midwest was where several weather systems and phenomena met, creating something extremely unique, and a lot of other places got the scary fallout from that, so Juniper supposed it would make sense that there were pockets that got all the advantages.

Like fireflies in October.

She couldn't wait for the Firefly Ceremony! It was utterly magical! It had always been one of her favorite things, and she remembered not caring about trick-or-treating, or much else around Samhain, except visiting the grandmothers.

How had she ever thought she was going to go visit them and not bring Tomas? He'd been to Ever After a couple of times with Juniper when they were kids, but as they grew up his interest in going had waned and hers had only intensified. He'd never been at Samhain.

This was something that would bring at least a little awe back into his life. He needed it. Furthermore, so did she.

She got to her feet, and shed the jacket, holding it carefully in her arms as she began to pack.

Like she should've done the night before.

Or any other day in the past week, but she'd procrastinated.

Along with being Queen of Happily Ever Afters, Juniper Blossom was also a champion procrastinator. She held numerous gold medals and silver, as evidenced by all the books she'd written in massive jags of typing and crying the week before they were due. She never missed a deadline, and she always said she'd never do that to herself again, but the next contract always ended up with her mainlining coffee and existing mostly on gummy candy and whatever she could bribe Tomas into making for her.

Why should packing be any different?

After she'd showered, packed, and snacked, she was ready to go when Tomas knocked on the door.

He was empty-handed.

"I thought you were bringing enchiladas?"

He rolled his eyes. "That's the greeting I get? You're not happy to see me unless I have food?" Tomas teased.

"It's like you forgot that you know me. Hello?"

"It's why I left them in the car." Before she could question him, he added, "Along with the gummies. I got extra for the grandmothers."

"That's why they love you."

"That's why you love me. That, and my skills in the kitchen."

"Truth." She nodded and handed him the garment bag that held her dress and his jacket.

He reached for her other bag as well, and Juniper let him carry it down to the car. She locked her apartment and followed him down.

The enchiladas were on the seat, with a folded napkin and a fork on the top of the container. In the footwell was a large bag of snacks for her inspection. She knew it held road trip treasure.

"I should really do something nice for you."

"You should," he agreed easily. "I have an idea."

"Oh yeah?" She was determined *not* to think about all the favors she wanted him to ask of her.

Determined.

She would not fantasize about giving him a BJ for enchiladas.

Nope.

Plus, there's no way that was a good idea, even if he did ask. His green sauce was hotter than the sun, and if her mouth was on fire in that special way that only his food could deliver . . . well, she knew it wouldn't end well.

But wasn't that the point of fantasies that were better left in the realm of brain fiction than reality? It didn't have to be realistic.

"Yeah. Tell me where to turn before I'm about to pass it."

She rolled her eyes and ignored the disappointment that settled in her gut. "I'll try."

Juniper snatched up the treats, putting the bag of goodies in the back, and settled in with the plastic container of enchiladas on her lap.

"What did I get? Chicken, beef, cheese? Oh, pulled pork?"

"Two of each. Obviously."

"God, I love you."

"I know." He smirked.

But she didn't mind. She was glad that he knew she loved him. The enchiladas, the tamales, and all the other things he did for her were how she knew he loved her, too. He didn't have to say it with words, because his actions proved it over and over again.

She was mid-bite when they rolled to a stop at the end of her street and she thought she saw a pink spider skitter across the windshield.

"What's wrong?" he asked her.

"Nothing." Had to have been her imagination.

"Juniper, I know it has to be serious if it made you stop before the food made it into your mouth."

She laughed. "Yeah, okay. It's not serious, I just thought I saw a spider on the windshield."

"It happens."

"Yeah, but for a second, I thought it was pink."

"Actually, I thought I saw one when I was packing the car that was bright yellow. Maybe it's some new species. She was pretty, though."

"How did you know it was a she?"

"Because she was so bright and plump. Usually, the males are small and rather plain."

He turned onto the street and tapped a button on his steering wheel, and the speakers came alive with the road trip playlist.

The sky was blue and the sun was bright, and the long ribbon of road stretched out before them. She sighed happily.

"It's been a long time since we've gone on a road trip," he said.

"Much too long. Remember the drive to Vancouver?"

"The mama bear and her cubs we saw at Yellowstone? I'll never forget it." He strummed his fingers on the steering wheel to the music. "We should set a date for the Galapagos trip. We keep talking about it. We should do it."

"Okay. Let's do that when we get back. Check out some tour packages. I've been saving since we decided we were going to do it."

He flashed her a half smile. "Me too."

"Since we've been saving so long, what do you think about adding on Machu Picchu?"

"And Easter Island." He nodded along.

"Oh!" she cried out as they passed a pair of white passenger vans whose windows had been painted over. "Murder van."

"Murder van," he agreed.

She pressed her face against the window, trying to get a better view. This was a game they always played on road trips, and something just when they were out together. They liked to imagine the lives of people they didn't know. They made up stories about them.

And of course, a popular topic was where to hide the bodies.

When they passed various abandoned buildings or train yards, or anything else that was dark and spooky, the conversation inevitably turned to corpses. She supposed it was a little grim, but they both had very active imaginations.

Something skittered in the corner of her vision. Something yellow.

"Hey, I think I saw that spider, too."

"Oh no."

"Don't say it."

"I have to."

"Please?"

"We're already there."

"Fine." She steeled herself for the memory.

"The rental car in Florida."

She shuddered. "I'm surprised we survived. If I'd been driving, I'd have killed us both."

"You almost killed us both when *I* was driving."

"And the rental car company didn't believe us until I showed them the video on my phone of the dash swarming with baby spiders."

"You want to hear something horrible?" he asked.

"No."

"Yes, you do."

"Let me eat this last bite of enchilada. Let me enjoy it, horror-free."

He waited for her to finish and then he said, "Someone is driving that car right now."

"You're terrible."

"I wonder if any of the spiders stayed?"

"I wonder if we're going to have a swarm of baby yellow spiders halfway to Ever After."

"We might." He looked over at her and dropped his hand down next to her leg in the seat, his fingers splayed wide, his palm arched, so it looked like a giant spider.

"No."

"Yes." He wiggled two fingers at her like a spider checking out its territory.

"I'm going to take us both off the road, and we're going to die a fiery death because you think you're funny."

He wiggled his fingers again, and she squealed and slapped at his hand.

He laughed. "Honestly, your spider thing makes zero sense to me. You'll catch them and put them outside, you tell them how pretty they are, and then if one gets on you, you scream."

"Primal instinct. I can't help it. They're just little creatures going about their business. They have as much right to be here as I do. I just don't want their little legs on me."

They passed several more hours talking, laughing, and singing along to their favorite songs. When she saw the sign for the first exit looming, she said, "Take this exit."

"Which one?"

"The one that says Highway Ten."

"I don't see it."

"It's right there! To the left."

"It's a left exit?"

"You're going to miss it!"

He narrowed his eyes, and just in time, he got over into the lane and took the exit.

"Are you okay?" she asked, concerned because the sign had been right in his line of vision. And huge. She didn't know how he couldn't see it.

"I'm fine." He shrugged.

"Okay, there's another exit coming up pretty fast. It'll be on the right. It's Ten East."

Tomas squinted. "Maybe I should get my eyes checked when we get back."

The sign was clear as day.

He still didn't see it.

She didn't understand what was going on, but it scared her.

"Hey, I'm fine. Don't worry about me," he reassured her. "We should probably worry about those clouds. Check the weather app, will you?"

Out of nowhere, the sky suddenly turned gray, but the clouds were getting darker every second. There was a green tinge to the sky that almost always was a precursor to tornadoes. The clouds were moving fast, and they were fat and dark with rain.

She grabbed her phone and checked the weather app. Nothing was expected. In fact, the weather app still said it was sunny and clear.

October wasn't even storm season.

Lightning split the sky, and a torrential rain crashed down upon them.

Chapter 7

Petty's loud, wicked witchlike cackle was muffled by the clap of thunder.

"You take much too much joy in your cackling, Petunia." Bluebonnet shook her little yellow head and tried to bind the three of them more tightly to the car.

"We're going to get washed away in this downpour, and then where will we be?" Jonquil shook her head and added her spinning to Bluebonnet's.

"Washed away, obviously." Petty realized she should probably be spinning. "But listen, the spiders weren't my idea, they were yours. *I* wanted to be invisible."

"We can never hear the conversations as clearly when we're invisible," Jonquil complained. "We spend the whole time like the three witches with one eye. Except we only have one ear."

Petty knew she was right about that. But spiders? She weaved faster.

They'd secured themselves rather tightly when Petty realized they were attached to the windshield wiper.

"Oh dear," she cried as they were suddenly flung to the right, then to the left.

"I'm going to hurl!" Bluebonnet cried as the furious whipping of the wipers smashed them to and fro.

"You better not," Jonquil squealed.

Petty was about to use magic when she saw Juniper's face

get uncomfortably close to the windshield. "Gird yourselves, sisters. We can't let her see us."

Tomas's face followed suit.

"Oh hell, can they see us?" Jonquil hollered to be heard above the rain. "I really don't feel good."

"Just hold on until we can untangle this. If you spew, I'm going to spew. Then Petty will definitely spew and we all just had way too many ice cream sodas."

"I had key lime pie at that last truck stop," Petty confessed.

"With too much whipped cream on top!" Jonquil cried.

"Oh no!" Bluebonnet gulped.

Petty would never do anything as undignified as . . .

She closed her eyes as they swung and waited for inspiration to strike. Then she realized that they'd been overthinking this. Of course being invisible, they wouldn't be able to hear them outside.

The sisters needed to be *inside* the vehicle.

Obviously.

In lieu of a snap, she rubbed her legs together to summon the magic, and the godmothers found themselves warm and dry in the back seat of the car, ensconced in a soundproof invisibility bubble.

"There's a Tupperware up my tush," Jonquil squawked.

Bluebonnet giggled.

"This downpour is ridiculous. I hope it lets up soon," Tomas said.

"I'm still not even seeing anything on the radar on the weather app. How strange," Juniper said.

"We may have to stop somewhere and ride this out," Tomas sighed.

"That wouldn't be so bad. We haven't gone over our game plan for dealing with the grandmothers, yet."

Bluebonnet tittered again. "I love how they think they're getting away with something."

"I love getting this out of my butt," Jonquil grumbled, and flung the container to the floorboards.

Juniper swiveled around to look in the back seat, presumably to see what had fallen. "Speaking of weird . . ." She turned back around, rubbing the gooseflesh on her arms. "I just had the weirdest sensation."

"Yeah. Me too."

"Your mama would say we're cursed, probably."

Petty laughed. "Oh, if you only knew."

"She would. She'd tell us to pull over right now," Tomas said.

"I think we should take her advice." Juniper kept rubbing her arms. "Next place we see, yeah?"

Tomas nodded.

"Hmm," Jonquil said. "It looks like there's a place up ahead." She drew a sigil in the air with her wand. "It's very clean. Lots of vacancies. Totally respectable."

"Totally not fit for our needs," Bluebonnet supplied.

Petty zapped the sign so that "vacancy" became "no vacancy."

"Ohhhh! Look! It's a filth barn!" Bluebonnet shrieked gleefully.

"That was my ear," Petty said.

"It's something," Jonquil snorted. "Goddess have mercy, look at it."

Petty did, and she saw it was indeed a barn. Eroti-Barn. Why? "That might be a magic wand too far."

"It's some kind of wand too far, that's for sure," Bluebonnet agreed.

Their two charges in the front seat didn't seem to notice.

"What else?" Petty asked. "We need something nicer than a motel but not a reputable hotel."

"I doubt we're going to find a W out here," Jonquil said.

"What do you know about the W?" Petty snickered.

"Plenty." Jonquil lifted her chin. Then she cackled. "They

have a sex cabinet in the rooms. Where you can buy condoms, lube, edible undies, and a plethora of other things. You use the key to the minibar."

"A smut bar in the room?" Bluebonnet's eyes went wide.

"It makes a kind of sense. I don't know why all hotels don't have that." Petty nodded.

"The rooms were very nice. The suites, even better. It's really too bad we can't just zap to a W and lock them in for . . ." Jonquil pretended to look at a watch on her arm that wasn't there. "Three days would probably be long enough."

Petty arched a brow. "I mean, we could. But I don't think we'd get the final result we want."

Jonquil sighed. "I suppose you're right."

"Sisters. I think we're trying too hard," Bluebonnet said.

Petty nodded. "Yes, I thought so, too. But what is it we've overthought this time?"

"We're fairy godmothers. We don't need to zap them to a W. We can make our own." Bluebonnet looked at them pointedly.

Petty palmed her forehead. "Duh." Then, "Ow."

"You've been spending too much time with Zeva. Instead of your good habits influencing her, she's got you smacking yourself silly," Jonquil said. "Although, it does sometimes save us the trouble."

Petty snorted. "As if."

"See?" Bluebonnet said.

Petty couldn't help but smile thinking of their FG in training. When she looked at her sisters, she knew they were thinking the same thing.

"I miss her," Jonquil was the first to admit.

"Me too." Bluebonnet squeezed her hand.

Petty tapped her wand on her hand. "Ladies. Back to the task. We all miss Zeva, but this is Juniper. Our actual granddaughter." She pressed her lips together. "A million greats down the line, but whatever."

Jonquil and Bluebonnet nodded eagerly.

"Okay, so. We need to build a sex hotel," Petty said.

"You've seen the W, Jonquil. I think you need to conjure it. I'm thinking a cross between the W and one of those tacky places in the Poconos." Bon-Bon's eyes were alight with mischief.

"Oh, that's so perfect," Petty said.

"Anything else?" Jonquil asked. "I mean, I might as well give their room a mind of its own like Phillip's castle."

"I know you were being sarcastic, but I think that's just the thing," Petty said.

"Of course you do," Jonquil sighed. "I'm going to need to steal some of these gummies to keep my magic up."

"We'll get some on the way home. Don't you dare steal those cola gummies before Juniper gives them to us. She'll feel bad and think she lost them," Bon-Bon said.

Jonquil rolled her eyes. "Fine. Fine. Okay, make some room." She pushed up imaginary sleeves and closed her eyes. She looked like she was about ready to conduct an orchestra.

Petty giggled, but she supposed that's exactly what Jonquil was going to do. It would be an orchestra of magic to build something from nothing and bend it to the purpose for which it was built. She put her hand on Jonquil's left shoulder and Bon-Bon the right, to lend their magic for this great undertaking.

Although, she probably didn't need it. Not with all the love that pulsed in the car between Tomas and Juniper. It charged the godmothers right up.

"It's done," Jonquil finally exclaimed.

"And . . . we passed it. Tarnation!" Bon-Bon swore.

"I've got it." Petty zapped a sign and an access road into existence.

"Love Nest?" Juniper wrinkled her nose. "Oh no. This is either going to be the worst, or the worst."

Tomas laughed. "It doesn't look too bad. It looks like it

probably has room service. We'll get some fries and a hot shower and wait this out."

"Room service? Good move, Jonquil." Petty nodded.

Jonquil buffed her nails on her collar. "I think so."

"Love Nest, though?" Bon-Bon asked.

"It's a theme," Jonquil explained.

The car pulled up to a large white building that, on the outside, looked like a Colonial-style mansion on steroids.

"Maybe we won't have to stop after all. It looks like the rain has stopped!" Juniper was obviously ecstatic.

Petty palmed her forehead again, but this time, she didn't almost knock herself back in the seat. She zapped the sky and it opened up again with a downpour.

Tomas just looked at Juniper.

She shrugged.

"I'll go in and see if they have any vacancies. You wait here. No point in both of us getting drenched for no reason."

"Guess I could've given them an awning, huh?" Jonquil made a face.

"No, no. This is perfect. They'll have to change out of their wet clothes, won't they?" Bluebonnet wiggled her eyebrows.

"Diabolical, of course." Petty clapped her hands together.

Juniper turned around in the seat again and stared directly at them. Her eyes narrowed, and she seemed to almost be able to focus on them.

Juniper believed in magic.

She'd always believed. From the time she was no taller than a duck, to now, she believed. That made Juniper so special because without ever seeing magic, she knew it was there.

It would be time to tell her. It was past time, actually. But it had never seemed like they needed to tell her what she already knew in her heart. Before this was over, their little boo was going to need every weapon in her arsenal to stay the course. Her most powerful weapon would be her faith in love, and knowing the truth about magic would only fuel her fire.

"Can she see us?" Bon-Bon whispered.

"I think she knows something is here," Petty answered.

"It's getting to be that time, isn't it? I love telling them," Jonquil said with a sigh.

Juniper's brow furrowed, but then she turned back around, muttering to herself. "I must just really be missing the grandmothers."

"Aww," the sisters said in unison.

"We miss you too, punkin." Petty wanted to reach out and stroke her hair, but she might actually feel it and the poor girl would lose her mind.

Tomas came back out to the car and was dripping wet when he popped back into the driver side. His hair was plastered to his forehead, and rivulets of water dripped down his face. He blinked, and he wiped away the droplets that clung to his long black lashes.

Petty had to say he was quite the handsome guy.

She could feel her sisters' agreement.

"Don't tell me, they're full, too?" Juniper said.

"They have a vacancy. But just one."

"Heee heeee," Petty cackled out loud.

"This should be so obvious to her," Bluebonnet said gleefully. "She did this in her last book to get the hero and heroine to admit they have lusty feelings for one another."

"Shh. I haven't read it yet," Jonquil confessed.

"How dare you not put down that serial killer skunk mystery to read our granddaughter's latest," Bluebonnet admonished.

"I know. But I really need to find out if they're going to catch him," Jonquil said.

"Of course they're going to catch him," Bluebonnet drawled.

"Maybe not. He got away in the last book. By the way, it's a serial-killing, demon-possessed wombat. Not a skunk."

"You're ridiculous." Bluebonnet laughed. "And I love it."

"Is that the one where he was a lab animal and the priest stole him?" Petty asked.

"Uh-huh."

"Guys. Shh." Bluebonnet grabbed both Petty and Jonquil by the wrist to quiet them.

"It's not a double. It's a king-size."

"Whatever. We shared a bed on that Vancouver trip." She shrugged.

"Things are a little bit different than when we went on the Vancouver trip," he said.

Petty watched as Juniper swallowed everything she wanted to say.

"No, it's not," Juniper replied. "Not at all."

"Oh, Petty!" Bluebonnet cried. "Did you see her expression?"

"Poor dear," Jonquil added. "This was her chance."

"Not to worry," Petty said to rally her sisters. "She has fairy godmother grandmothers. She has as many chances as she needs."

"Too right," Bon-Bon agreed.

Jonquil sighed. "You'd think this would get easier. But it doesn't. Every single match we make, it's like this. We're on the edge of our seats, and we fret and fuss, but it always works out in the end."

"But we don't know which thing is going to be the one that works! They still have free will. So of course it doesn't get easier," Petty said.

"True. And if it did, we'd probably be bored," Bluebonnet confessed.

"Can you imagine retirement?" Jonquil said with horror.

"Goodness no," Petty gasped.

The three of them were startled when the car door closed and they realized that Tomas had gotten out of the car and was getting their bags.

Hopefully, they hadn't missed anything important!

"Did you do the thing with the room?" Bluebonnet asked.

"Of course," Jonquil snorted.

"We should probably go . . . ," Petty offered, leaving it open ended.

"Or we could just take a quick peek at their faces when they see the nest that Jonquil made for them."

This time, all three of them cackled.

"Will you do the honors, Pets?" Jonquil asked.

"Oh yes!" She waved her wand and zapped them inside the room and it was . . . awful.

Which was wonderful.

It had a red heart-shaped hot tub in the corner. Mirrors on the ceiling. A big-screen TV that dominated the far wall. A wet bar with champagne on ice. There was a fireplace on the opposite wall, and some kind of animal skin splayed out before the roaring fire.

And the bed.

Oh goodness, the bed.

It was one of those four-poster numbers, and the bedding was a rich wine velvet. Only, the posts had metal rings that Petty rather imagined were to secure shackles.

The three of them giggled.

"Best not forget the gift basket with condoms. We don't want more grandbabies until they want grandbabies!" Petty said, and zapped a giant basket full of various brands, flavors, and textures of condoms by the bed.

Jonquil scrunched up her face at a chair that was positioned by a writing desk. "Can't have any of that. There's only one bed, but there needs to be only one place to sit." She zapped the desk and chair out of existence.

Bluebonnet sighed happily. "Perfect."

"No, wait. I have one more trick up my sleeve," Jonquil said. She held up her hands, as if framing the television from a distance. Then she flicked her wand in a series of sharp motions. "That should do it."

"What did you do?" Bluebonnet asked. "Is it what I think it is?"

Jonquil crossed her arms. "Probably."

"Tell me!" Petty demanded.

Jonquil gave her a sly grin. "Let's just say the programming on every channel has been carefully curated."

"You didn't!" Petty said with a laugh. "Oh, our little darlings are in for it, aren't they?"

"Only if they're lucky!" Bon-Bon laughed.

"I think it's time we made our exit," Petty said as she whisked her sisters and herself out of the Love Nest.

Chapter 8

"*¡Hijo de puta!* What fresh hell is this?" Tomas swore as he put down their bags and took in the room.

There was so much happening in that space and so much that was wrong with every part of it. It looked like the set for a bad porno from 1983.

"Well, we were warned," Juniper sighed.

"How were we warned?"

"The Love Nest? We're lucky it's not worse."

Tomas considered. "You're right."

"Mm-hm. But look, we got complimentary champagne! We were able to order our food at the desk, and it's on the way. It's not that bad, really."

"You're not the one who has to sleep on the floor." He closed his eyes and shook his head.

"Don't be dumb. Why would you sleep on the floor? That bed is huge. We could both starfish on that thing and still not touch each other."

Except he wanted to touch her, and he was pretty sure she wanted to touch him, too. Sleeping in the same bed was not a good idea.

But when he looked at the floor, and remembered that news special where they investigated various hotel chains with a black light, there was actually no way he'd get any sleep. He'd have to sleep in the bathtub.

She nodded knowingly. "Remembering that black-light thing, huh?"

He nodded.

She hopped up on the bed, her feet dangling a little off the side. "Wow!" She bounced. "This is awesome." But then Juniper paused and studied him. "So I guess we should talk about it, huh?"

For the first time probably ever, he didn't want to. He wanted to pretend nothing had changed between them. It had been easy to make that pact where they promised to talk things out, but since there were zero palatable solutions on the horizon, talking about it wasn't going to help anything.

In fact, he was pretty sure talking about what they were feeling would only amplify the problem. More fuel for the fire.

"Yeah, I don't really want to, either." She took a deep breath. "Things are getting weird and awkward, and I don't want to lose us."

"We won't lose us."

"You didn't want to sleep in bed next to me. Did you think I was going to pounce on you in your sleep or something?"

He realized he'd hurt her feelings and felt like an ass. "No, of course not."

"I got the message last night," she said softly.

"Oh, hey . . ." Oh, hey, what? What was he going to say?

"Yeah. It's fine. I mean, we decided. And I didn't even mean it that way, but I guess I did?" She huffed. "I'm not expressing myself well. It was just . . ."

He had to go to her. Had to touch her. He had to make it okay. So he sat down next to her and put his arm around her. She was stiff against him until he pressed his lips to the crown of her head.

How was it she still smelled like hydrangeas?

"I understand. It was like that for me too, okay? It got twisted."

"Then why can't we talk about it?"

She looked up at him, and there was something in her eyes. It was a sadness, but it was something hungry, too. Something that threatened to devour them both.

"Because it only makes this burn that much hotter. Do you really want to hear what I'm feeling now? What I want? The things I think about doing to you?"

"Oh God, yes." Then she laughed. "I mean, no."

He raised a brow. "See what I mean?"

"I thought last night I'd damaged us, which is dumb, because nothing can damage us, right?"

Tomas knew that she was looking for reassurance from him that no matter what happened, they'd always have each other. He couldn't imagine his life without her. Didn't want to. "Right."

He didn't voice the other thoughts in his head. The ones that argued that if nothing could damage them, then why didn't they just let themselves have this thing that they both wanted so much?

What was he doing anyway? She'd invited him in last night. She'd made her choice. So why was he holding out? It was what he wanted, too. Juniper was a grown woman who could make her own choices.

Except those thoughts were splashes of ice-cold water down his spine.

It wouldn't be fair of him, that was why. And he knew it.

Juniper's feelings were worth more to him than a good fuck. Except, as good as it would be, Juniper could never be "just a fuck."

"Now, see what *I* mean? We needed to talk about it. It's better, right?"

"Right."

She leaned closer to him and pressed a kiss to his cheek. "I'm going to take a hot shower and put on some dry clothes. Maybe the food will be here by the time I'm out."

Juniper slid to the floor and padded toward the bathroom.

"Juniper?" he blurted.

"Yeah?" She turned to look at him over her shoulder.

"I don't think we're going to get out of this unscathed."

"Me either," she said softly.

"I know why I think that, but why do you?" He needed to hear her answer, but he was afraid of it, too.

"The same things we already talked about." She took another step toward the door. "And I think despite our best intentions, we're going to cross that line that we can't uncross. But luckily, we've agreed that we can always go forward. That we *will* always go forward."

She didn't wait for his reply but grabbed her bag and headed into the bathroom. Which now he had to wonder, was it a den designed for sin, too?

Of course, any room that Juniper was naked in was designed for sin.

"Hey," he called as he walked to stand close to the door.

"What now?" came her muffled reply.

"Is the bathroom like the rest of the room?"

"Come in and find out." The door opened.

He stepped through the opening, and saw Juniper was sadly and wonderfully not naked.

She arched a brow at him as if she knew the direction of his thoughts. Of course she did. She was teasing him. Daring them both to cross that line she'd been talking about.

If she'd been naked, he would have. If she still wanted to have that experience with him.

"You think you're funny," he said.

"You rose to the occasion."

And he had at that. He was harder than stone.

"This is surprisingly normal. I guess whoever designed the Love Nest thought lovers might need a reprieve."

"Or maybe, still waters run deep." She pulled open the cupboard underneath the sink to reveal . . . toilet paper.

"That's buck wild right there. Something to tell our friends about."

"Actually, it kind of is. Can you imagine telling anyone about this?"

He laughed. "I guess it is pretty funny."

"Okay, now get out." She shoved him back out through the door and closed it behind him.

He took the moment to observe the room again. It was odd that there was absolutely nowhere to sit except the bed.

Unless he wanted to splay himself out on that rug in front of the fireplace. Which wasn't a bad idea. Not the splaying part, but the fireplace. The air had taken a chill, and he didn't want Juniper to get sick.

It seemed to be a gas model, and he found a trio of remotes on the nightstand. He found one that had a little fire logo and deducted that was the one he wanted. After pressing a few buttons, he had a nice fire roaring in the hearth.

Tomas flopped on the bed and examined the other remotes. He found one that seemed to be for the bed.

He looked at the remote.

At the door to the bathroom.

Back to the remote.

Screw it.

He pressed the power button and the bed began to rattle like it was possessed. Just when he would've turned it off, something inside the mattress began to move and massaged precisely into that knot just under his shoulder blade.

In that moment, he decided he didn't care what the room looked like. He might just move in. A loud sigh escaped him and the pleasing motion continued.

When he sighed, the rattling of the bed made it sound like he was talking through a fan. It amused him. He hadn't done that since he was a kid, so he did it again. And again. And again.

Until he was lying there, letting the bed shake him like a

maraca and with one continuous moan coming out of his mouth punctuated by the shimmy of the bed.

"Uh, Tomas? Is it safe to come out?" Juniper called.

"Why wouldn't it be?" he called back, still making the voice-through-the-fan sound.

The door opened, and she stepped out. Her hair was wrapped up in a towel, and she was wearing a long T-shirt, her standard sleeping attire.

Which had somehow gone from comfortable to sexy. He found he liked it better than any lingerie.

"Come here! You have to try this," he said.

She laughed and got a running start to flop on the bed next to him.

Juniper must have landed on the TV remote because as soon as she hit the bed, the television flashed to life.

Normally, it wouldn't have given him pause.

Except, by slow increments he was becoming increasingly aware of what was on the screen.

The first moan had them both turning to look at each other, eyes wide and laughter welling up deep in their bellies.

"Oh no," Juniper said, with a giggle.

"I hope we don't get charged for a rental," Tomas said.

"Ever practical, my friend." She shook her head.

They both stayed prone and another moan whined from the television.

"I'm not looking," she said.

"Me either," Tomas said. "Guess we're just gonna let it play?"

"Turn it off!" She was still laughing.

"It's going to be awful. I know it is."

Sounds worse than moaning filled the room.

"*Madre de Dios*, where's the remote. I can't."

Juniper rolled around, trying to grab it from beneath her, but wasn't having much luck. They scrounged and squirmed until Tomas reached beneath her, his hand precariously beneath the hem of her nightshirt, but he pulled away as if burned.

They righted themselves, but when he lifted the remote to turn off the dirty movie, something unbelievable happened.

The music had changed from bow-chick-a-wow-wow to something elegant.

The background wasn't someone's green-carpeted romper room.

The images on the screen weren't actors.

They weren't posed for the camera.

The scene was set in Juniper's apartment. The two people on the screen were completely absorbed by each other. Every touch, every whisper, every kiss.

And those two people were Juniper and Tomas.

The only reasonable answer for this was lust poisoning. It had turned into something viral and it had infected his brain.

They'd never done those things on the screen.

That wasn't them.

It couldn't be.

This had to be a hallucination.

He looked over at Juniper, and her mouth had fallen open, her face was flushed, and Tomas could see her breath quicken by the rise and fall of her chest.

She turned to look at him. "I'm going to ask you a really stupid question. Whatever the answer is, I'm going to need you to not tease me."

He shook his head slowly. "Thank God. It's not just me."

"How is this happening?" she whispered.

"I don't know. Maybe we've been poisoned," he said softly. "Maybe they sprayed the sheets with some kind of erotic hallucinogen."

"But we're having the same hallucination."

"Maybe it's a glimpse of the future," he said.

"Oh," she gasped.

And the breathy noise she made after sounded just the same as the image on the television.

He wanted to hear it again.

They turned to look at each other.

She wet her lips.

And just when he was going to lean in to kiss her, she grabbed the remote from his hand and flung it at the television, shattering the screen, and it crashed down off the wall.

"Problem solved," she said.

"I guess that's one solution."

She bit her lip. "I'll chip in halfsies to pay for the damages?"

He nodded. "I was just going to get up and go turn it off."

Of course, that was most likely a lie he'd told himself. He couldn't have budged from that spot to do anything but recreate the carnality from the screen on the bed with her.

Juniper shrugged. "Well, it's fixed now."

Tomas was sure it was far from fixed.

"I should call down there and see about those french fries."

"And I should text the godmothers to tell them that we're not going to get in until tomorrow because of the storm."

"Although listen," he said, serious. "If that thing comes on again, storm or no storm, we're going to get the hell out of here."

"That is most definitely a deal."

They looked at one another at the same time. "Cursed," they said in unison, and laughed.

Just as Tomas reached over to pick up the in-room phone to call down to the desk, a knock sounded through the door.

"Room service."

Tomas hopped up off the bed and checked the security peephole before opening the door to let the server inside.

The server entered carrying a tray with a silver dome and beneath was a ridiculous mountain of thick-cut fries. Ketchup, mustard, and mayo were offered in silver dipping cups.

"Will there be anything else, sir?" the server asked.

"No, this is great. Thank you."

The server presented him with a leather-bound booklet that contained the check, and he signed it, sure to add a generous tip.

"I'm sorry about the TV. We had a bit of an accident. We'll take care of that before we leave."

"What TV, sir?" He sounded genuinely confused.

Tomas looked over to where the thing was clearly in pieces on the floor and gestured.

The server clearly didn't see it, or perhaps he was simply being polite.

"I'll take care of it with the desk."

"As you say." The server accepted the booklet back from him. "Thank you. Have a good evening and a pleasant stay."

The server exited, and Tomas closed the door behind him, engaging the security locks.

"Oh my God, what the hell was that?" Juniper cried. "How did he not see the TV?"

"Maybe he was trying to avoid a confrontation, but I'm telling you, one more weird thing in this place, and I'm out."

Juniper nodded. "Agreed."

A flash of lightning accompanied by a crash of thunder filled the room.

"Storm or no storm," he continued. "We can sleep in the car."

"It's freaky, but let's not be hasty. Your car is nice and everything, but this bed is better." She slipped her legs beneath the covers.

"You are not eating these fries in bed."

"Yes."

"No."

He put the tray on the floor on the "bearskin" rug. Tomas was pleased to have realized it was polyester instead of actual animal.

"I'm not sitting on that thing."

"It's nice. Come on. Picnic." He gestured to the fire.

She laughed. "I didn't even realize you had the fire going. I was a little distracted."

Juniper got out of the bed and joined him on the rug, sitting next to him with her legs crossed, and she popped a fry in her mouth.

"These are actually not bad."

"Do you want some of that champagne? It's complimentary." He shrugged. "Might as well."

"Yes, I think I do. I need some liquid fortification."

He leaned over and grabbed the bucket and glasses and poured for them. "Do you realize that we drink a lot of champagne?"

"There are worse habits." She ate another fry. "Your hair is still wet, and you're still in damp clothes. You should probably go shower."

"Ha. Nice try."

"What?" She wore an innocent expression.

"I'm eating these fries first."

She laughed. "I'm not going to steal your fries."

"You won't mean to. It'll start small. You'll see one you just have to have, and then another, and then another, and before you know it, they're all gone." He ate another one as he poured the champagne.

"As tacky as this place is, it's not too bad, you know?"

He looked around the room and realized the fire gave the place a bit of ambiance. Everything was softer. Colors, shadows, the overall effect of even the heart-shaped tub was subdued.

Just being there with Juniper and feeling like things were normal and good in his world once again was priceless.

Tomas realized his entire body had been clenched all day. His shoulders and neck were tight, and when his muscles released, he was suddenly aware he'd been holding his breath.

She'd been right. They had desperately needed to talk this out.

"Yeah." He nodded in agreement. "Not too bad."

She lay on her stomach and put her chin in the bowl of her hand. "I can't wait to show you Ever After."

"I don't remember it at all."

"Childhood memory is such a weird thing. Those moments that choose to tattoo themselves on your brain and those that just disappear as if they were nothing."

"Hey, that's pretty profound. It's almost like you should be a writer or something."

"Dork." She threw a fry at him.

He opened his mouth and caught it, much to his own surprise. "It's been a long time since I've seen the grandmothers. I think it's been years."

"It's only been a few months for me, and I miss them terribly." She threw another fry at him. "I'm glad you're coming with me. And not just because of the . . . *misunderstanding*."

"Me too. I'm really interested to see the Firefly Ceremony. Do they really believe that bugs can carry messages to the dead?"

"I know you don't believe, but your mama leaves cakes and wine on your grandmother's grave for Day of the Dead."

"That's more for herself than Abuela."

"Maybe it's the same for this. All grieving rituals are for the living."

"It's so strange that they still have fireflies in October."

"I think it's pretty magical."

"That's one of the things I love about you, Juniper. You see magic in everything, and you believe. No matter what, you keep believing."

"It's probably all kinds of naïve, but I don't care. I can't imagine living in a world where there's no wonder." She rolled onto her back. "No awe. What an ugly place."

Tomas considered her words carefully. He couldn't remember the last time he'd found wonder in the world. The last time he'd been filled with awe.

Yes, he could. It had been at the benefit when he'd seen her in that dress.

All of the wonder in his world, all of the awe, it was all wrapped up in Juniper.

"Maybe I'll find something to marvel at in Ever After."

"Probably not." She laughed. "It's all fairy-tale kitsch. You'll hate every second of it. Except the food."

He didn't know why, but her response left him cold. Even though he was lying right next to her, Tomas had never felt more alone.

Chapter 9

The look on Tomas's face when they drove into the city limits of Ever After confirmed her statement from the night before.

He looked completely disgusted.

Of course, his displeasure might've been slightly influenced by his inability to see any of the signs or turns leading to Ever After.

Juniper would've been worried he'd had some sort of health event, if not for the fact he seemed to be able to see everything else just fine.

"Are you kidding me with this?" He gestured to the sight of the town square and all the quaint and whimsically styled shops.

"I think it's fantastic."

"Of course you do."

"You're not going to be like this with the grandmothers, are you?" She eyed him.

"No. Never," he swore.

She crossed her arms over her chest. Juniper knew that he would find Ever After to be cheesy, but there was something about his reaction that rubbed her the wrong way.

It was okay that Happily Ever After wasn't his thing.

Wait, maybe that was the problem. She kept telling herself it was okay that it wasn't in his particular wheelhouse, but what about how she felt about it? Wasn't that okay, too?

Juniper studied him further with a hard eye.

"I can feel that stare in my kidneys. What's up?"

"Just thinking."

"Obviously."

She decided to just tell him. "We've spent a lot of time focusing on your opinions about love and commitment. Your thoughts are not a secret. It's fine that we don't think the same way about them, but I feel like I have to qualify my opinions to you. Apologize for . . ." She gestured out the window. "Explain that I know how hokey it is but that I love it anyway. It's not hokey. It's hope. It's love. It's all the good things that humans are supposed to feel. It's okay if you don't want them, but I do. So stop shitting on them."

He pulled into the grandmothers' driveway, and when he put the car in park, he turned to look at her. "I never meant to do that. I'm sorry."

"I know it's coming at you from all directions. I'm sure you feel under attack. The grandmothers and our mothers, your bosses . . ."

"That doesn't mean I should take it out on you. Or be derisive about the things that matter to you."

She swallowed hard. He understood, and she wasn't sure if that made it better or worse. "Thank you."

"So you forgive me?" He gave her a half smirk.

"Just be nice to the grandmothers. I love them dearly, and they love you, too."

"I promise." Tomas squeezed her hand.

She peered out of the window to see if the grandmothers were going to pounce on them, or if they were going to let the two of them make their own way into the cottage.

Tomas must've been thinking the same thing because he said, "I see a flash of pink in the window."

"That will be Petty."

"I thought her name was Petunia?"

"It is. But Petty is Petty for a reason."

"Because she's petty?"

"You have no idea."

"Good thing I don't have any illicit intentions." His half smirk bloomed into a grin.

"That will be what she considers a problem, I'm sure. Are you ready to be absolutely coddled and adored?"

"Always." He got out of the car, and came around to open her door.

Juniper could see the grandmothers fussing and fretting by the windows waiting for them to come inside.

She couldn't wait to hug them all.

The door to the little cottage opened as they approached and Petty stood there, holding out her arms, looking just as she had the last time she'd seen her. Right down to the same pink dress with lace trim, and the fat, loose bun on top of her head. Come to think of it, Petty, Jonquil, and Bluebonnet never seemed to age.

For that, Juniper was grateful. She didn't know what she'd ever do without her grandmothers.

Juniper found she wanted to launch herself into Petty's arms the same as she had when she was little. It was like that every time she saw her. She couldn't wait to be wrapped in grandmotherly goodness.

When Petty hugged her tight, all of her cares and worries flitted away like busy little bees with better things to do to occupy their time. She was quickly passed to Bluebonnet, who petted her hair and kissed her forehead. From there, it was Jonquil's turn, and she gave Juniper a mighty squish.

She saw that Tomas had been subjected to the same treatment, and he took it in stride, smiling and laughing and generally allowing the godmothers to make a perfect fuss.

They ushered Juniper and Tomas inside to the table in the kitchen that was covered in wedding-planning frippery.

"Oh, is this for Betina's wedding?" Juniper asked.

"Yes! You did bring those copies of *Phoenix*, right?" Bluebonnet wore a hopeful look.

"Of course. They're in the car. I can't believe she wanted to give those as bridesmaids' gifts. I'm so happy to be included in her Happily Ever After," Juniper said as she thumbed through some of the drawings of the bouquet and the dress.

"Did you both remember to bring costumes for the Firefly Ceremony?" Petty asked.

Bluebonnet perked. "That reminds me. When you two go out for lunch, you can drop them off with Rosebud at the dress shop. She said she'd get them cleaned and pressed and ready to go. Top priority." Bluebonnet grinned. "Aside from the bride, of course."

"Of course," Juniper readily agreed. "Wait, we're going out for lunch?"

"Yes, dear. We've fallen a bit behind, so we're going to need to run to the shop to finish a few things before tonight. We thought you could show Tomas around and have a nice lunch at Pick 'n' Axe." Jonquil nodded.

She found an illustrated plan for the Firefly Ceremony and sighed happily. "I can't wait for this."

"So tell me again about how it works?" Tomas asked, peering over her shoulder.

"We spend the day of Samhain crafting our messages to our beloveds on the other side. We write them on leaves and burn them in a great fire. As the fire burns down, and the smoke fills the air, we release thousands of fireflies that carry those messages in the smoke to the beyond," Bluebonnet said with a soft reverence.

"It was always my favorite thing as a child and why I never cared much about trick-or-treating. This was where the real treat was," Juniper said.

"And you knew you were going to get treats anyway." Petty patted her on the shoulder.

"Speaking of treats, who needs an ice cream soda?" Jonquil asked.

"I do! Pumpkin, if you have it," Juniper said.

"Actually, we do have pumpkin, but we have a lot of cherries, too." Petty looked at Jonquil and Bluebonnet, and they all shared a secret smile.

"An embarrassment of riches, really," Jonquil replied.

"Okay, cherry it is, then." Juniper was easily swayed. Everything the grandmothers made was delicious.

"Such a good girl," Bluebonnet said. "Tomas, would you like one?"

"It's a little early for sweets for me."

Juniper furrowed her brow. "You eat pancakes and waffles at breakfast. Those are sweets. And don't even at me with that whole-grain nonsense."

He laughed. "I just can't ice cream yet."

"Hmm," Petty said, as if she'd just discovered something very sad.

"Mm-hm," Jonquil echoed.

"What?" Juniper asked.

Bluebonnet nodded sagely. "I see."

"What?" Tomas was obviously curious as well.

"Tell us, how did you find the drive?" Petty asked.

What did the drive have to do with anything?

"Fine," Tomas said.

"Really?" Petty pressed her lips together. "No complications? None?"

"I did have some trouble seeing a few signs," Tomas admitted.

"Hmm," Petty said again.

"Mm-hm," Jonquil added.

Bluebonnet just sighed.

Juniper's attention wandered back to the wedding plans. "Wait, why is the castle black? Don't tell me you painted the thing just for the wedding?"

"Oh, no! That's new construction," Petty said. "Castle Blackheart."

"Blackheart?" Tomas asked in a disbelieving tone. "That's not very Happily Ever After, is it?"

Petty pushed her glasses up on the bridge of her nose. "I think it is."

"Not everyone's Happily Ever After looks the same. Some are white castles and roses, some are bats and moonlight, and others are something else entirely," Jonquil counseled.

"What made you three decide to go into the wedding-planning business?" Tomas asked.

"I love this question," Bluebonnet said as she gathered the things together to make the ice cream sodas.

"Love, of course," Petty said. "That's the simple answer."

"But what specifically about love," Tomas prodded.

"Why not love?" Petty replied. "Why does there have to be something specific about it?"

"It's too broad an answer," Tomas answered. "It's generic."

"I don't know, what is it about dissolving unions that used to be made of love that appealed to you in your chosen profession?" Jonquil asked.

"That's easy. I wanted to make sure no one went through what my mother did when my father left us. I wanted to make sure people lived up to the promises they made to each other."

Bluebonnet handed Juniper her soda but then put her arms around Tomas. "Oh, honey. You're doing so good, aren't you?"

From anyone else, that might have sounded like condescension, but from Bluebonnet it was all care and concern.

"I like to think I am," Tomas replied softly.

Petty studied him for a long time before she spoke. So long that Juniper wondered if Petty was considering smiting him. She wasn't sure what her grandmother would do to him, but she knew in her bones it would be ugly.

"The same can be said of what we do. Love is the source

of all things, my little darling. We must plant it, cultivate it, feed it, and sprinkle it all over the world so it can continue to grow. Giving people their dream weddings, bringing friends and families together to celebrate love, to bask in the love they have for each other while they embark on new journeys . . . it's a ray of light in a scary and unsure world," Petty said.

"I can be on board with that," Tomas said.

"Since you're going to marry our granddaughter, I should hope so," Jonquil chastised him.

Juniper had forgotten for a moment that the grandmothers thought that they were engaged.

"Sweetie pie, can you come with me for a second?" Jonquil nodded toward the door.

"Sure." Juniper got up from the table and did her best not to look at Tomas as she abandoned him to deal with Petty and Bluebonnet all on his own.

Jonquil led her outside onto the back deck, where she handed Juniper a watering pot and took one for herself and began to water the herbs that sat in various pots and planters.

"I wanted to ask you, did you manage to get the ring off? Or has it been stuck on your finger since we talked?"

"Stuck."

Jonquil paused her watering and took Juniper's left hand to inspect the ring and her fingers. "It doesn't seem to be too tight. There's no swelling in your fingers."

"No, it's mostly fine. It feels weird to have it there, though."

"It's a beautiful piece. But I can't say I'd be too thrilled if I couldn't get it off." She clucked her displeasure. "Having him try to take it off didn't help, either?"

Juniper flushed, thinking of the incident in the office. "Zero help. In fact, it was awful."

"What happened?"

Juniper considered telling Jonquil the gritty details but decided that maybe her sweet grandmother didn't need to hear about that particular misadventure.

"It just didn't go well," she said.

"Hmm," Jonquil murmured.

"You've been doing that all day, Gramma. Out with it. What do you know that you're not telling me?"

Jonquil smirked. "I'm old. There's lots of things I know that I'm not telling you. That you just have to learn for yourself."

"Hmm," Juniper replied.

"Hmm, indeed."

"Were you ever in love, Gramma?"

"Lots of times." A soft look crossed her face.

Juniper debated this next question, but against her better judgment, she asked anyway. "How did you know?"

"You just know."

"No, but . . . you can love someone and not be *in* love with them." Juniper sniffed. "What I mean to say is, there can be . . . physical attraction, mutual respect, and love that's not romantic love. So what's the difference between that and true love?"

"It's about your soul, baby. The way the parts of yourselves that no one else sees fit together like puzzle pieces. Your broken pieces are jagged to the wrong person, but to the right one, they fit with their pieces to build a whole new beautiful picture."

"It seems so easy in the books that I write." She poured a bit of water on the rosemary.

"It is, and you do it so well." Jonquil gave her a soft smile. "It's because you can see all the puzzle pieces. You craft these characters to belong to each other. Don't you think fate has done the same to you?"

Juniper dropped the watering can, and it bounced on the deck before splashing their feet. "Holy shit, that's terrifying." Juniper bit her lip. "Sorry!"

As she bent down to pick it up, and was going to refill it with the garden hose, Jonquil put a hand on her arm.

"Why is that terrifying?"

"Because I have actually zero clue what I'm doing when I start. I just sit down and the words come from somewhere, I don't know where, and the story appears on the page. It doesn't stop in the conscious part of my brain."

"Yet, somehow, it's still whole. It still hits every mark, and your lovers earn their Happily Ever Afters," Jonquil reassured her. "Are you having doubts about Tomas?"

Juniper waited for the recrimination, for empty platitudes, but reminded herself that her grandmothers weren't like that. Jonquil was the most practical of her grandmothers, and if anyone would understand, it would be her.

Deep down, she knew all three of them would understand. Sometimes, they just got so wrapped up in their matchmaking and wanting good things for everyone around them, they tended to get a bit hyperfocused.

"We have different opinions," she said.

"I see." Jonquil took the watering can from her and put it on the railing. "Different opinions lead to different perspectives and that's wonderful. It can open up a whole new world for both of you. The question isn't about opinions, but about morality."

"What do you mean?"

"Do you have different moralities? You can have an exciting relationship by stepping into each other's shoes and experiencing your shared world and space in different ways. Sometimes, I think that makes for the strongest relationships. Differing moralities, however, will make you incompatible. Is Tomas a good man?"

"He is the best of men, Gramma. The very best. He refused to accept a client who he believed was a bad person. He didn't want to use his skills to give that person an advantage over someone who needed it more."

Jonquil smiled softly. "Then it's about what you want, isn't it? Does he have different ideas of what the future should look like?"

While she'd expected Jonquil to understand, she hadn't expected that she'd see so clearly.

She nodded.

"You know what you have to do here, don't you?"

"Talk about it." Juniper sighed.

"Not necessarily. Not if you've already talked it to death. Sometimes, you just have to let things play out until the point of no return. Then you have to make a choice. Either this is something you can live with, or it's not."

"I don't want to imagine my life without him."

"I don't want to poop on your parade, my love, but you may have to."

This was definitely not the advice she'd been expecting, and it was like a punch to the solar plexus. "What?"

To her surprise, Jonquil smiled. "Follow your heart. Have faith in yourself. Even when it's scary. If this doesn't work out the way you wanted it to, the way we all want it to, then make peace with the fact that it's what's best for you both."

"I don't think I can be that Zen, Gramma."

"Oh, it'll suck, for sure." Jonquil grinned wider. "But such is life. Ten years from now, you're going to look back on this moment and you'll know I was right. Wherever you are, however this works out, it will be where you're meant to be."

"What if where I'm meant to be is not with Tomas and I still can't get this ring off?"

Jonquil laughed so hard she wheezed. "Oh, sweet girl. You don't worry about that."

Juniper couldn't help but worry about it. She'd become a quivering ball of anxiety. It was ridiculous. Although, Jonquil's sage words soothed her and shored up her aching heart.

"Thanks, Gramma Jonquil. You're the best."

"That's what I'm here for, don't you know?" She patted

Juniper's arm. "Run along now and finish your ice cream soda. Then you can take Tomas into town and show him around."

"Juniper, lovie!" Bluebonnet called from the door. "We forgot to tell you. We had some rain damage upstairs, so we booked one of the mushroom cottages for you and Tomas. You can drop your things off and get settled in."

Petty poked her head out behind Bon-Bon. "I have an idea. Tomas said he might need to return some client calls tomorrow. While he's doing that, would you like to help with the wedding planning?"

Juniper was thrilled at the idea. Especially excited that she was being asked to help with someone else's wedding and not her supposed wedding to Tomas. "I'd love to!"

"Fantastic! You'll get to meet Zuri," Bluebonnet said.

"She moved here with a broken heart and married Phillip Charming, the B and B owner," Jonquil said with a knowing spark in her eyes.

"I suppose you three had your paws in that?" Juniper asked.

"Us?" Petty said, faking an innocent expression. "Of course we did." She laughed.

"He used to date Gramma Petty. It's how she got the nickname Petty," Bon-Bon stage-whispered.

"I . . . how old is he?" Juniper blurted. "I mean, it's just . . . you know. You're my grandmothers."

Petty wasn't offended. She simply laughed. "I promise I'll tell you the whole story before this visit is over."

Bluebonnet hugged herself. "Oh, I can't wait to tell you everything."

Juniper didn't know why, but she suddenly had the most overwhelming sensation that everything was about to change for her in a big way.

Chapter 10

Tomas had promised Juniper to rein in his skepticism, but he couldn't help it. Ever After was beyond ridiculous.

It wasn't just the kitschy shops, although that gave him big eye-rolling energy. It was the mushroom cottages that looked like something out of a cartoon; it was the names of all the people running the shops; it was even the freaking woodland animals who flittered to and fro and seemed to understand every word he said. Someone had put in a lot of effort to train these creatures.

He hated it.

It was like a fairy tale threw up and this was what was left.

No, that was wrong. If it was just what was left, he could work with that. One could say that his career was made up of what was left after fairy tales threw up. No, this was taking all that ugly and painting a pretend veneer over that puke with frosting.

His stomach churned thinking about it. Tomas decided he needed a better analogy. All this talk about vomit was doing a number on his guts.

Although, when he turned to look at Juniper, her eyes were bright, her face was flushed, and he could see the happiness glowing on her face. She loved it here.

For her sake, he tried to tamp it down. Tried to push his negative thoughts back into the far reaches of his mind where they wouldn't intrude. Juniper had asked him, specifically, to just let her have this. She hadn't asked him to suspend disbelief, she'd simply asked him to not destroy hers.

But he couldn't help it.

"We should drop off our costumes with Rosebud before we go to Pick 'n' Axe," Juniper said, pulling him out of his thoughts.

"Pick 'n' Axe, huh?"

"They have fantastic food. You'll love it. Everything is super close together. It'll just take us a minute."

"On the plus side, it looks like we'll get in a lot of walking." He pulled the car into the parking space in front of the single most ridiculous cottage he'd ever seen.

It was squat, fat, and looked exactly like a giant replica of a fairy-tale mushroom. Or something that had been yanked right out of *Super Mario Bros.* The main part of the cottage was the white stem, the roof the red-and-white mushroom cap. Bright, cascading flowers hung from beds attached to each window, and he had trouble reining in his disdain.

The interior wasn't much better. Once inside, there was a small metal spiral stairway that led to the upstairs where he assumed the bedrooms would be.

Madre de Dios, he hoped it would be more than one bedroom.

The hotel room had almost killed him.

A big smile bloomed on Juniper's face. "I could stay here forever. Look at this!" she cried, running over to the small, white distressed desk by the window.

"I can see you've already set up shop."

Her happiness was infectious, and he found himself smiling along with her.

"Just wait until you see upstairs."

"Have you been in this one before?" he asked, curious.

"No, but I'm sure it's going to be fantastic."

A fat cardinal, fatter than any bird had any right to be and still fly, sat on the sill of an open window. It looked at him, cocking his head from side to side as if the bird couldn't make heads or tails of *him*.

Juniper caught sight of the bright red beast and cooed, "Who's the prettiest boy?"

The bird looked at her and hopped back and forth on the sill, seemingly pleased with her attention. Of course, the hopping was more like the bouncing of a giant red ball. That cardinal was ridiculous, like everything else in Ever After.

He chirped a little tune as he looked at Juniper.

"You! That's who! You're the prettiest boy. What a pretty song. Thank you."

As if the silly creature understood her. He shook his head.

Juniper darted up the stairs with her bag, and Tomas followed behind her, doing his level best not to look at her delectable ass.

On second thought, he should've waited to follow her up the narrow, winding staircase. His own fault, he supposed.

The bird chirped, and it sounded like a chortle.

Of course that had to be his imagination. Maybe Ever After was starting to get to him. He shook his head and continued up the stairs. To the right was an open door and beyond was a bedroom where Juniper had launched herself onto a dainty white bed and proceeded to spread herself out like a starfish on top of the quilt.

For a moment, he considered launching himself on the bed next to her, and in the past, he'd have done it without a second thought. Only this wasn't the past. This was now.

She propped herself up on her elbows to look at him.

When he met her eyes, time stopped.

They were wide, guileless, and yet, so inviting. As she smiled wider, he was sure that would bring him back to his senses, but it didn't. It only made her more appealing.

His legs moved without his permission.

Bastards.

They launched him onto the bed with her, and before he

knew what was happening, they were a tangle of limbs on a creaky, old bed, and he wasn't sure it would hold them both.

Juniper laughed. It was loud and deep. Hearty. She didn't hesitate to curl right against his chest like a kitten completely sure of her welcome.

"I'm glad to see you getting into the spirit. Although, I think we're too old to be jumping up and down on this bed," she said.

"You know, for the grandmothers being so keen on matchmaking, you'd have thought they'd have stocked the place with sturdier beds."

She squeaked a laugh that became a full-blown cackle. "You're right." Juniper looked up at him with her dark eyes full of mischief. "Wouldn't they just die if I said so?"

Tomas considered the old dears and tried to imagine the expression on each of their faces. "I don't know, I don't think they'd be quite as scandalized as we'd like to believe."

"You're probably right." She turned to look at him. "But you know what? I think that's fantastic."

"You do?" He wasn't sure he wanted to hear this, but curiosity had him shifting, so he was propped on his hand and looking down at her.

"Yeah. They're old, not dead. And that's one of the best parts of life, right? Connecting with other humans?"

"Connecting . . . ," he considered. "That's one way to put it."

"Okay, fine. I'll be blunt. Sex is one of the great experiences of being human. It's not the only one. It's not even the most important one, but it's pretty great. Why should age mean you stop experiencing the world and the people around you?"

Tomas gazed down at her face, which was a mistake. He was so close to her now. Close enough that if he wasn't vigilant, it would be so easy to kiss her.

And oh, how he wanted to kiss her. He'd start with her lips, then he'd taste that tender spot where her jaw met the edge of her throat, and he'd travel down to her collarbone, then to the plump top curve of her cleavage while his hands were filled with her breasts—

He had to exorcise these thoughts from his head. It was like he was possessed by a lust demon or something.

Tomas found his hand on her face, his thumb grazing the edge of her jaw. "We're not even old and we're missing out, aren't we?"

Christ, but his voice was a harsh whisper, choked by this damn desire.

"I don't know if waiting for the right person could be called missing out," she said quietly. "You can have all the sex in the world, and it can even be good sex, but for me, without that deeper connection, it pales in comparison."

"Tell me, which of your lovers did you feel this with?"

"None," she confessed.

"Then how do you know?"

"I just know."

For a second, only a single moment, he wanted to be the one who showed her. He wanted to be the one who proved her right. And Tomas wanted to know for himself, too. He wanted to feel everything she promised. Juniper knew him better than he knew himself, and if he was honest, he'd never let any of his partners past all of his defenses. Not like Juniper.

He wondered what it would be like to do more than fuck. To be naked in all ways with her.

It terrified him.

It intrigued him.

His cock was rock-hard, and it was getting more difficult to resist the siren call of this thing between them.

Her eyes were suddenly half-lidded, and the way she looked at him was a blatant invitation. Her chest rose and fell with an increased rhythm that was evidence of her desire for him.

How long could they hold out?

"I'll prove it to you," she whispered.

He wanted those words, they were the answer to all his desires, but he knew he should say he didn't need any kind of proof. That what was true for her was not a universal truth and that—

"How?" he said, before his logical mind could save him.

She didn't speak. Instead, she pulled him down to her, and it was like being caught in an undertow. Tomas couldn't have resisted if he'd wanted to. He knew they were both drowning, but it would be a good death.

Their lips met in a rush of fire, and he found himself positioned between her thighs, pushing her down into the bed, with his hands eagerly questing over flesh that was all at once both familiar and new.

Yes, he felt this kiss on a cellular level. Deep, primal, and it was, in fact, better than any other kiss he'd ever tasted.

The way she melted beneath him, the give-and-take of her tongue against his, and the fugue of sensation that overwhelmed him.

She pulled back. "Tell me that wasn't the best kiss you've ever had. I dare you."

His mind scrambled for something witty to say, some sharp sword of verbiage to duel with her, but his brain had mostly shut down.

"If I say it wasn't, you'll never forgive me."

"Wasn't it?" she demanded.

He grinned. "Of course it was, Juniper, but—"

"But we have to go drop off the costumes with Rosebud and go get some lunch." She shoved him off her and hopped to her feet. "You ready to go?"

It was as if the last few moments hadn't even happened. He knew it was for the best, but how long until it wouldn't be?

Tomas wasn't thinking about that culmination with fear. It was a longing that burned deep inside of him. He wanted Juniper more than he'd ever wanted another woman.

It was obvious she wanted him, too.

He'd already known it would be good between them, he didn't need proof. Neither did she. She'd wanted to kiss him as badly as he'd wanted to kiss her. They were speeding past the boundaries they'd set for themselves just like they both knew they would.

"*Corazoncita*, you are playing with fire," he warned her.

Tomas watched as she gave a delicate shiver and then the corners of her mouth turned up in a smirk. "Am I?"

"Two can play this game, and I play to win," he said, as if she needed the warning.

She licked her lips. "Do you think I play to lose, Tomas? I know exactly who you are."

"Then you know exactly why we should talk about this now."

"I'm tired of talking. At some point, we just have to let things unfold as they're meant to." She fiddled with the ring on her finger, absently twisting it in circles.

"If we were letting things unfold as they were meant to, you wouldn't be over there while I'm over here."

Her smirk became a full-bodied grin. "Oh yes, I would. Do you really think all you have to do is say that you want me and I'll fall on my back like a desperate turtle?" She crossed her arms over her chest. "Please, son. Do you know how many times I've written this exact situation?"

"I'm a real flesh-and-blood man, Juniper. I'm no storybook hero."

"Yes, you are. If you weren't, we'd have already had each other six ways from Sunday and a couple bonus rounds."

The confidence in her words terrified him. The weight of her expectation, her belief in him crushed his ribs together.

"That's too much to expect from any man."

"But you're not any man, are you?"

It was hard to argue that without telling on himself. If he said he was just any man, he'd be devaluing himself. He'd worked hard to be the person he'd become. As her best friend, he wanted to be the one she trusted, the one she depended on. He'd proven over and over again that he was everything she believed about him. Yet, somehow, he still found some part inside himself lacking.

He didn't know what to say.

"Am I still playing with fire?"

"You're going to burn us both," he promised.

"If you're not already on fire, then I'm doing something wrong."

She'd been right to try and take the easy exit. Neither of them were ready for where this conversation was going to go. Not yet. Not even as much as he longed for it.

"So what do you usually eat at Pick 'n' Axe?"

She gave him a soft look. "We need to drop the costumes off first."

Something in her voice told him the night of the masque was when it would happen. When there would be no turning back.

Hell, he knew there was already no turning back. No rewind. They'd tried that, and it had failed spectacularly.

Why was he fighting this so hard? They were adults. They'd been honest with each other. Why shouldn't they enjoy each other if that's what they both wanted?

Well, he knew *damn* well why.

Tomas followed her downstairs, and the fat red cardinal was still on the windowsill.

"Such a pretty boy," Juniper said to him again, and the cardinal ruffled his feathers and preened for her. "I wonder if there are any snacks in the kitchen we could give him?"

"He doesn't look like he needs any more snacks."

The cardinal's head seemed to swivel as if he were an owl so that he could fix his black eyes on Tomas.

Tomas held up his hands. "Whoa, sorry there, little guy. My bad."

He didn't think birds could sniff with indignation, but this one did.

Juniper found a tin of birdseed and a small scoop, and she shoveled a bit onto the sill for the creature. The bird would eat a bite, then glare at Tomas, eat another bite, and glare at Tomas.

"I think you may have made an enemy," Juniper said.

"It's almost like he understands me."

"Animals understand more than we think. But they also understand the universal language."

"Love?" Tomas snorted.

"Kindness, jackass. But same thing."

He noticed that *her* feathers seemed a bit ruffled, too, and he couldn't help but reach out for her hand and squeeze. It was as much for her as it was for him.

She squeezed back, and for a moment, everything was right in his world.

Until they stepped outside and began the short trek to the dress shop, where the dressmaker would see to cleaning their costumes and getting them ready for the masque.

When his foot touched the grass, it was like a record scratch in a movie when all the action stops and all attention is focused on someone who is usually committing a mighty faux pas. All the animals stopped what they were doing to focus on him.

Squirrels stopped throwing nuts at each other to look at him, birds landed in branches silently, two dogs and a cat on leashes in the park stopped what they were doing to stare at him. He'd swear even the bugs had gone silent.

"What did you do?" Juniper asked.

"I don't know, but I'm sorry. Heartily sorry."

A loud squawk sounded perilously close to his ear. He turned, just in time to see the fat-bastard cardinal attempting to fly over around his head and struggling mightily. The cardinal wheezed, and it was only because of his wheeze that he saw the horror the bird was about to inflict on his person.

The cardinal had obviously eaten his share of gooseberries before the seed Juniper put out for him, and Tomas knew this because the bird had dropped a giant, wet, green bomb that was headed straight for him.

He ducked out of the way, and the poo missile landed by his foot, resulting in another vengeful squawk from the bird.

"I swear he did it on purpose!"

"I think he did," Juniper agreed. "Looks like Ever After feels the same way about you that you do about it."

"Towns can't have feelings."

Juniper looked around across the green grass at all the animals that were still staring at Tomas. "I wouldn't be too sure of that. Ever After isn't like other places."

"Yeah, other places don't have people to train their 'wild' animals." He scanned the skies for the cardinal.

"Maybe you should let me carry the garment bags? Just in case the squirrels get froggy," she teased.

He could feel their beady eyes focused on him like lasers.

"No, I've got it," he said, but he started walking at a brisk pace toward the dress shop. Or what he assumed was a dress shop. The building that looked like a giant dress was his first clue.

Juniper shrugged and walked with him toward the building.

He couldn't get out of this town fast enough.

Chapter 11

Juniper didn't know if Tomas was going to make it.

She'd never seen the animals take such a dislike to someone. If they were out to get him, there was no way he was going to survive the long weekend with the charade intact.

Of course, maybe that would be for the best.

Things had quickly spiraled out of their control.

She considered what had happened between them only moments ago. Part of her wished they were back in that moment now. Juniper studied his profile and found she no longer saw just her best friend.

Now that she'd seen him as a man, no . . . not just a man. But a *man*. She couldn't unsee it. She couldn't stop thinking about the shape of his mouth and what it felt like to melt under his kiss. To have that hard, sensual mouth on her body. His strong, sure hands all over her skin.

It occurred to her all those nights they'd spent together so innocently they could have been doing a lot of other things.

Delicious and wicked things.

Something deep in her belly clenched, and heat bloomed, an aching, visceral need.

Yes, if she could go back to that moment in the bedroom, she wouldn't have stopped for banter. Or to let themselves talk each other out of what they both wanted. Instead, she'd be brain-dead with bliss right now.

At least they'd have gotten something out of all this angst.

His warning echoed in her head. She was playing with fire? Juniper didn't want to play anymore. She just wanted to burn.

She stuffed it all down as they approached the door to Cinderella and Fella and put on a happy face for Rosebud.

When they entered the shop, a small bell overhead gently announced their entry. Juniper couldn't help but notice the place smelled like sugar cookies.

Rosebud came to the front of the shop to greet them. She was willowy and blond, with an absolutely perfect complexion, of which Juniper had always been slightly jealous. Stick pins and safety pins were all stuck haphazardly in the otherwise lovely and delicate pink dress she wore, but she had a large, unhurried smile for them.

"Juniper! It's so lovely to see you! And who is this fine gentleman? It can't be our little Tomas?" She held open her arms and embraced them each in turn.

It occurred to Juniper that like the grandmothers, Rosebud seemed ageless. When she was a little girl, Rosebud had sewn her frocks to play dress up in and had allowed her free rein in the little dress shop.

"I'm sorry, I don't remember you," Tomas apologized.

Rosebud seemed to take it in stride. "You will." She turned to Juniper. "Bon-Bon tells me that you two have quite the busy day ahead, so I won't keep you too long. Let's see those costumes!"

Tomas presented the garment bags, and Rosebud directed him to carry them to the dress rack, where she unzipped them and admired what was inside.

"Oh, this suit is gorgeous." She fingered the material. "The dress matches the pocket square? You guys are so cute." Rosebud looked up. "Promise me you'll let me design your dress and tux for the wedding?"

"I don't—" she began.

"We'd be honored," Tomas interrupted.

Juniper desperately wanted to look at him but didn't dare

because she wouldn't be able to keep the *What the eff?* expression off her face.

"Of course we would," she agreed. "We haven't set a date yet, and it might be some time."

She waved her hand in a way that was reminiscent of Gramma Petty. "Pish posh. It's no never mind to me, my darlings. Love does what it will. I just want to be part of it when you do."

"Definitely," Juniper replied.

"I can see it already. How do you feel about pink?"

Juniper arched a brow.

"Obviously not a garish pink, but something soft and pale. It would contrast so beautifully with your black hair."

"As long as you don't put me in gray, I'm fine," Tomas said.

This time she couldn't help it. She whipped her head around to fix him with a stare.

He shrugged. "What? Gray looks awful on me."

"I would never," Rosebud promised. "I'm thinking a moss green for you."

Juniper rolled her eyes.

Rosebud took her hand and examined her ring. "Oh, the godmothers were right. This ring is truly something special."

"It's magic," Juniper said. "Or so Mama Estella says."

Rosebud clasped her palms around Juniper's hand. "She is absolutely correct."

For a moment, it seemed as if Rosebud was trying to tell her something more, but then the moment was gone, and Rosebud dropped her hand and turned her attention back to their costumes for the masque.

"I'll get these taken care of, my darlings, and you're going to look amazing the night of the masque. I promise. It's going to be the best night of your lives." She grinned. "Aside from your wedding night, of course."

"Of course," Tomas agreed.

Just then, the fat cardinal that had been harassing Tomas

earlier flew in through an open window and landed on Rosebud's shoulder.

"There's my sweet Bronx!" Rosebud kissed his head.

"That beast is yours?" Tomas blurted.

Instead of taking offense, Rosebud laughed. "He's a bit on the grumpy side these days. He didn't crap on you, did he?"

"He tried."

"Bronx, that's not nice."

But the smug bird simply rubbed his head against her cheek.

"Let's get you some tasty grubs, okay?"

"I already fed him some birdseed," Juniper volunteered.

She'd swear the bird narrowed his eyes at her words. But that was just silly. Wasn't it?

"That's okay. Bronx works hard, don't you, boo?"

He continued nuzzling Rosebud's cheek.

"Make sure you stop in the bakery! It's under new management. Red and Gran have moved out to the country because Gran wanted to retire. Although, she's performing weddings now. Anyway, I think you'll really like Gwen."

"I can totally see Gran performing weddings. I'll miss her Aztec cocoa, though."

"I bet if you asked nicely, Gran and Red would be thrilled to have you out at the ranch for cocoa."

"Red and Gran? You guys take this fairy-tale thing pretty seriously, eh?" Tomas said.

Rosebud obviously wasn't bothered by this, either. "You'll see, little Tomas." She patted his cheek with a soft expression on her face. "You'll see."

From the way his brow began to climb up into the beautiful dark waves of his hair, Juniper knew it was time to go.

Beautiful dark waves? Hell on a cracker, she needed to get herself together.

"I think we're going to be late for lunch. We better go." She linked her arm through Tomas's.

Rosebud grinned. "If you're going to Pick 'n' Axe, make sure you try their mutton stew. It's the best thing you've ever eaten."

"We will! Thank you again!" Juniper dragged him toward the door.

"That fucking bird," Tomas muttered.

The bird in question squawked loudly, almost as if he'd heard and understood Tomas's words.

"Juniper, slow down."

"Nope. Not until we get to the pub."

"I'm not going to lose it. I promise."

"I don't know, I think you were pretty close."

"Not on Rosebud, even though it was slightly condescending of her to treat us like we're children."

"I think to her, we probably are. Don't you remember that summer you came when she let us play in the attic of the shop?"

Tomas stopped walking. "You know, I don't remember anything about visiting Ever After. Nothing. It's almost like it didn't happen."

"That's really weird."

"Nothing could be as weird as that hotel."

"I don't know. Just wait until you meet Shandy."

"What's Shandy, besides a beer?" Tomas shook his head. "Wait, let me guess. He owns the pub."

"He does! Along with his six brothers."

"For fuck's actual sake," Tomas muttered.

Once they made it to the door of the pub, Juniper's phone rang. She was tempted to ignore it, but something told her she needed to answer it.

It wasn't a number she recognized. She hoped to hell it wasn't another one of those calls asking about her car's warranty.

"Hold on, I think I need to get this." She swiped to answer. "Hello?"

"Hello, Juniper. This is Helen Williams. Do you have a moment to chat?"

She mouthed *Helen Williams* to Tomas.

He furrowed his brow and shrugged, as if to answer the unspoken question of wondering why Helen was calling her.

"Tomas and I were about to have lunch, but I can spare a quick moment. How can I help you, Helen?"

"I wanted to talk about your future."

A stone the size of a mountain dropped inside her gut.

She was tempted to just hang up. Oops, bad signal. But she knew whatever Helen wanted to say, she'd still want to say it when they got back from Ever After.

"It'll just take a moment," Helen promised, as if sensing her displeasure.

"Okay," she managed.

"First, I'm so happy you'll be joining our little family. I think you could help us do great things at the foundation, the same way Tomas has done great things for the practice. Your marriage is going to be the frosting on the cake."

"Thank you?"

Helen laughed. "I'm sure you're overwhelmed, and I'm hoping instead of adding to that, that our chat can lend you some peace of mind."

Peace of mind would be good. She wasn't sure how Helen was going to accomplish that, but at this point, Juniper would try anything.

"I'm sure Tomas has told you that after you're married he'll make partner."

"Yes."

"There are other incentives, too, I thought you should be aware of. I know how scary it is when you're first starting your lives together as a couple. But I want you to know, I've been where you are."

You've pretended to be engaged to your best friend so he

can make partner and get your grandmothers to stop trying to set you up? Doubtful, but we'll roll with it, she thought.

"Oh really?" was all she could manage.

"When my husband and I met, he was with a little firm much like ours now. They had the same incentive structure in place, and it made planning for the future so much easier. In fact, I got a call much like this one after we got engaged."

She wondered if Pick 'n' Axe had enough tequila for her to deal with this.

"Oh?" Apparently, that was the limit of her available words for the day.

"Don't worry, is what I'm trying to say," Helen said in a motherly tone. "After Tomas makes partner, he'll be making more money and have a better retirement, but we also have bonuses for other milestones as well. With the birth of each child up to three, the practice will open a trust for that child with fifty thousand dollars. For every five years of marriage, you will get a onetime bonus of a paid vacation to a destination of your choice. I can't believe I almost forgot the most important parts!"

"Oh?" She shook her head. "I mean, what would that be?"

Helen laughed. "I know it's so overwhelming. But the biggest perks we offer our partners are paying off any leftover student loans and any help you may need to buy your first home together."

"I . . . I don't know what to say."

"Say that this is wonderful and you can't wait to start your life with Tomas."

Juniper swallowed. "This is wonderful, and I can't wait to start my life with Tomas."

"Fantastic. I'll let you get back to your visit. Now that you have my number, call me if you need anything."

"I will, Helen. Thank you."

She put down the phone and looked at Tomas, feeling a little numb.

"What did she want?"

"To tell me about all the financial perks of getting married."

"What?" He narrowed his eyes. "Are you serious?"

"Did you know they'll pay off your student loans?"

"Yeah, actually I did know that." He managed a half smile. "There's more? Might as well tell me everything."

"Bonuses for every five years of marriage. Trust funds for each kid, up to three, of course. Any more than that"—she shrugged—"fuck them kids, I guess." She couldn't help the snarl in her voice. Juniper shook her head. "With this kind of pressure, no wonder you feel the way you do."

"It's not just the pressure, Juniper. It's everything."

She pressed her lips into a grim line. "I understand. I do."

He studied her. "Do you?"

His voice was low and soft, and it reminded her again of things she shouldn't be thinking about on the wholesome streets of Ever After.

Or maybe she should. This was a town that was supposed to celebrate love, and carnality was definitely part of that for many couples.

It would have to be part of it for her.

"I do," she said.

Just as she said that, the door to the pub swung open, and a short man with a bright red beard stood there and gave a mighty laugh.

"Don't be saying your vows just yet, me girl. Come on in and give ol' Shandy a hug."

She leaned down to squeeze him with a laugh.

"And you're the groom, eh?" Shandy eyed him. "Might as well come along. What's your pleasure today? A bit of this mutton stew and some cider?"

"That sounds great," she agreed easily, and Shandy led

them inside the darkened pub and to a table off in the corner, far away from the pool tables.

Tomas looked around the place as they were led to their table, and after his first sip of the hard cider that was put in front of him, he nodded approvingly. “Okay, this place is living up to its reputation.”

“See? I told you. You should trust me when I tell you things.”

He looked at her over his mug, and she realized it sounded like she was talking about more than just their choice of where to eat.

She bit her lip, knowing she should qualify her statement but deciding not to.

“I do trust you.”

She held his gaze for a long while, not only unsure of what she wanted to say next, but if she was ready for the fallout.

Then her mouth made the choice for her. “You know, maybe we should just do it.”

“What? I don’t think I heard you correctly.”

“You did.”

“I didn’t.”

“But you did.”

“But I’m so very sure I didn’t.” He took another long pull from the cider. “Because if I did, you just proposed to me.”

“I’m already wearing the ring that doesn’t seem to want to come off.” She wiggled her finger at him. “Why not?”

“You just said you understood, Juniper.”

“I do. But hear me out.”

His brow did that thing again where it crawled up his head like a wandering yet well-clipped caterpillar.

“You’re not going to make partner until you’ve signed a marriage contract.”

“I know. And I’m considering leaving the firm.”

She swallowed. “That’s valid, but consider this. We’re already basically married, so why not reap the benefits?”

"This is even more insane than pretending to be engaged," he said.

"Well, yes." It was. It was completely batshit. "But we spend all our free time together, we don't see other people, our lives really won't change that much except for that our mothers will be really happy, you'll be really happy because you'll make partner, and I can take more risks with my work as well. And I get to see my best friend all the time. You could say we're giving in to the pressure, or it could be the best prank we've pulled yet."

"If I thought you believed like I did, I would say this was the best idea you've ever had. But you don't. You believe in true love and happily ever after. Why would you take that away from yourself? For me? I can't let you do that."

"How about we rewind to the part where this was my idea? You can't *let* me? Who do you think you're talking to?"

He laughed then and nodded. "Fair enough, but what about . . ." Tomas shrugged and went silent.

He didn't need to put it into words. She knew what he meant.

"What about it?"

"It looks too much like what you want, only you've dressed me in a cape that doesn't fit."

"I haven't. I know full well who you are, Tomas." She did, and it was at that moment she knew . . . everything. The knowledge steamrolled over her like a Mack truck.

It was what their mothers and her grandmothers had known all along. It was what that voice in the back of her head had been trying to tell her. It was what she'd been trying to deny for so long now.

Tomas Rivera was her person.

She'd been low-key in love with him for years. It had started with a stumble, that time under the stars when she'd been so sure he was going to kiss her. How oddly bereft she'd felt when he only touched his lips to her forehead.

Then the remaining years in between had been a slow, yet steady fall.

The ring on her finger seemed to burn her skin, and she twisted it round and round underneath the table as her epiphany rose up in a tsunami that threatened to spill out of her mouth.

There had never been anything she couldn't tell Tomas, but now there was this thing. This beautiful, glorious, powerful thing, and she should've been able to speak this truth to him.

Yet, she couldn't.

Because she knew he didn't want it.

He loved her, she knew that, but he didn't believe in romantic love. These feelings coursing through her, he'd say it was simply a biological imperative.

She supposed he was right, in a way. He was vital to her in ways he couldn't and didn't want to understand.

"And who am I?" he asked. "In this equation, who do you want me to be?"

That was the question, wasn't it?

"You're my best friend. I've never wanted you to be anyone but who you are." She took a drink of her own cider. "You love me. I love you. Why not?" Juniper forced a smile. "We could take that Galapagos trip for our honeymoon."

"Why not? Because when you wake up and realize this farce isn't what you really want, I'm going to lose you. And I can't have that, Juniper."

Her bottom lip quivered. "Don't be silly. You could never lose me. I'm a fungus. For life."

Except hadn't she already had this conversation with herself? The one where she'd been adamant she'd never settle for anything less than everything? He knew her. He knew the parts of her that she didn't want to face.

"Some fungi are symbiotic. What happens when you don't get what you need?" His expression was earnest, and she'd swear it was almost haunted.

"I know what I'm asking for," she whispered.

"Galapagos it is," he said softly.

What had they done?

Nothing, yet. It was what they were going to do that was the problem.

And the way she was going to break her own heart. She knew it was coming. Juniper had the sure knowledge that every step forward was another down toward a special kind of torture that was going to hurt more than anything in her life ever had.

Yet, she accepted that was the price she'd have to pay.

Chapter 12

Something in Juniper changed at Pick 'n' Axe and Tomas couldn't help but think it was something he'd done.

He'd agreed to what she wanted, even though he knew it was a bad idea. So he didn't understand why she was so muted, defeated.

It occurred to him that he was already losing her.

They couldn't go back, not now.

The only way forward was through, and he didn't know if he was strong enough.

He'd been so sure that they could survive anything, but if this was the thing that broke them? His mother would say that if they could be broken, they needed to be. Tomas didn't agree.

For a moment, he reconsidered what she'd said about being married. How their lives wouldn't change, but the two of them were already changing. The easy silences they'd always been able to share seemed to have become a thing of the past.

Yet he thought about coming home to her every night. Having her near him always. Never having to say good night. A forever sleepover. Seeing her with her deadline hair, in her dirty T-shirt, and having to silently make her enchiladas while she cried and typed toward the end of her deadline, the way she mouthed dialogue along with her characters and made their facial expressions as she wrote.

He grinned.

"Okay, what?" she asked.

"I was just thinking, maybe this marriage in name only won't be so bad."

"Gee, thanks." She snorted.

"No, really. I get all the . . ." He cleared his throat. "*We* get all the marriage perks without the hard parts."

"I wouldn't say that's a good thing," she teased.

He rolled his eyes. *Hard parts.* "Listen, if you want those hard parts you can have them. You did agree to buy the whole pig." The words were out of his mouth before he could think better of them, or perhaps his filter had simply disengaged. Or maybe it was those self-same hard parts doing the talking.

"Oh, can I? Thanks." She snorted. "Your powers of seduction are first class, Mr. Rivera."

She didn't look impressed, not that he expected she would. "You're the one who wants to be Mrs. Rivera," he teased back. "I warned you."

"I've changed my mind. I'm running for the hills."

Just then, their food appeared seemingly out of nowhere. Two baskets of warm, dark bread and tiny cauldrons of butter, along with huge bowls of the mutton stew.

"After I eat," Juniper continued. "I need to fortify for all that running."

He knew she was kidding, but her words kicked him in the guts. Even joking about her leaving sliced him in ways he couldn't bear to think of. It was his worst fear made flesh, and even as a joke, it cut deep.

Tomas couldn't let her have the last word, either. "Fine, I'll show you. Are you ready for this fully operational seduction station?"

"God, no." She cackled and wheezed. "Was that a Star Wars reference?"

"You bet, baby." He winked at her.

"Yeah, we'll see."

"Won't we just?" he promised.

She snorted again.

Well, he'd show her. He abandoned his stew, and slid around the booth until he was sitting next to her and wrapped his arm around her waist so he could lean into her. "That wasn't the kind of sound you were making earlier when your thighs were wrapped around my hips, *corazoncita*."

She stiffened, froze.

Tomas wondered if he'd taken it too far.

Fuck, what was too far when they'd just decided to get married for real?

Juniper turned to look at him slowly, and as she did, her hand slid to his thigh. Her fingers were perilously close to the "hard parts" she'd referenced earlier.

"Why don't you remind me?"

It was his turn to freeze. Her eyes were half-lidded, and her words had been a sultry purr. There was no doubt about what she meant. She'd put it all on the table.

He wasn't going to say no this time.

"Right here?" His lips brushed the shell of her ear as he spoke.

"If there was a tablecloth, I'd dare you." She grinned. "Bathroom?" She nodded toward a door in the back.

She wasn't actually going to go through with it, was she?

"Yeah, okay. You go first, and I'll follow."

"No, *you* go first."

He raised his eyebrows but then shrugged, and casually walked back to the door of one of the two unisex bathrooms. All the while, doing his best not to adjust his package. When he'd bought these slacks, he hadn't allowed for moments like this.

Tomas couldn't believe this was happening.

It couldn't happen.

They'd just gotten carried away trying to outdo each other. It happened all the time. Just not with sex.

This was how they'd ended up driving to Glacier National

Park in one solid go, only stopping for fuel and road snacks because neither one of them had wanted to let the other outdo them on drive time. Of course, they'd spent the first day of their vacation sleeping.

It was also how they'd ended up tying in a hot-dog-eating contest at one of the firm's charity events.

And also how they'd both ended up vomiting the rest of the night away.

This wasn't so much different.

Tomas rolled his eyes skyward. "*Madre de Dios*," he whispered. "Don't let her find out I compared sex to vomiting. She'd kill me."

The door eased open, and Juniper stood there, still wearing that damn expression he was going to see in every fantasy he ever had from now until he was dead. "Why would I kill you?"

"How do you know I was talking about you?"

"The only time you talk to the Virgin Mary is when I frustrate you." She grinned. "Or scare you."

"You don't scare me."

"I should work on that, then." She advanced on him.

Suddenly, he felt like prey, and Tomas had to say he liked it.

Only, he wasn't sure who the woman was in front of him. He'd never seen this side of her. When he would've embraced her, she pushed him back against the sink.

"Oh, no, Tomas. This is my turn. I'm going to show you exactly what you've been turning down."

Sirens blared in his head, and a panic seized him. He needed to get away from her before this went too far, but the part of him that wanted this—that wanted her—it muted all those feelings so they were nothing more than a memory of a dream.

They were here now.

No more fighting the inevitable.

"Put your hands on the sink," she commanded.

He did as she instructed.

"Don't move them."

"I hope you don't think you get to be this bossy in the bedroom all the time," he teased.

"You like it," she replied, her mouth curling into a smile.

"So far."

"Remember what I said. Hands on the sink."

He obeyed, but she couldn't possibly mean to—

Juniper sank down to her knees and her hands went to his belt.

It was surreal, seeing his best friend on her knees for him, yet the culmination of every secret fantasy.

Her hair hung over her shoulder, a dark curtain, but did nothing to obscure his view. If he'd thought the sight of her divine, the first touch of her fingers on his cock convinced him he was either in heaven or hell. It was too good. He wasn't going to last for shit, and then she'd win.

Of course, he couldn't say that it wouldn't be a win for him, too.

But then he'd have even more to prove to her.

His brain flashed with images of what that would entail and he got even harder. He hadn't known that was possible. Tomas was sure if he fought the pleasure her lips brought for too long, the damn thing was going to snap in half.

Her mouth was hot and sweet, driving him to the brink, and holding him there with expert skill.

The porcelain of the sink was cool and solid under his hands, and he tightened his grasp. He wanted nothing more than to tangle his fingers through the dark waves of her hair, but he complied with her edicts.

She was the one in control.

As if she could read his thoughts, she paused in her work to say, "All you have to do is surrender."

"If I surrender, it'll be over." He was talking about more than just the carnality of the moment, and it was obvious that she knew it.

"No, it won't. You still have to best me, don't you?" She went back to her task, taking him deep into her mouth.

Juniper knew exactly what she was doing.

He was out of his league. She'd warned him. She'd reminded him that this was what she did for a living. Not sucking his dick, but crafting these moments between people. These irrefutable and unbreakable bonds.

Yet, he was afraid he would be the one to break the unbreakable.

Because she'd see him then.

That he wasn't enough.

He wasn't the person she believed him to be.

Only when she looked up at him again, her fingers digging into his thighs and her mouth working his cock, all of that fled. It was silenced, smothered by the expanse of the space she filled inside of him.

Juniper was the beginning, she was the end. She was everything.

His body tightened and flexed, but he couldn't hold back the storm of pleasure she wrought in him.

Everything about her demanded his surrender.

The look in her eyes.

The emotion he could read on her face.

The way she teased, stroked, and laved at his body, giving him anything he would have of her.

She tightened her grip on his thighs, and when he would've pulled away, Juniper took him deeper.

So he surrendered.

He gave himself over to the sensation, to the waves of bliss that carried him out of space and time, and at last, to Juniper herself.

A loud, clamoring knock on the door yanked him back to reality.

He wasn't ready.

Juniper licked her lips, holding his gaze, as she said, "Just a moment." Then to him she said, glancing at his belt and slacks, "You better saddle up."

She went to the sink and washed her hands, acting as if she hadn't just given him the best blow job of his life, then exited the bathroom while he frantically tried to right himself.

When he opened the door, he was relieved to see whoever had come knocking had the decency to wait elsewhere. Tomas went back to the table and saw Juniper calmly buttering a piece of the dark bread. He couldn't take his eyes off her mouth.

Her delectable, beautiful, talented mouth.

She ate slowly, chewing each bite carefully. She reached for another roll, smeared the golden butter across it, and then offered it to him.

His brain wasn't back to full capacity yet, and he found all he wanted to do now was watch her mouth. He couldn't yet summon words.

She shook the roll at him, and he realized that her mouth was moving and sound was coming out, but he couldn't hear a damn word she said. He wanted to, but his brain was not cooperating.

That was when she laughed. "I fucked you up. Admit it."

He found his voice. "I was not going to deny it."

An expression of obvious self-satisfaction bloomed on her face. "I win."

That was when his brain kicked back into gear. "Oh, I beg to differ, *querida*. I haven't yet had my turn."

"Promises, promises," she said, as if she didn't believe him.

"Promises, indeed." He took a drink of his cider. "When have you ever known me to break a promise?"

She shrugged. "There's a first time for everything."

"It's not going to work."

"What?" She schooled her features into a mask of perfect, but utterly false, innocence.

"You're trying to goad me to make my play now, but I'm

going to wait until you least expect it. Until you're least prepared. Until you're hot, wet, and begging."

"I. Can't. Wait."

She downed the rest of her cider.

His stew had gotten cold, but it didn't matter. He couldn't taste it. Tomas shoveled it down and began plotting his counterattack.

Just then, his phone buzzed. Tomas wasn't going to answer it, but he saw it was the firm. When he picked it up, something cold settled in the base of his spine. When his mother had that feeling, something bad always happened.

He put it back down without answering, which was completely unlike him.

So it shouldn't have surprised him when they called back.

"Aren't you going to answer?" she asked.

"Nope. It's the office." He switched his phone off and put it back in his pocket.

"You better be careful. The world might end," she teased.

As if his world hadn't just crashed and burned around his ears only moments earlier.

He shrugged. "I'm trying new things."

"Good. You should actually take your days off."

"I do." Noticing her raised brow, he said, "Most of the time."

Then Juniper cocked her head to the side. "Now that I think of it, our phones have been suspiciously silent."

Their mothers. They hadn't texted or called in a day. That had to be some kind of record. Unless they were up to something.

He and Juniper shared a look.

"They couldn't possibly be up to something, do you think?" Juniper asked.

"Well, it's always a possibility."

"It couldn't be as simple as we finally gave them what they

wanted and they're leaving us alone, because if I knew it was that easy, I'd have tried it years ago."

Tomas narrowed his eyes. "I bet they've been plotting with the grandmothers."

She fiddled with the ring on her hand, as he noticed she'd taken to doing when she was concerned or upset. "What could they possibly have to plot about?"

"Oh no," they said simultaneously. "A wedding!"

"No, I draw the line here. I don't care how happy it makes them. We gave them the engagement, they can wait," Juniper said.

"Change your mind, did you?"

"About what?"

"Doing it for real."

"No. But I'm not doing this again, so it's going to be how we want it, when we want it, and they, and everyone else who has a stake in this, are just going to have to wait."

He swallowed the panic that surged in his throat. "Don't lie. You know you'd do anything for those ladies."

"Which ones?"

"All of them," he said with a gentle knowing.

Her shoulders slumped. "You're right. I don't want you to be, but you are."

It was part of what he loved about Juniper. How she cared about other people. "It's okay. We'll figure this all out. We always do."

"Meddlers. The lot of them." She sighed.

"The lot," he agreed.

"I have an idea." She held up her mug for another cider.

"To get drunk?"

"No . . . maybe. No. Listen, what if we do some digging and meddling of our own."

"I like the sound of this. Go on," he encouraged.

"All of them, the moms included, have meddled with no

repercussions long enough. Look at how we've done everything we could to please them, and they just won't stop pushing. Maybe, if they had some drama of their own to deal with, they'd leave us in peace."

He fixed her with a skeptical look.

"At least for a little while." She laughed but then sobered quickly. "At least while we figure things out for ourselves."

"So we're going to matchmake? I have to say, I'm probably the least qualified person to do that."

She tapped her chin. "I object."

"On what grounds?"

"I'd say you might be the most qualified. You know what people are like when it doesn't work, so that has to give some insight on what does."

He didn't want to be the one to tell her that nothing worked. Not long term. Not forever. Contrary to her staunchly held beliefs, life wasn't a fairy tale. Not the good parts, anyway.

"Overruled. This is your wheelhouse."

"Maybe you're right. It's in my blood, after all."

"So what's the plan?"

"I'm going to need a few days to really chew on it, but I'm going to set up the grandmothers. And I think, with just the right amount of inspiration, I may be able to get the mothers to turn on each other, too. Then *voilà*, peace and quiet."

"You should've thought of this before we played fake fiancé," he suggested.

"No, we would've had to do that anyway. To get them to let their guards down. Now, they're going to see just how they like being meddled with."

Like many of the other occurrences of the last few weeks, Tomas was sure this was going to end badly.

Yet, that didn't stop them from galloping down the very same path toward disaster.

Chapter 13

They spent the rest of the day out. The grandmothers kept finding errands for them to run, or last-minute things to do to help prepare for Betina and Jackson's wedding.

And Juniper was grateful.

She wasn't quite sure what possessed her in Pick 'n' Axe.

It was literally like she'd been possessed. It was her voice speaking, her body carrying out the actions, but the logical part of her had been locked away in a box and stuffed in a dark corner.

Juniper wasn't sure she knew the person driving the bus, but she'd made quite a mess of things, hadn't she?

Why couldn't she have at least made sure that Juniper got hers?

Although, she supposed Batshit Juniper had it right because if she'd just decided to jockey him like a pony, that would have been that and they would've gone straight to the fallout.

She knew there was no way to miss the fallout completely, but at least this way, they were taking the longer route to get there.

And she knew that Tomas wouldn't be able to resist trying to one-up her.

Trying.

She shivered with anticipation.

"Are you cold?" he asked, as they walked across the softly lit square back to the mushroom cottage.

"A little." Which was the correct answer, instead of, *Oh, I'm just thinking about your sword in my velvet sheath.* Yeah, no.

He put his arm around her as they walked.

Butterflies were on a rock 'n' roll stadium tour in her guts as they got closer and closer to the mushroom cottage.

He'd promised he'd wait to beat her at the seduction game when she least expected it.

But she didn't want to go to her own room tonight.

When they got to the door, he unlocked it and held it open for her. After they walked inside, another awkward silence hung over them like a storm cloud.

Until he put his hand on her waist and drew her to him, his other hand coming up to cup the back of her head. She was so sure he was going to kiss her.

And he did.

Only not like she wanted. He pressed a chaste kiss to her forehead and held her against him.

Juniper was overwhelmed with her love for him. She wanted nothing more than to tell him, but she couldn't say the words. Those words that had always come so easy between them had become something forbidden, something she had to keep secret.

"Good night, *corazoncita*."

The word meant little heart. She'd always enjoyed that he called her that. He'd said a hundred times that she was his heart, only now, it had taken on a different meaning.

It was the stark, constant reminder that they were only friends.

He was her best friend. Now, he'd become her lover. How couldn't it mean to him what it did to her?

She didn't understand.

She needed to talk.

Any other time, if she needed to talk about something like

this, he was the one she talked to. He was the one who made everything okay.

She couldn't talk to her mother. Not about this, because of her deceit.

Maybe she could talk to Jonquil. Jonquil would understand.

She pulled away from his familiar embrace slowly, savoring the scent of him, the heat of his hands, the sense of home she always felt when she was close to him.

"Good night."

"You're not going to bed? We have another early day tomorrow."

"No. I think I'm going to walk over to Fairy Godmothers, Inc. and see if Jonquil is still working on Betina's bouquets. I saw the lights were still on."

"Shall I walk you?"

"No. I'm perfectly safe. This is Ever After. Bad things don't happen to good people here."

He grinned. "I'm not saying you're not a good person, but the town might take offense you've got matching in your heart when it comes to their resident fairy godmothers."

She grinned. "Nah, I bet even the squirrels think they have it coming."

"I'll see you in the morning."

She turned and fled as fast as her legs could carry her without breaking into an outright sprint.

When she got to Fairy Godmothers, Inc., she flung open the door and called, "Gramma Jonquil?"

"No, honey. It's just Zuri tonight," a woman with an enviably perfect dark complexion, wide brown eyes, and a genuine warm smile said as she emerged from the back of the shop.

"Oh! I'm sorry to bother you. I thought Gramma Jonquil might be here."

Zuri looked her up and down and shook her head. "Love trouble?"

"Uh . . . I . . . no. Of course not." She coughed.

Zuri flashed her a knowing smile. "Why don't you come in and help me finish up these centerpieces?"

Juniper was led to a back room where bloodred roses and black baby's breath were being tied together in surprisingly elegant sprays.

"I knew there had to be a reason the godmothers wanted me to stay late and do this by hand."

"They wanted you to be here?"

Zuri smiled again. "Sometimes they do know what they're doing."

"Not if you've been on the receiving end of their meddling."

Zuri gave a loud hearty laugh. "Oh, but I have. And I've never been happier."

Juniper felt her lip curl. "Really?"

"I won't say I enjoyed it while it was happening, but it was worth it." Zuri pushed wire, tin snips, and flowers toward her. "Start wrapping, and I'll tell you about it."

Juniper stared at the flowers in front of her for a long moment before slowly picking up the tin snips.

"Oh, how could I have forgotten? Gwen left some cookies to fortify us." Zuri pulled out a box and pushed that at Juniper as well. "The frosted kind. There's coffee, too."

Juniper demolished a cookie and then watched carefully as Zuri wrapped the flowers together. She picked up her supplies and began wrapping.

"So my grandmothers helped you fall in love?" she began.

"Indeed. More like pushed me down the hill kicking and screaming, but we got there." Zuri finished one spray and began on another, a wistful expression on her face. "I didn't want to fall in love." She looked up to meet Juniper's eyes. "I didn't believe in it."

A tiny kernel of hope kindled in her heart. "What happened?"

"I used to dream of weddings. When I was a little girl, I designed weddings for my dolls. For my friends. For actresses in my teen magazines. For me. It was all I ever wanted to do. Then I found out the man I wanted to spend the rest of my life with was the groom in the wedding I was planning."

Juniper's heart broke for Zuri, and she must have gasped or maybe the expression on her face gave her away because Zuri nodded.

"I know. It was awful. The bride took her wedding gown off during the ceremony and lit it on fire."

"Wow. That's a powerful woman."

"I know, right?" Zuri shook her head. "She took her bridesmaids on her honeymoon and never looked back. Me? I came to hide in Ever After. I didn't think I could still be a wedding planner. I didn't know what I was going to do with my life, but my sister, Zeva, she said I was going to come to Ever After and I was going to make a new life. A better one. I, of course, doubted."

"As one does," Juniper agreed.

"Yes, as one does," Zuri said gently, as if she was now in possession of some kind of secret knowledge no one else had. "They were convinced that Phillip Charming was the man for me. Ever After? Prince Charming?" Zuri snorted with the derision that anyone would have given to those words, especially after a breakup. "Yet, I persevered. I kept believing even when I wasn't sure what there was left to believe in, and I got it. I got my happily ever after."

Juniper's eyes welled with tears. "Thank you."

"For what?"

"For reminding me that I do believe."

"Of course you do. You couldn't be their granddaughter if you didn't. Don't forget who you are. It's easy when our hearts hurt to forget what makes us special." She grinned. "*Magical*. But don't let anyone take that away from you."

"Can I tell you a secret? Something you won't share with the sweet old dears?"

"Of course!" She passed her another cookie. "It's what you came to talk about, isn't it?"

"That's exceedingly irritating that you and the grandmothers know so much about other people's feelings."

"Damn. Sorry. I try really hard not to do that because it irritated me so much in the early days. It's just that we have hope. We believe in your Happily Ever After, too."

Juniper crossed her arms over her chest. "Well, when you put it like that." She huffed. "First, I'm going to matchmake them. See how they like it."

Zuri's eyes grew wide and she clapped her hands together. "That's one of the best things I've ever heard. If you need more hands, I'm in."

"Definitely. I need to choose who I'm going to match them with. Any ideas?"

"Not at the moment, but I can find some. We may have to call in Ravenna Blackheart. She'll have the goods."

"Blackheart. Hmm. As in Castle Blackheart?"

"Yes. Do you know her?"

"I know of her. She was always the scary blond lady at the bank who didn't give kids suckers at the window."

Zuri laughed again. "I could see that. Actually, I could see her taking candy away from kids at the window to add it to her hoard."

"I thought she was terrifying when I was a kid, but if she can help me fight fire with fire . . ."

"This is a firefight?" Zuri asked. "Not just because you want them to fall in love?"

"I want them to be too busy dealing with their own love lives to meddle in mine."

"If you're engaged, why would they need to . . . Oh, I see."

Zuri nodded. "You and your Tomas aren't really engaged, are you?"

"It's that obvious?"

"Only to me, I think."

"I hope?" Juniper squeaked. "That would suck if all of this angst was for nothing."

"If you're not interested in each other that way, what is there to angst over?"

Juniper just stared at her. "Isn't it obvious?"

"Talk it out, you'll feel better," Zuri promised.

"We thought it would be funny," she began. "It would be a way to get our mothers off our backs, my grandmothers, and it would get his bosses to leave him alone and finally give him the partnership he's worked so hard for."

"That seems like a win-win. The problem?"

"It was all fine until our mothers came over while we were having our usual Friday night not date." She rushed to explain. "Tomas and I have been best friends since we were children."

"Oh, I see. Go on."

"And the grandmothers told our mothers about the engagement, and they came over, and well, one thing led to another and I kissed him." She held up her hand. "I'm also stuck with this magic ring. It's supposed to fit perfectly if Tomas is the one for me. It won't come off. Not even with bacon grease, and Tomas's pulling."

"Wait, wait. Magic ring?" Zuri took her hand to examine the ring in question.

"It's obviously not really magic, but I can't get it off."

"If you're sure about that."

"Of course, I'm sure about that. Magic isn't real."

Zuri simply raised one expertly groomed brow. "Interesting you should say that."

"Why is that interesting? It's common knowl—" Then she realized who she sounded like.

Tomas.

That was how he felt about love.

His feelings weren't a revelation, but for a moment, she'd thought Zuri was losing her mind, implying magic was real. That must be how Tomas felt every time she brought up the subject of romantic love.

It was a cold splash down her spine, and humiliation burned. The idea that he would think . . . that he didn't believe her.

Or *in* her.

It churned her guts.

"Hmm," Zuri said knowingly.

"Well, that's uncomfortable." She flopped back in the chair. Hot tears burned behind her eyes. "And stupid."

"It's not stupid, Juniper. Not at all. It's going to be okay."

"How do you know?"

"If it's not Happily Ever After, it's not over." Zuri patted her hand. "A wise fairy godmother once told me that. She also said that happily ever after might not look like I expected it to, but that doesn't make it any less magical."

Juniper blew out a heavy breath.

"Tell me, what is your Tomas to you?"

"Home," she whispered.

"Does he feel the same way?" Zuri shook her head. "Without all the great confessions and pronouncements of love. Are you his home, too?"

"I thought so."

"Just keep the faith, then."

She gulped. "We agreed to get married for real today."

"He's in deep."

"Him? I'm the one that flung us into the deep end without knowing how to swim."

"If you could go back, would you?"

Juniper stopped to really consider the prospect. Would she

go back if she could? Would she undo this knowledge she had? These feelings she only just now understood?

"No. It took all of this for me to realize that my feelings for him are why it never worked with anyone else."

"He just needs to catch up and get with the program." Zuri finished another bouquet. "You'll bring him around."

"I don't want to bring him around. I want him to realize it on his own." She started tying her own flowers. "I've already been the one who has initiated everything. From the kiss to . . ." Juniper trailed off. "I'm not going to chase him forever."

"You shouldn't chase him forever. My guess is that he's going to have to learn what it's like without you. Then he'll get himself right."

"More angst. I don't want it. I just want him to look at me, realize I'm it, and we get the carriage ride, the wedding bells, and the delicious cake. More important, we get tomorrow. A lot of tomorrows."

Zuri put her flowers down and took Juniper's hand. "We all want it to be that way, but that's not how it works. You, more than anyone, know that. You're a Happily Ever After engineer just like your grandmothers. Would you let your characters get away with that?"

"No," Juniper pouted. "Maybe I should."

"Whyever would you do that?"

Juniper laughed. "You're right. Some days I am kind of like the sipping tea with Satan meme. I take great joy in putting my characters through hell. It makes the good parts better. I guess I can't be a bitch about it if fate decides to do that to me, too." She pursed her lips. "To be honest, I have it coming."

Zuri laughed, and so Juniper did again as well. She found her heart light and her troubles sliding away.

"You know, you're pretty good at this fairy godmother thing."

"I mostly leave that to my sister, Zeva. However, I'm pretty sure the godmothers wanted us to meet and wanted you to hear my story."

"Or they just knew that you're a wonderful person and that we'd get along so well. They were excited for me to meet you."

The bells over the door to the shop jingled, and Juniper wondered who it could be at this late hour. Just as she turned, she saw a tall blond man with wide shoulders and the greenest eyes that were practically inhuman. They had to be contacts.

"Oh, hello. Juniper, I didn't expect to see you here."

"You know me?" She was sure she didn't know him. She'd have remembered those eyes.

"I'm Phillip. You used to play by the fountain, like all the kids in Ever After. We're all so happy for your engagement."

"Thank you," she said.

"Our Juniper here has a magnificent idea."

"I have a magnificent idea, but I'll let you share first." He winked at Zuri.

She rolled her eyes. "Anyway, Juniper wants to matchmake the godmothers."

Phillip choked and snorted. "You do know that your grandmother Petunia is called Petty for a reason, right?"

"Wait, wait, wait!"

Zuri and Phillip both stared at her.

"You can't be Phillip Charming."

Phillip looked down at himself, around the room, then back at himself. "I'm not anyone else."

"You can't be a day over thirty. Gramma Petty said you two dated."

Phillip was obviously fighting laughter. "I'd say that I like older women, but that doesn't quite explain it, does it? You're going to have to ask your grammies about that one."

"I'm asking you."

"Oh no. I've already been on the wrong end of that woman. I'm not risking it again. You're just going to have to wait for them to explain it. It'll all make sense," Phillip said.

"It really will. I promise," Zuri swore.

"I'm stealing my wife away. She's done for tonight. You can lock up?" Phillip said, sweeping Zuri up into his arms.

"You know how I feel about being carried. So if you start this, you're going to have to carry me all the way back to the castle," she teased.

Phillip's expression grew serious. "It would be my greatest honor."

"Stop it." She smacked his shoulder. "All of your courtly nonsense."

Juniper, for her part, could only sigh and stage-whisper, "Don't stop. It's obvious she loves it."

"I know, right?" He grinned. "I've got the best part of this deal, though."

"And don't you forget it." Zuri leaned her head against her husband's shoulder. "I'm serious," she said as he carried her toward the door. "I want you to carry me all the way to the castle."

"I know," he said, in an indulgent tone that melted Juniper's heart.

Zuri had her Happily Ever After. She'd earned it. And it was beautiful.

Maybe Juniper could still have one after all.

And maybe, just maybe, she should leave her grammies alone.

Or not. Who was she to deny the matchmaking fire in her blood?

They'd brought this on themselves, after all.

Chapter 14

The next day dawned bright and early with a frantic group text from Petty.

We need you both at Blackheart Castle!

Followed by: *!!!*

And then*: !!!!!*

He scrubbed his hand over his face. It was much too early for this, whatever it was.

Tomas hadn't slept well. He'd gone to bed, but he hadn't been able to even pretend to sleep until he heard Juniper come in. Her steps had been quiet on the stairs, and he'd heard her stop just outside his bedroom door.

He'd wanted to invite her in, with every fiber of his being, but his mouth wouldn't obey him. So he'd lain there, long into the dark, silent night with regret on his mind, yet unable to summon the courage to take that step.

He'd tossed and turned, exhausted, but still unable to drift off to sleep. Dawn had already started to creep pink and soft across the sky when he'd finally gotten to sleep. He might've been asleep for three hours, at the most.

Then he heard Juniper's phone ring through the thin walls.

It wasn't long before she knocked on his door and opened it. Juniper looked as tired as he felt.

"Did someone die?" he asked.

"No, but they need us. There's been an incident."

"What now?"

"I know, right?" She rubbed her eyes sleepily and padded over to the bed, where she flopped next to him.

It was second nature to pull her near, to wrap them both together in the blankets. He was immediately at peace, and ready to go back to sleep. This, her, was what he'd needed all along. The fact wasn't a surprise to him.

"I just want to go back to sleep," she murmured.

"You look how I feel," he said.

"Thanks." Her tone was dry.

"No problem."

She smelled so good, he just wanted to bury his face in her hair and drown there.

"We should get moving. The grandmothers need us."

"What happened?"

"You didn't read the rest of the text, did you?" She sighed. "So the wedding tonight? The groom wanted to surprise his bride by flying her aunt in from France. They thought she wasn't going to be able to come, but Jackson made it happen for her."

"Oh, do they need us to go pick up Auntie from the airport? Maybe we can get some breakfast on the way." His stomach rumbled in favor of the plan.

"Not exactly. Jackson and Betina left for the airport early this morning. Their rental broke down on the way back and they're waiting for someone to bring them another car. The problem is that Betina and Jackson were both cutting it close with final fittings with Rosebud, and a final walkthrough of the ceremony tonight. They need us to stand in."

A cold wash of something ugly splashed over him. He swore. "They just can't leave us alone, can they? They won't stop until they have us trotting down the aisle for real."

Juniper stiffened and pulled away. "Are you serious right now?"

He sat up and scrubbed a hand over his face and through his hair. "Are you blind? This is obviously some sort of scheme on their part to get us in the costumes and to perform their little play."

"First of all," she began, her hands on her hips, "the play isn't theirs but ours. We're the ones who told them we were getting married. So whatever they believe, that's on us. They don't think it's a *little play*."

"Juniper—"

"Not your turn to talk yet. I'm not done."

Juniper rarely got upset with him, but this was one of those times that he could tell he'd hurt her feelings. He couldn't believe that she didn't understand that they were both being manipulated into something neither of them wanted or were ready for.

Yet, when he looked into her eyes and saw not only her anger but the wealth of sadness, he was immediately sorry. Tomas wanted to tell her so, but he waited for her to finish.

"Do you really think that my grandmothers have some kind of magical powers that could cause a radiator to crack? Further, do you think they'd be that malicious? This could ruin the wedding. Why would they do that? Is that what you think of them?" She pressed her lips together and shook her head. "Is that what you think of me?"

Tomas felt awful. He couldn't stand that he'd hurt her, and worse, that his words had made his regard for her change for even a second.

His irritation faded. "I'm an asshole?" he offered.

Her shoulders sagged. "You're not an asshole, but . . ." She wrinkled her nose. "Okay, you're a tiny bit of an asshole this morning. You want to talk about it?"

Not particularly, no. But she deserved an explanation. "It's absolutely no excuse to take it out on you, but I'm a little overwhelmed, and tired, and . . ." He decided to lay it all out, because he owed her that. He owed it to their friendship to come clean. "I didn't realize that being here would feel so bad."

She sank back down on the bed to sit next to him.

"What do you mean? What feels bad?" She searched his face, obviously waiting to hear what he had to say.

"I am completely out of my element. This place makes no sense to me. It feels like I've been yanked out of reality and stuffed into some pocket universe where none of the rules I've been taught my whole life make sense."

"It's just a kitschy small town. It seems like you feel like it's out to get you."

He pointed at the window. "Explain the bird that kept trying to shit on me."

She laughed and the sound soothed him. "Okay, maybe he knew what you were saying. He was obviously Rosebud's pet. Some birds can have the vocabulary of a four-year-old."

"It's not just that. It's everything else, too. It's how everyone is planning out the rest of our lives. It's Helen calling you and giving you the reimbursement tier for decisions that should have nothing to do with bonuses. It's that everything here is geared to make me believe something I don't."

She nodded slowly. "I didn't realize it would be so bad for you. I thought it was just going to be a fun weekend with some nostalgia while we ate way too many sweets."

"There's one more thing."

"I know about that thing." She gave a small huff. "It's hard for me, too."

"Yes, it is," he confessed in a faux whisper. "Constantly."

She swatted at his arm. "Shut up," Juniper said in a light tone.

"That's the problem, though." He was serious again. "It's this place. It's this pretend. And it's the very real way that we've changed."

"Change is inevitable. Nothing stays the same forever."

"That's what I'm afraid of, Juniper." He shook his head. "You know what I do and why I do it. This inevitable change is never for the better. It's never together. That's why romantic love is a lie."

She exhaled heavily, her shoulders slumped. “You’ve told me that a million times, and it never really hit me like it just did. Maybe I wasn’t listening like I should have been.”

Her phone buzzed again, and she quickly tapped out a message, presumably to the grandmothers.

“I’m going to tell them you’re not feeling well and can’t make it. If you want to go home, you can. I understand.”

She’d given him the out he thought he wanted, only once it was there on the table, he didn’t want it. “I’m not going to leave you out here. How would you get home?”

“I can rent a car. Don’t stay because of me.”

“I only came because of you. Of course that’s why I’d stay,” he said softly.

“Don’t blame me, then, if you’re uncomfortable or unhappy.” She frowned. “Or the grandmothers.” Juniper stood again. “I have to get going. They need me.”

“Do they still need both of us?” he offered.

“Not if you don’t want to be there.”

He didn’t want to be there, but he found he couldn’t say the words. “I’ll do it.” He flashed her his biggest, brightest smile. “With a smile.”

“Okay. Gramma Bon-Bon said we should eat the doughnuts they left in the kitchen for us. The trek up to Castle Blackheart is a bit of a hike. They say we need fortification.”

She checked her phone again. “Oh, it’s almost like they are a little bit magic. Petty just texted to say that the kitchen at the castle will be open and after the fittings and rehearsal, they’ll feed you a traditional breakfast.”

“I can be bribed with food,” he agreed easily.

“You know what I want?” She grinned at him.

“Enchiladas for breakfast?” He knew damn well she could and would eat them at any time of the day or night.

“Enchiladas always. *And* tamales.”

“Both? So greedy,” he teased.

Although, enchiladas might be exactly what they needed.

They were safe. They were familiar territory, a place that was so them. It was a flag of all that was normal and good.

"If Snow's Market has what I need, I could be persuaded."

"Really?" She bounced on the bed and landed a fat, sloppy kiss on his cheek. "That makes the whole world brighter. It really does. Thank you!"

He realized then that he'd never actually thought about how happy his cooking made her. He knew she loved it, but Tomas had thought she was just as food motivated as he was, but there was a kind of pure joy she exuded every time he cooked for her.

It had gotten to be part of their thing, so he didn't think much about the weekly tamale offering, or when she requested the enchiladas. It was like the backrubs she was always so willing to provide for him.

"Maybe I could make them for the grandmothers before we leave."

She grinned even wider. "That's the only reason I'd be willing to wait another day. They would love that." Juniper flung herself at him again, this time to hug him tightly.

"Everything is going to be okay, you know."

For a moment, he allowed himself to believe her. After all, she'd never lied to him before. Juniper's promises were the forever kind.

But later that afternoon, when they'd made the hike to Castle Blackheart and he found himself standing in a suit, a reproduction of Gary Oldman's black suit with braided gold embellishments from *Dracula*, complete with top hat and cane, he knew nothing would ever be okay again.

Storm clouds had gathered overhead, blocking out the sun, but no one seemed concerned that there would be rain. People darted to and fro, building complete set pieces around each other. Rosebud fiddled with the sleeves of the jacket while an older, white-haired woman, wearing a suit and a red bow tie, stood at the ready on a riser in front of him. The sight of her there, holding a leather-bound book, looking ready to commit two people together forever terrified him.

He must not have hidden it well. The woman leaned over. "I hear you got three grammies already. This place is rotten with 'em. But that's my name. Grammy. Ain't nothing to be scared of, young man. I don't bite." Then she guffawed. "Leastways, not tonight."

"I'm Tomas."

She eyed him up and down. "You got some wolf in you, too."

"I'm a lawyer," he confessed.

Grammy cackled. "'Course, you are. A divorce lawyer, I hear tell."

"Yes, ma'am."

"This must be hell for you. Good for you for seeing it through."

He narrowed his eyes, wondering just what exactly she knew about it.

"You didn't have to tell me anything. You look like an opossum that's about to be roadkill. And here comes your Mack truck." She nodded to the end of the rose-petal-strewn red carpet.

Somehow, the clouds overhead became even more menacing, thicker, darker.

The candelabras lining the path flickered to life and there, in their warm, sweet glow, stood Juniper.

His brain simply shut down.

There were curses on the tip of his tongue, but so were words of praise and joy. Although, he tended to think they must be curses, too.

Or maybe the grandmothers were witches.

No pretend fairy godmother would be so cruel.

Or dress their charges so provocatively.

If he'd thought she was stunning in the dress she'd worn

to the fundraiser, this was a completely new and different animal that had yet to be classified.

She was a siren.

A witch.

A goddess.

Juniper stood, the soft light washing over her pale, perfect skin. The contrast of the bloodred dress, the shiny ink-black fall of her hair in tousled waves, and those pale, pale swells of flesh drew him in, captured him, and devoured him whole.

He'd been told the dress was also a costume reproduction of Mina Murray's dress, but it seemed it had been made for Juniper. The plunging neckline, the cinched bodice that clung like a lover to her ample curves. The bustle that called attention to her already shapely figure.

She'd be happy he knew it was a bustle, he thought dumbly.

Something glittered on her finger and managed to draw his eyes away from the vision as a whole to focus on that silver glint.

The ring.

His ring.

On his bride.

His Juniper.

"I'd tell you to close your mouth because you're going to catch flies, but that's the sweetest reaction I've ever seen from a groom on first glance at his bride."

"We're not . . ." He trailed off.

"Oh, I know. Not yet. But you can't help but picture it, can you?"

Grammy's words were far away as he watched Juniper take the first tentative step toward him. However, he couldn't help but think she was right. What he was feeling right now, he could have it for real. She'd offered it all to him on a platter, and he'd taken it without much thought. He'd said might as well.

As if that could ever quantify what this woman meant to him. As if those words were even worthy of trying.

Her face had been painted with cosmetics as if she really were the one getting married today, with heavy mascara to accentuate the wide, dark pools of her eyes. Her lips were a red that matched her dress, and there was a touch of pink on her cheeks that deepened when she looked at him.

She moved forward, floating on a cloud, as the theme music from the movie began to play.

When he'd first heard about the Dracula-themed wedding, he'd thought it trite and silly. Two little kids playing dress-up and trying on angst.

Yet he found it all coming together in an elegant way he hadn't expected.

She met his gaze, and as she walked toward him, everything inside of him had tuned to a single word.

Mine.

It reverberated through his mind, a song on repeat. It thundered in his bones, and it danced, a dark ballet in his blood.

When she reached him, he held out his hand and she slipped her fingers into his.

"This is incredibly beautiful," Rosebud said, tears in her eyes.

Tomas had forgotten she was there. He'd forgotten the rest of the world existed at all when she'd been walking toward him.

Sounds, smells, sights, it all rushed back in at once, reminding him where he was.

Who he was.

And that this was all pretend.

"Okay, I'll begin the ceremony." Grammy looked up. "Hansel, do you have the lights figured out? The soft glow on the bride was stellar, but make sure you're not blinding anyone who will be seated in the back. That was a problem in the first rehearsal."

"Oh! I'll go check," Rosebud chimed in, and darted to the back row of chairs that had been set up. She quickly put her hand up to her eyes. "It's still a problem."

The lights were moved, and Rosebud gave a thumbs-up.

Action continued to happen around them, but Tomas felt like they were in some kind of strange bubble every time he looked at her.

"I think I need one of these dresses. I could wear it to conventions." She was still holding his hand.

No, that dress was the last thing she needed.

The last thing he needed.

But his stupid mouth wouldn't comply with his stupid brain. "Uh-huh," he managed.

She reached out and ran her other hand down his arm. "This looks fantastic on you. When we get back home, you should consider something like this for next year's fundraiser. Can't hurt to get an early start."

How was she talking about something so mundane as their clothes when their whole world had been shoved on its ass?

"The bride!" Grammy cried.

They turned to look to see what Tomas assumed to be Betina and Jackson standing at the start of the plush, red carpet.

Betina put her hand to her mouth and even at a distance, Tomas could see the emotion in her eyes.

Juniper let go of his hand and caught the skirt of her dress to lift it enough so she could dash toward Betina, who she immediately hugged. Tomas followed behind her slowly.

"I can't believe how beautiful you look!" Betina said. "Oh, thank you so much doing this. I don't know what we would have done."

Tomas found a hand thrust in front of him and he shook it.

"Yes, thank you. You're lifesavers," Jackson said.

"And now the emergency has passed, I think I'm about to get fangirl squee all over you," Betina whispered.

Juniper gave her an easy smile and wrapped her in another hug. "Don't do that, you'll get it all over your beautiful dress."

"Not only is my favorite author at my wedding, but she did this for me?" Betina sniffed. "Oh no, I said I wasn't going to cry."

"If you cry, I'll cry. I don't know if I've ever been anyone's *favorite* author before."

Jackson turned his attention to Juniper. "And you're mine, too."

"Really?" Her joy was electric.

"I'll admit, I didn't think I was going to like it, but when I met Betina, you know she was reading one of your books. I told her I'd read it and loved it, and would love to talk about it with her over coffee. So I had to go buy it and read it."

Juniper laughed again. "That's fantastic. I'm glad it wasn't a chore."

"No. I was surprised how much I loved it."

Tomas decided this was a safe subject and one he could speak on. "Juniper is a master at what she does."

"You're the Tomas? The one she dedicates every book to? I can't wait to tell my book club I met you, too." Betina sighed. "And you're every bit as dreamy as we all decided you were. What a relief you're hero material."

But he wasn't, was he?

And that was the root of the problem.

Juniper seemed to sense the change in him, or maybe his need to flee. She put her hand in his again.

"We should go get out of your wedding clothes now that you two are here. Tonight is going to be beautiful, and I can't tell you how much it means to me that I get to be part of your Happily Ever After," Juniper said.

"We wouldn't be here without you." Betina teared up. "Thank you. For everything."

"No, *thank you*."

She gave Betina and Jackson each a soft look, and it seemed as if she wanted to hug them both, but she had a death grip on his hand and she didn't let go. Instead, she dragged him off toward the dressing rooms where they could change back into their normal clothes.

"So, the plan," she said, as if all of that hadn't just happened, "is that we'll get dressed, go back to the grandmothers' house for dinner, then we'll get ready for the Firefly Ceremony."

"Are we walking back up to the castle after dinner?" Tomas didn't think that was going to go over well.

"Definitely not. Pumpkin carriages. We'll walk over to the square, and there will be the pumpkin carriages to transport guests up to the castle."

"Of course pumpkin carriages." He shrugged. "Why not?"

"I like them. I think they're whimsical and fun. But these won't be like the traditional Cinderella carriages. They're going to be black and red, like a poison apple."

He thought that was fitting. The poison part. But he kept it to himself.

She narrowed her eyes, almost like she heard what he was thinking.

"What?"

"You know what. Do not ruin their night for them."

"I wouldn't do that."

"Good. Then don't ruin it for us, either."

"That's all I've been trying to do this whole time, Juniper."

They parted ways at the entrance to the changing tents, but he quickly found that there was to be no reprieve.

Chapter 15

As soon as she entered the changing tent, she remembered that someone had had to help her get into the dress, and now she needed someone to help her out of it.

She bit her lip, wondering if perhaps she should try to find someone—anyone—but Tomas to help her.

Which was stupid. He was just undoing the buttons on the back of the dress.

And untying the corset.

His fingers would be on her bare skin.

Nope, she wasn't going to think about it like that.

It wasn't anything she hadn't asked him to do before.

That time he'd gone with her to one of her convention book signings, he'd helped shovel her into something similar. It hadn't been a big deal. She'd even had him untie the thing after the event.

Same thing, right?

Wrong.

She clenched her hands into fists. This was so frustrating. She was over feeling this distance between them, this fear that at any minute they were going to break.

Or that crossing that line again was bad.

No matter what it was, it was bound to happen. The minute they started acting like things were wrong between them, that's when they would be.

If she wouldn't have hesitated to ask him this in the past, she wasn't going to start now.

Summoning her courage, she went to his tent.

A slight breeze ruffled the opening, and Juniper got a glimpse of his bare back. She sucked in a deep breath. "Tomas?"

"Yeah?"

"I need help with the dress. All these buttons. I can't reach them myself."

"Okay, come in." His voice sounded strangely tinny.

She didn't mean to rake her eyes over his body, but she couldn't help it. His skin was the most beautiful shade of gold, and she knew how hard he worked to sculpt his body. It was art and should most definitely be admired.

Yet, she wanted to do more than admire it. She wanted to touch him everywhere.

She remembered the way he'd looked when she'd pleasured him in the bathroom. The way the cords on his neck had stood out, the veins in his hands and forearms, the thrust of his hips . . .

Why was she doing this to herself?

"It's still just me, *corazoncita*."

"Same," she said, and presented her back to him.

Same? Yeah. That was articulate. Some fucking writer she was. She should've had some kind of witty reply, some sharp quip, something that wasn't "same." Lame.

He began moving his fingers over the tiny scarlet pearl-seed buttons. Her chest grew tight, and her breath caught. The brush of his warm fingers on the bare skin of her back caused her to gasp.

"Sorry," she mumbled. "This corset is killing me."

"Same," he murmured, tossing her own word back at her.

And it broke the tension as they laughed, but only for a moment. Only until his finger dipped into the valley of the ties of the corset.

"If this were one of your books, what would happen next?" he whispered.

"Well, if I were the author, I'd say that the hero owes the heroine one, don't you think?" she said, breathless.

"And how would he pay that debt? Would it be here, in these changing tents where anyone could come in? Would it be another one-upmanship where she has to try to stay quiet and he has to try to make her come so hard she screams?"

"I might've done that in *Dark Captive*."

"I know."

"Just because I wrote it doesn't mean it's my fantasy," she said. "I write a lot of things that I'm not interesting in doing."

"Like what?" He untied the first knot.

She struggled to find something, anything, that she didn't want him to do to her. Right now, if he said he wanted to act out all 237 sex scenes she'd ever written, Juniper wouldn't say no. In fact, it sounded like a good start.

It was easier to think about the need her body had for him instead of the need in her heart.

Seeing him waiting for her at the end of the aisle was almost too much. The way he'd looked at her, like she was his everything. Like this was for keeps. Like she was the answer to his every wish. It made her want it to be real all the more.

She hated that she felt that way. Not because there was anything wrong with wanting those things, or wanting them with Tomas, but because *he* didn't want those things. He didn't believe.

She couldn't expect him to change who he was, or what he wanted, simply because those things didn't line up with her dreams and desires.

And yet, it was desire where they did meet on an even playing field.

"You haven't answered," he said. "Does that mean you don't want to play?"

"This is like a game of Fuck Me Jumanji. I don't think we get to stop playing until we beat the last level."

He laughed. "We can stop any time you give the word, Juniper."

She didn't want to stop. She wanted this.

Well, what she wanted was everything, but she'd have to settle for this.

Juniper swallowed hard.

"Tell me what you want." His voice was harsh, ragged, and filled with a fatalism she couldn't bear.

"Everything," she confessed. "I want everything."

Juniper turned to face him, the dress falling off her shoulders. "There is nothing that I've ever written about I wouldn't do with you."

His eyes darkened, his pupils dilated. "Then take off your dress so I can pay my debt."

She stepped out of the dress and hung it up with shaking hands. He made short work of the rest of the corset and she hung that up as well and slipped out of her panties.

Her nakedness didn't cause the swell of doubt that rose up inside of her, it was the vulnerability.

Yet, whatever happened between them, she trusted him. Juniper was willing to give him anything he wanted. Anything he could imagine.

"I'm going to kiss you."

He pulled her close to him and she felt incredibly decadent being so bare while he was still mostly clothed. She felt very much at his mercy and she loved it.

When he kissed her, it was just as intense as before, like a supernova. She could drown in him, in sensation. This was a new side of Tomas, commanding and primal. She'd initiated all of their past kisses; it made her feel better somehow that he was in the driver's seat. It wasn't only her who was pushing the handcart to hell.

Heaven.

Wherever they eventually ended up.

He lifted her easily to perch her on the edge of the makeshift vanity, and she didn't hesitate to push her fingers through his dark hair when his mouth moved to her throat.

"*Besarte es como ver las estrellas*," he murmured against her skin.

To kiss you is like seeing stars.

"*Eres divina*," he said, as he moved to the valley of her breasts.

You are divine.

She arched into him, the scalding heat of his mouth, his touch.

He spoke other words that she didn't understand, but they were obviously praise. His appreciation of her body was in the reverence of his touch, the dark depths of his eyes, and the way that every single thing he did took her higher than she thought she could go.

Tomas dipped down to her stomach, kissing her, caressing her, and cooing praise all the way until he dropped down to his knees.

She looked down at him, a hedonist in the midst of his work between her spread thighs, and he turned his face into her thigh to kiss her there, too, all the while holding her gaze.

When he finally bent to her cleft, she thought the first touch of his tongue was the pinnacle of all sensation. Then it was the second.

The third.

Her hands were on his shoulders now and she knew she'd never touch him in any casual way again and not remember what this felt like.

The crisp bite of fall, the scent of cinnamon and cloves in the air, and the feeling of her hands on his body while he took absolute delight in repaying her in kind.

He was too good, too focused. It was going to be over

much too soon and then they'd descend back into the hell of uncertainty and fear.

What she'd done with him in Pick 'n' Axe had done little to nothing to diminish the tension between them. Obviously, it had only upped the ante.

She knew he wouldn't take this to the ultimate culmination here because then they'd have nowhere left to go, except to that place they both feared, each for different reasons.

Wave after wave of bliss washed over her, both sating her fierce desire and yet still, driving it higher and higher.

"Tomas!" His name was torn from her lips on a ragged cry.

He intensified his ministrations until she was mindless with pleasure and the storm took her over the edge.

As the after tremors ricocheted through her with all the force of a cannonball, she clung to him. He rose up to hold her against his chest, his hands gently stroking up and down her spine.

For a single moment, she was in heaven.

This was everything she wanted.

And nothing.

Tomas loved her, but he wasn't in love with her. He never would be.

She wanted to tell him her secret so desperately. Juniper wanted to be free to tell him, without consequence, that she loved him.

Not just that she loved him, but that she was in love with him.

That he was her one, her only, her forever.

It was then she remembered something her high school creative writing teacher had told her. Ms. Gibson had warned her that being an author wasn't all it was cracked up to be. "Those who can, do," she'd said. "And those who can't, will teach creative writing to ungrateful freshmen."

Against all odds, she'd managed the author part, but when

it came to love, well, she supposed she was stuck teaching ungrateful freshmen.

Or at least writing heroes who she, and other women like her, could fall in love with until the real thing came along.

That was when the awful knowledge hit her like a wrecking ball.

She'd thought Tomas was the real thing, but he couldn't be. Not if he didn't believe.

At least, not the right one for her. Maybe there was another woman out there who felt exactly as he did, and maybe she was his One.

She tightened her arms around his waist and buried her face there in his chest like a baby bird hiding under a wing from a storm.

The longer she stayed there, the longer it was until they had to face the fallout of what had happened between them.

And what was still coming.

He seemed content to have her there as well.

Oh so slowly, the outside world began to intrude.

"Darlings, darlings!" Rosebud called. "I need the wedding finery! Are you almost decent?" She snickered and then mumbled to what she obviously thought was only herself. "Might be a while before I can get those. Good thing I'm magic with a needle."

"Youse bet yer cute patooty it is," a male voice answered. "Think they're doing the dirt right now?"

"Don't be filthy, Bronx."

Bronx? Wasn't that the name of that fat cardinal that kept trying to shit on Tomas? No, no way.

Her eyes widened.

"What?" Tomas whispered. "She won't come in. You're safe."

"Did you hear that?"

"Rosebud?"

"No. The guy."

Tomas fixed her with a curious expression. "No."

"Shitballs. I think she heard me," Bronx said.

"Did you hear *that*?" Juniper asked.

Tomas smirked. "I rang your bell so hard, you're hearing things. Points for me."

He looked ridiculously pleased with himself.

If he were any other man, she'd assume he was just being a dick about hearing Bronx, but she could tell from his reactions that he really hadn't heard anything.

"Darlings?" Rosebud asked again.

"Yeah, we'll be out in just a moment. Sorry. We were . . ." She coughed. "Talking."

"No worries, dears. I have to run along and fix a tear in one of the bridesmaid dresses. That should give you a chance to finish your conversation," Rosebud said without guile or sarcasm.

"She's a gem," Tomas said.

Juniper bit her lip and looked up at him. God, but she wanted to kiss him again.

"Keep looking at me like that and we're going to have another *conversation*."

"Threaten me with a good time, why don't you?" She grinned and ran her hands up her sides and then curled around his back to pull him closer. "We could have a more in-depth conversation right now. It would have to be fast, but I think we could manage it."

"No, I don't think we could. See, you know how we like to talk things to death?" He nodded but pulled her hips forward so that his erection was pressed against her. "We have to explore every avenue. Make sure we get each detail correct. Short conversations are for the uninspired, and that's not us."

"Damn, but I love you." The words slipped out of their own accord, but after they were out, she was careful to school her features to a sexy smile. Or at least, what she hoped was a sexy smile. That would be all she needed—to think she was giving him some come-hither smile, but, really, she looked like a derp fish.

To her relief, he didn't seem to notice anything out of place about her words. Instead, he simply said, "I know."

She rolled her eyes. "If you're going to be like that, I just won't tell you."

"I think we can both find better things to do with our mouths."

"No. You don't deserve it. Tell me I'm amazing, then we'll see," she teased.

"You weren't paying attention, then. I've already told you that you're the most beautiful woman I've ever seen, that your body is made of stars and rivals heaven. You need to learn more Spanish, *mi amor*."

"I knew some of it. You were talking with your mouth full." She agreed, though, she should learn more Spanish. "But I do like it. Your mother is right. Everything sounds better."

"Can we not talk about my mother right now?"

That was fair. She didn't really much want to talk about his mother, either. Hers, too, for that matter. "Okay. New task. Can you get my clothes from the other tent?"

"Of course." He released her, dropped a kiss on the top of her head, and went to get her clothes.

He was only gone for seconds, but in that time, she'd had ample opportunity to start a freak-out loop in her brain.

Namely, what had they done? What did this mean for them? When could they do it again?

When he came back in, he paused, staring at her. She suddenly felt even more vulnerable than she had before they'd done this.

"What?"

The way his gaze roved her body, it was like a physical touch, and she wasn't sure if it was good or bad.

"You're just so goddamn beautiful. How did I not know this?"

"I'm not sure if that's a compliment or not? Like, am I stealth pretty?" She'd never thought she was ugly, but Tomas saying he didn't know she was pretty confused her.

"You know the power of words more than anyone. I didn't say pretty. I said beautiful."

She couldn't meet his eyes then, and she looked away, biting her lip. "Then kiss me again."

"Woman, we do not have the time," he teased.

But then he did. He took her in his arms and he pressed his lips to hers. She could taste herself on his mouth, and that got her hot all over again, but this kiss was about something more.

It was about making a memory in the aftermath.

It was about telling him how much she loved him in word, in deed, and for a moment, feeling their hearts beat as one—before they went back out into the world where what had happened between them meant nothing.

Chapter 16

"You're filthy," Jonquil accused, pointing her wand at Bluebonnet.

Bluebonnet smacked the wand down with the palm of her hand. "Don't point that thing at me." But then she crossed her arms over her chest. "I am, aren't I?"

Petty thought Bon-Bon looked rather smug about it all. "What did I miss?" she asked as she fiddled with the firefly cages.

"Your sister and her . . . sex magic."

Petty perked. "Sex magic?"

"Well, what would you call it?" Jonquil demanded from Bon-Bon.

"I don't know. But so what? What's wrong with that?" Bluebonnet wiggled her nose in obvious indignation. "Honestly, it was intended to be a gift for the bride and groom."

"What was a gift? Oh goddess, what have you done?" Petunia demanded, but then she put her hand over her mouth to stifle a laugh. "Please, don't tell me you did what I think you did."

Bluebonnet huffed. "Betina, the dear, confided in me last night that she's a little nervous about tonight."

"Whyever would she be nervous?" Jonquil squinted. "It's not like . . ." She gasped. "It is like?"

Bluebonnet nodded emphatically. "Yes. She's a virgin. They both agreed to wait until they were married. I thought it was rather sweet. I'd think you'd adore it, being as old-fashioned as you are, Jonquil."

"Well, Bon-Bon, as we know, that ship has usually sailed." Jonquil nodded at her.

"Yes. Well."

Petty straightened her spectacles. "Our dear Betina," she sighed.

"Our dear Juniper," Jonquil corrected.

Bon-Bon giggled. "I have to say, I'm sure it's turned out for the best."

"I still don't know what you did," Petty reminded her. She was dying to know what kind of sauce Bon-Bon had put on that dish. Mostly so she could remember it was a tool in their arsenal should the need arise again.

Arise. She tried not to giggle to herself. Petty was an adult, and a professional. She was supposed to be above dick jokes.

Yet, for all her trials and tribulations, she was not. Much to her own chagrin.

"Oh! I just bespelled the wedding clothes to heighten their desire for each other, and before you tsk-tsk me, I sweetened the spell with honey and rose quartz so it was all done with sweet, sweet love."

Petty thought that was kind and dear. "Sweet, sweet Bon-Bon!"

"Thank you," Bluebonnet said, obviously pleased with herself.

"You may have to redo it, because my sources tell me that Juniper and Tomas used it *all* up," Jonquil said.

"Your sources?" Bluebonnet snorted.

"A little bird told me."

"If it's who I think he is . . ." Bluebonnet trailed off.

"Don't you dare. If you fat-shame that bird, I'm going to smite you," Jonquil threatened.

"I wasn't going to say anything about his chonk. Just that you know how Bronx likes to stir the pot."

"As if we don't?" Petty interjected.

The three sisters looked at each other and cackled.

The fireflies buzzed happily in their cage and flickered their lighted behinds in time with their happy cackle.

"Oh, my darlings. You have such important work tonight," Petty cooed at them and watched as they buzzed toward the magic in her wand.

"Yes, yes. That's tonight. We need to get back to the task at hand. With Juniper," Jonquil directed.

"Yes, of course. What is it you want me to do?" Petty asked, focusing back on their mission.

"Well, according to my calculations, they weren't supposed to do the deed until after the masque. Everything is off course," Jonquil said. "The sexual tension still hasn't been resolved." She held up some of the flower centerpieces, and every single one of the roses had transformed into a pussy willow.

Petty giggled, setting off a chain reaction of giggles among the sisters, and Jonquil swung the bouquet of pussy willows around like floppy swords.

"En garde!" Jonquil cried, swatting Bon-Bon.

"I hope you know," Bluebonnet said in a staid tone, "this means war." She brandished a centerpiece of her own and shoved it at her sister.

Jonquil parried, thrusted, and defended herself against the surprisingly limber and battle-ready Bon-Bon.

"Wait, wait, wait!" Petty cried. "How can our calculations be off?"

Jonquil, startled by the question, froze mid-thrust, and Bluebonnet took the strategic advantage to shove the long, furry, cylindrical flower right into Jonquil's open mouth.

Jonquil's eyes narrowed, and she spat out the offending plant. "War, you say?"

Petty had to take a solid clock minute to compose herself

before she could speak again, but Bluebonnet gave no such mercy.

Her cackles and snorts had devolved into the sound of a truffling pig.

Which seemed to have given Jonquil an idea because she raised her wand.

"Jonquil!" Petty cried. "No!"

But it was too late.

Where Bon-Bon had once stood was now a very large, very pink, and very upset squealing sow.

Wearing Bon-Bon's kerchief.

There were even little holes for her ears.

"Now you've done it," Petty whispered, unable to keep the awe out of her voice.

The pig, for her part, pawed at the ground, reminding Petty of a bull about to charge. Then, that's exactly what Bon-Bon the pig did: she charged Jonquil.

But Jonquil was laughing much too hard to defend herself.

Petty couldn't quite distinguish the shrieking laughter from the squealing pig.

That was when things got juicy.

Bluebonnet must have tried to work some kind of magic because she got bigger. Big enough that she could carry Jonquil, and carry her she did. She charged to and fro, snorting and roaring, making a wild attempt to fling Jonquil into the sun. Or so that's what Petty surmised.

She used her wand to zap them both up into the air and held them, flailing and squealing, mid-flight.

Petty wondered just what kind of hell she might have unintentionally unleashed because it was very common to swear upon the eventuality of pigs flying.

Bon-Bon, at this very moment, was a porcine aeronaut.

Jonquil was still laughing.

Petty did her level best to bring them both back down to

the ground gently, and oh so slowly Bluebonnet became her normal, if furious, self.

"Oh my goddess," Jonquil wheezed. "This is the best thing that's ever happened. The best." Just when it seemed that Jonquil had quieted herself, she'd take a few deep breaths and school her features and then, she'd cackle all over again.

Petty was sure her tummy had to ache like the devil.

Which was why Petty had strict control of her cackle. She knew once she started, she wouldn't be able to stop. They still had a mission to accomplish.

And Bon-Bon would be intensely hurt.

Bluebonnet found her wand and raised it, and Petty knew her sister so well, she knew exactly what was going through her mind. She was considering turning Jonquil into something much worse than a pig.

But because she knew her sister so well, she made no move to stop her. She was ninety percent sure that Bluebonnet wouldn't go through with it.

She'd get Jonquil back in other ways.

It might take her a hundred or so years, but she'd do it.

Jonquil held up a quivering hand. "Listen, I'm . . . Whooo . . . Oh goddess." She lowered her hand and then raised it again. "I am actually sorry." She pressed her other hand to her chest as she continued to wheeze with laughter. "I didn't mean to. It was a stress misfire."

Bluebonnet sniffed with indignation and righted her kerchief.

Which Jonquil found to be even funnier.

"Stop. I'm literally going to die. Don't look at me," Jonquil pleaded.

Bluebonnet glared harder but then turned back to Petty. "As you were saying about our calculations?"

If Petty lived to be 2,020, which she probably would, she'd never forget Bon-Bon the pig and she had to cast a quick spell on herself so she could cackle later, in the privacy of her room, where Bluebonnet could neither see nor hear her.

Jonquil finally settled and cleared her throat. "Yes, as I was saying. Weren't we planning for them to consummate at the hotel?"

"Oh, no. At least, I wasn't," Petty said. God, that would've been awful for them to give in to carnal desires in that cheap den of sin. No, she just wanted to bring awareness of those desires to the forefront was all.

"Do you think that maybe you should have shared that with the rest of us?" Jonquil said.

"I thought it was obvious?" Bluebonnet said.

"We definitely need a vacation," Petunia said. "Our wires are starting to cross. Wand misfires." Petty pondered. "Oh, I see now."

"What?" Jonquil asked, casting another sly glance at Bon-Bon and pushing the tip of her nose up with her finger and making a pig face at her.

"You're going to die a slow death in the belly of a . . ." Bluebonnet paused. "No, no. I've decided the form of your destructor."

Jonquil was suddenly young, blond, thin, and wearing an eighties-style workout ensemble. Complete with leg warmers. "Like, I'm so sure." She chomped her gum a few times, bopping her head back and forth from side to side.

Then Jonquil was herself again.

"A misfire, huh? Seems like you've got great control now," Bluebonnet accused.

"Sisters!" Petty demanded. If she didn't intervene now, who knew where they'd end up? Definitely not peak fairy godmother, and Petty was determined they'd achieve the pinnacle of success.

"She started it," Bon-Bon grumbled.

"She did," Petty agreed. "But . . . I need you both to stay

on task. Just another couple of days and we can run away to Pirate Island, or whatever."

"Drake Gregorian," Bluebonnet sighed.

"Whatever," Jonquil groused.

Petty gritted her teeth with frustration. Her usual motivators weren't working. "Fine. I'll let you figure out the timing threads all by yourselves."

At that, the other two sisters scrambled to appease her, just like Petty knew they would. She didn't pull out the "I'm Taking All My Toys and Leaving" strategy very often, but it was effective in times like this. Petty's special gift was seeing the threads of fate. She could pluck them from the ether and watch the different paths hearts could take.

"We're sorry," Jonquil said. "Tell us."

"We're listening," Bluebonnet encouraged.

Petty fixed them both in turn with an appraising look before continuing. "So, at the hotel, all signs pointed to the big bang."

Jonquil blinked. "Can you . . . not?"

"What?" Petty grinned. "Big bang?"

Bluebonnet giggled.

Jonquil just sighed.

"Anyway, if they'd done the deed then, we'd already be to the hard part." Petty snickered at her own phrasing. "The part where they're sad and they can't be together."

"I'm frankly amazed they've held out this long. And maybe a little disappointed," Bluebonnet confessed.

"You know that even with our help, everything in its own time."

"Everything in its place, and everything has its time," Jonquil replied dutifully.

"So, the whole shebang should go down tonight," Petunia said, as she examined the silvery thread in front of her.

Then she saw something that caused her great concern.

"Oh. Oh no."

"What?" Bluebonnet and Jonquil said at the same time.

"Their Happily Ever After isn't the only outcome." She pulled at a thread and tugged it forward to see where it split in half. "It's possible he won't have the epiphany he needs."

Bluebonnet and Jonquil both put their hands to their chests, as if the very idea was too much for their hearts to take.

"How can this be?" Bon-Bon gasped. "Poor Juniper."

She studied it further. "No, not poor Juniper. Not at all. I mean, for a while, she'll be heartbroken. Devastated. But she'll heal." Petty looked up to meet her sisters' questing gazes. "She'll fall in love again. With . . . eww. No. That can't be right." She peered closer.

"What? Who?" Jonquil demanded.

"You're killing us here, Pets."

She'd forgotten for a moment that her sisters couldn't see what she saw. "I'm sorry, darlings. I just got lost in the maze." She let the thread snap back into place and focused on the real world. "If Tomas doesn't get himself together, Juniper will end up with Roderick. It seems she likes lawyers."

"Why did you say eww? I thought we liked Roderick?" Jonquil asked.

"We do, but we like him for Gwen. If Juniper and Roderick end up together, Gwen will never fall in love again. She won't miss it; she'll be happy here. But Tomas won't fall in love again, either."

Bluebonnet nodded knowingly. "And he will miss it, won't he?"

"Not to be too dark, but he'll die alone and full of regret," Petty shared.

"Our little Juniper, will she be happy with Roderick?" Jonquil asked.

"Oh, yes. But not intensely. Not the way she would be with Tomas," Petty said.

Jonquil shook her fist at the sky. "Get your shit together, Tomas!"

"We may need to activate the mamas," Bluebonnet said.

"I don't know. I think at this point, any more pushing is going to break him. Ever After itself seems to want to eject him. He wants to eject himself, too. I think we're going to have to let it ride," Petty said unhappily. "I hate it when meddling doesn't help."

"Me too," Bluebonnet huffed.

Jonquil was usually the one who advocated for less meddling, but this time, she said, "What, exactly, constitutes meddling?" She blinked several times, as if that alone could prove her innocent of the whole affair.

"Sometimes, I do like how you think," Bon-Bon praised grudgingly.

"I think we've got one last shot at dinner tonight. The rest is going to be all up to them," Jonquil said.

"So what are you thinking? Love amplifier in their food?" Petty asked. "We did that with Ransom and Lucky and it seemed to work pretty well."

"Hmm, I don't know. We've already amplified things with the enchanted costumes," Bluebonnet said.

"I think perhaps good old-fashioned meddling might work this time. No magic. Just us, being our doddering, old, grandmotherly selves," Jonquil said.

"What if we got them to stay a little longer?" Petty said. "We could get to the root of Tomas's problem."

"Or, I could just hit him with something heavy." Bon-Bon shrugged. "It worked on Captain Gregorian."

"Bon-Bon," Petty began in a very serious tone.

"What?"

"Captain Gregorian is dead. He's a ghost."

"I know." Then her eyes widened. "I didn't kill him if that's what you mean."

"To be fair, you did suggest hitting Tomas with something heavy," Jonquil said, conciliatory.

"To rattle his brain a little so it makes the proper connections. Not to kill him," Bluebonnet huffed again. "Geez. Talk about going dark."

"I don't like this uncertainty. I mean, I know I'm always the one who says we should leave things be, but this . . ." Jonquil shook her head. "I just can't leave this alone."

"We're not going to." Petty looked up at the sky. "Fiddle-faddle! We need to get back to the cottage and make dinner."

"You mean this dinner?" Bluebonnet swung her wand in a series of delicate arcs. "It's in the oven. It'll be ready to go by the time we get back."

"Can we please float back to the cottage in a time keeper?" Jonquil begged. "I'm so tired. I need an ice cream and a nap before I deal with all of this. Today has been too much. Using all that magic drained me a little."

Bluebonnet narrowed her eyes. "Oh, you're tired? You're not the one who shape-shifted today."

Jonquil yawned. "I know. But I am the one who laughed so hard I deprived myself of oxygen for a solid five minutes."

"You're not even ashamed."

"Maybe a little. I really am sorry, Bon-Bon." Jonquil did seem contrite.

"I think we could all do with the nap in the time keeper before tonight's festivities. We still have to write our messages to send across the veil," Petty said.

"No rest for the wicked," Bon-Bon said. "So it's a good thing we're awesome fairy godmothers."

"To the nap!" Petty cried, ready to lead the charge.

Meddling was hard work. They needed to rest up to deal with what was coming for them next.

Chapter 17

Tomas wasn't sure how he was going to make it through dinner, let alone the rest of the weekend. The walls seemed to be closing in around him, and he could see no escape.

He was trapped in fairy-tale land and the inmates had taken over the prison, so to speak.

Yet, when he looked around at what was beginning to become a gilded cage, he felt guilty for thinking of it as such. The family who loved him were not shackles. The warmth that permeated everything the grandmothers did was not the ore used to craft chains.

Technically, no one had asked him for anything he didn't want.

Juniper had asked him not to harp on his disbelief, but she hadn't asked him to suspend it.

Everything that had happened thus far had been of his own free will. Agreeing to pretend to be her fiancé, coming with her on this trip to begin with, and everything that had happened between them. He'd been a willing participant.

Tomas could get up and leave any time he chose.

Except, looking at the grandmothers as they bustled around the kitchen preparing a meal for them, and Juniper as she sat at the table with a happy smile, he knew he couldn't choose to leave.

He wouldn't.

"I'm sorry we haven't gotten as much time together this visit," Petty said, as she pulled a piping-hot cherry pie out of the oven.

"It's okay, Grammas. I know that you're trying to launch your business. Weddings are hard work," Juniper said. "Although, I forgot to tell you that Tomas has promised to make us enchiladas and tamales! So you could've taken the night off."

Petty almost dropped the pie. "Estella's recipe?"

Jonquil and Bluebonnet both perked.

"I didn't realize it was famous outside of my mother's house," he said.

"Don't let your mother hear you say that," Juniper said.

"Well, that settles it, then," Jonquil said with a certain finality. "You just have to stay another couple of days."

Juniper grinned. "Maybe we will. I don't have to be back, but I think Tomas does." It was kind of her to leave him an out, even though he already knew that she wanted to stay.

"Pish posh," Petty said with a dismissive wave of her hand. "Work will always be there. Time with family is the commodity." She looked directly at Tomas. "Don't you think?"

He felt like the kid who had to sit in the first row in grade school. The one the teachers always chose to look at when they spoke and every question was a test. Luckily, he knew the answer to this one.

"Definitely," he said easily.

"So, it's settled. Another day." Petty grinned.

"I'll check my appointments. I don't think I have any Monday," he said.

Juniper beamed at him. "Yeah? Really? We can?"

"Sure. Why not? But let me double-check my calendar just to be sure." It wouldn't be a sacrifice to stay another day and let the grandmothers feed them, especially if it made Juniper so happy.

"You absolutely have to tell them about the dildo," Juniper blurted.

This time, Petty did drop the pie. Peach. It sounded like the plate shattered. Tomas popped up to go help her clean the mess.

Only, there was no mess. Jonquil picked it up with strawberry-shaped oven mitts.

"No worries, darlings. It just took a bit of a fall, but it's still pie, and only the bottom of the pan touched the floor," Jonquil said.

Juniper was looking back and forth between him and the pie; her eyes were wide. Her expression told him he should be seeing something incredible, but all he saw was pie. Which, to be fair, was pretty great, but it didn't warrant the way Juniper's eyes had bugged out of her head.

"Everything okay, Junebug?" Bluebonnet asked carefully.

"I . . ." She straightened. "I don't know."

"Oh," Jonquil sighed happily.

"It's time," Petty said.

"For what?" Tomas asked. "We still have a couple hours before we have to leave for Castle Blackheart." He didn't understand half the conversations that were had in this house, but it worked for Juniper so he'd try to roll with it.

"You'll see. We'll tell you later," Bluebonnet said.

"Tell me now," Juniper demanded.

Jonquil went to her and clasped both of her hands. "Believe."

Juniper looked at Tomas, her eyes wide and brimming with wonder, but all he could do was shrug. She looked back to Jonquil.

"Believe, my child, when you're on the darkest part of the road. Believe in the light inside of you and it will light the way home," Jonquil swore. "All your questions will be answered after the masque."

He had absolutely zero idea what was happening. Tomas picked up his cup of iced tea and sniffed it, searching for traces of something illicit that would make him hallucinate whatever the hell was going on. Finding nothing, he looked back at Petty and Bluebonnet, who were carrying on as if nothing out of the ordinary had happened.

It was official.

He'd lost his mind.

He was going to wake up in a hospital somewhere, and Juniper would be there holding his hand and he would know that it was her voice that brought him back from near death. Everything that had happened was a malfunction of his brain due to a head injury.

He'd wake up, and he'd tell Juniper everything. They'd laugh about it and life would go on.

Except it occurred to him he didn't want to go back to a world where he didn't know what it was like to feel her nails digging into his shoulders, the taste of her on his lips, and how perfectly she fit in his arms.

He took her hand, holding it while he could. While she'd let him.

At some point, she was going to want to talk, and she wasn't going to like what he had to say.

This thing between them was just biology. He refused to call it anything else. It was separate from the love he felt for her.

Romantic love didn't last. It wasn't real. When their hormones changed, when the biological imperative to stay together faded, so did love.

He couldn't fathom why she couldn't understand what they had was better.

"Aw, you kids," Petty said with a grin.

"Why don't you take a walk around the yard before dinner?" Bluebonnet encouraged. "Nothing like a little walk to get those digestive juices moving."

"Gramma Bon-Bon?" Juniper began. "Not the best imagery before dinner."

"Says the girl who wanted her fiancé to tell her grammas about a dildo," Bluebonnet responded in a sweet voice.

Juniper and Tomas both cringed.

"I . . . sorry. But I knew you'd appreciate it." Juniper shrugged.

Jonquil snickered.

"You two are terrible," Petty said, as if she wasn't snickering herself.

"*Corazoncita*, I am not telling your grandmothers any such thing. My mother would hear me from home and come wash my mouth out with soap. She would also tell me she didn't raise me to speak that way to women. You may tell it, if you wish."

Petty grinned. "Goodness, child. It's not like the three of us don't know what it is. You speaking of it isn't going to conjure the thing."

Jonquil raised her brow and Bluebonnet pursed her lips.

"Hush. Don't tempt fate," Petty said.

"That's all we're trying to say," Bluebonnet countered.

"Fair."

He swore they were speaking another language, but Juniper didn't seem to notice.

"Okay. So. He had a client who was fighting with his wife over a dildo," Juniper began.

"I would never have said this out loud to my abuela," he swore.

Juniper waved her hand. "Who do you think gave me the birds-and-the-bees talk?"

"Your mother and your grandmothers?"

Juniper nodded. "All of them. At least I got it over with in one fell swoop. Anyway. It has a name."

Petty widened her eyes.

Bluebonnet tittered.

Jonquil rolled her eyes. "One of those? Goddess preserve us."

"Heaven, it was called. None of these facts are the ones you're going to find shocking," Juniper began.

"Isn't she so good at storytelling?" Bon-Bon beamed.

"Yes, quite," Jonquil said. "I love how she does the buildup. Next thing you know, she's going to say the thing was made of pure gold."

Juniper bloomed under the praise. "Not gold, but silver. It was designed by a New Zealand silversmith."

"What?" Petty asked. "Wow."

"There's more. It retails for a half a million dollars."

Tomas didn't know exactly what reaction he expected from the grandmothers, but the three of them bursting into gales of laughter was not it.

"See? I told you they'd think it was funny."

"Oh, child!" Petty hooted. "This really might be too much for me."

"So wait, is this the client that you fired? Your mother told us that you're getting a promotion because you declined a client," Jonquil asked.

"That's the one." Had his mother told everyone all of his business? He loved the woman to the stars and back, and he was glad he made her proud, but it was disconcerting how much of his business she spilled everywhere.

"We almost forgot!" Bluebonnet shouted.

"*Oh!*" Jonquil and Bluebonnet shared a knowing look. "I'll just run and get it, shall I?"

Jonquil toddled off, and Bluebonnet and Petty clapped their hands together with glee.

"We hope you like it," Petty said when they returned with a small square box wrapped in a purple ribbon and set it on the table in front of him.

He looked at the box, then back up at the grandmothers, their faces bright and cheeks flushed.

Petty motioned for him to open the gift, but he wanted to sit with the moment just for a few seconds more.

He wasn't used to anyone but his mother and Juniper making such a big deal out of his accomplishments.

Juniper understood exactly what he was feeling and what he needed. She always did. She put her hand on his shoulder and squeezed.

"Open it."

He opened the box to find a watch from a designer he'd never heard of but wouldn't be out of place next to a Breitling. It was silver, with a strange iridescent blue face. The watch had no hands, so he wasn't sure how it was supposed to work.

Petty patted his hand. "Wear it for a few days. You'll learn how it works. A dear friend of ours is a watchmaker, and he swears it will tell you the time when you need it."

Tomas loved it.

He didn't care if it told the time or not. It was a thoughtful gift, and he liked the way it felt on his wrist. As soon as he closed the clasp, he felt so much more like himself.

"Happy promotion!" the grandmothers said together, and each kissed his cheek and hugged him.

"Now, you two go for that walk and when you get back, dinner will be ready." Jonquil herded them to the door and practically shoved them outside.

"I guess they wanted us outside," Juniper said.

"I can't believe you told them the dildo story."

"Eh? They read my books, so they've heard worse."

"I also can't believe they did this." He held up his arm with the watch.

"It's actually exquisite. There most likely isn't another one like it in the world." She fluttered her fingers over the watch face.

"They love me," he said quietly. "They barely know me and they love me."

"You're pretty lovable," she said softly.

"Can I tell you something?" Of course, he knew he could tell her anything, but he was building up the courage to hear the words himself.

She nodded.

"I don't think I knew that." His voice was barely above a whisper.

Instead of reacting with an embrace, or any other gentle thing he'd ask of her, she punched him in the arm. "Tomas Rivera, you shit."

"What? Me? Here I am baring my soul and you punch me."

"Of course I punched you. Are you serious? I have loved you with my entire being the whole of my life, and you just now realize you deserve to be loved?" She crossed her arms over her chest. "Wait until I tell your mother."

He grinned. "Come on, both of those are different and you know it."

"Not so much." She didn't return the smile. "By saying it's different, you're discounting the magnitude of the emotion. You're saying you didn't really feel it until someone else told you."

"You're right. But that's not ever what I meant."

That was when she smiled. "Good to hear. I knew that, but I wanted you to say it out loud so you heard it, too."

"You're as bad as the grandmothers."

"And yet, you still love me." She grinned wider. "Come on. Say that, too."

"Nope. You've meddled enough. All this self-realization. Don't like it. Don't want it. Not going to do it anymore." Of course, he didn't mean it. Not in the slightest.

"Okay. Suit yourself. I may just have to go to the masque on my own."

Tomas decided he didn't like that option at all. "*Madre de Dios*, fine. I love you."

"Was that so hard?"

He was tempted to say yes, but when he looked into her face, he found he couldn't. Not even to tease her. "No, it wasn't hard."

"Oh!" she exclaimed. "This is so wonderful."

Juniper stood with her hands out, and she was twirling in some invisible storm. She seemed to be holding something in her hands, but if she was, it was something he couldn't see.

He could smell cherry blossoms, but the cherry tree was bare and asleep for the coming winter.

She laughed again, and twirled some more, the scent of cherry blossoms wafting thicker with her every spin.

Again, he had to wonder just what the fuck was going on.

He turned to check the kitchen window, and he heard the grandmothers giggling like children who'd gotten caught with their hands in the cookie jar.

Juniper suddenly stopped, and her shoulders slouched. "You don't see it, do you?"

"I have to say, I have zero clue what you're talking about," he confessed. "You look slightly insane. I mean, we'll roll with it, but it's nuts."

"Not inside earlier when Jonquil zapped the pie back into existence, either, huh?"

He squinted at her, as if that would make her words make sense.

"Don't give me that look. I think you're just going to have to trust me."

"I do."

"But you don't believe what I'm saying."

"I think that we're both really tired and—"

"Look, I know you think that I've always got my head in the clouds, but I choose to put it there. When have I ever been the manic pixie dream girl who dances in rain that's not there?"

"Never."

"So why don't you have faith in me?"

"I do," he swore.

"You don't, Tomas. And that's where we have the problem." She turned to go back inside.

He followed behind her, unable to quiet the part of him that suspected she might be right.

Chapter 18

As Juniper slid into her dress for the masque, she remembered the last time she'd worn it.

The night of the fundraiser had only been days ago, but it seemed like a lifetime.

Her world had changed so much since that night. Nothing was the way it was supposed to be, but she knew that she couldn't worry about the way things were supposed to be, she had to deal with things as they were.

The realization that Tomas didn't believe in her had been a shitty one. A punch to the solar plexus if she were to keep thinking about it.

She understood why he didn't believe her about Jonquil, and she'd not even tried to explain the cherry blossoms that had burst to life from the great tree and showered her in their delicate bounty.

Things were starting to add up for her in other ways, too. She was becoming more and more convinced that the grandmothers, who used their fairy-tale schtick for matchmaking and meddling, might be what they said they were. Or something not of this world. At first, the thought had seemed even more batshit than suggesting she and Tomas get married for real, but she knew she could trust her own eyes, and her own memories. The grandmothers believed in her, and she could do no less than believe in them, too.

The grandmothers never aged.

The weather was always perfect in Ever After.

The animals, well . . . she'd chased squirrels and skunks and rabbits as a child, and they even let her catch them every now and again. It had always seemed like they were playing with her, not running from her. She knew she'd heard that bird talking, and Rosebud talking back to him.

Jonquil had zapped a brutally murdered pie back to perfect and delicious health.

And when she'd talked about her love for Tomas, the cherry tree had bloomed, and bloomed, and bloomed some more.

She remembered how Jonquil had told her that she only had to believe.

Her belief wasn't the problem. It was Tomas's. She couldn't believe for him. So she didn't understand how her faith, how her oh-so-painful hope was going to change anything.

Although, Juniper supposed that was probably why Gramma Petty had told her to keep believing.

She looked in the full-length mirror to study her reflection, and she saw sadness on her face, in the depths of her own eyes. Juniper didn't want to be sad. The Firefly Ceremony was her favorite thing, and she was determined to experience it with joy.

As she watched, her hair began to wave all on its own, silky, smooth, as if she'd just had a blowout and a Hollywood stylist take her in hand. Then she saw Jonquil standing behind her.

"Thought you could use a little help." Jonquil put her arms around Juniper and squeezed gently.

She had quite a grip for such a small woman.

"Do I have to be back by midnight?"

"Oh, no, dearie. It'll last as long as you're in Ever After, if you want it to."

Juniper, while she trusted herself, wanted confirmation. This must have been what they meant about it being time to tell her. She was surprised at how easily she believed. How willing she was to simply accept that magic was real. Maybe because she'd always known. It had always been alive deep in the stardust in her bones. "So this magic stuff . . ."

"This magic stuff." Jonquil nodded.

"Part of me wishes I'd known sooner, but there's another part of me that always knew."

"We were so sad when we had to stop wearing our wings around you. Oh, but you were a delight as a child. Most of our charges are, but you were so special." Jonquil leaned into her again. "I'm not supposed to say, but you're my favorite."

Juniper hugged her back. "I think it's allowed. I hope so, because you're my favorite, too."

"Petty is usually the most popular, and that doesn't bother Bon-Bon or me. We know we're loved. So I'm sure they'll feel the same."

"One question."

"Just one?" Jonquil sounded surprised.

"Well, to start. How are you guys my grandmothers instead of my godmothers?"

"You got lucky, kid."

"You know what I mean."

"I do, but that involves saying the name of him who shall not be named. Suffice to say, one of your ancestors got a bit of our magic and that makes you ours."

"I'm trying to believe, Gramma Jonquil. I'm trying so hard."

Jonquil patted her hand. "I know you are. It's all going to be okay. You'll see."

"I have a confession to make," Juniper blurted, and looked down at her feet. "We lied to you. I'm sorry." Damn, there went her plot for payback meddling. She couldn't very well plot against them while she was confessing her sins and hoping for forgiveness.

Jonquil patted her hand again. "Oh, honey. Did you think

that pretending to be engaged was your idea?" Her blue eyes sparkled with mischief.

"I . . . I actually did. Yes."

"Not at all. Sometimes, we do know what we're doing."

"I guess if you've been doing it long enough. . . ." Juniper shrugged.

Jonquil squeaked. "That's the best reaction anyone has ever had upon finding out they've been the recipient of our machinations."

"Trust the experts, right?" Juniper shrugged again. "Also, I need to know. Petty and Phillip Charming? I met Zuri, and they seem so ridiculously perfect for each other."

"Phillip Charming is *that* Prince Charming. He was courting Petty, and he kissed Bon-Bon. So Petty turned him into a frog," Jonquil said matter-of-factly.

Juniper's eyes widened. "You guys are even cooler than I thought you were. Cooler than the other side of the pillow."

"We like to think so. It's important work." Jonquil grabbed her arms. "I almost forgot!"

"What now?" Juniper cried. However cool this magic thing was, Juniper didn't think she could take any more surprises. She was still processing this one.

"It's nothing bad. In fact, it's a beautiful thing. The cherry tree. We know you saw it bloom." Jonquil reached up and cupped her cheek. "Oh, sweet girl. It only blooms like that in the presence of true, overwhelming love. In fact, the last time it bloomed like that, we had cherries the size of grapefruits. It was ridiculous. Poor Ransom got a concussion."

"That's not a surprise, Gramma. I know why it bloomed."

"Of course you do. You and Tomas are in love."

"He still doesn't believe in love. It bloomed because *I* realized he was my one. Even though we're pretending, I'm in love with him."

"I know." Jonquil squeezed her again. "He loves you, too."

"I need him to tell me."

"You need him to admit it to himself."

Juniper swallowed. "I noticed that you didn't say he would admit it to himself."

"We don't know what he's going to do, but whatever it is, you will be happy again. I can promise you that." Jonquil fussed with her dress. "If he's going as the Phantom, you need a certain type of dress to be Christine." She zapped her with her wand, and the dress was transformed. It had become a ball gown version of itself, complete with corseted bodice and all. "Okay, you look perfect. There's a carriage waiting for you and Tomas."

Juniper was pleasantly surprised to find that she could breathe in this ensemble. "Maybe I should go on my own."

"Or maybe you should go down and get in the carriage." Jonquil nodded toward the stairs.

"Okay, Gramma. I love you. See you at the ceremony."

Magic was real.

Her grandmothers were fairy godmothers.

And she was irrevocably in love with her best friend.

This was turning out to be one hell of a weekend.

Juniper descended the stairs and found her other grandmothers waiting like bridesmaids and Tomas in that suit that had first so captured her attention, with a half mask to cover the left side of his face. His hair was slicked back, and it emphasized the blades of his high cheekbones.

"A very dapper Phantom of the Opera, sir."

"Just don't ask me to sing," he said, then offered his hand. She put her fingers into his palm so that he could guide her down the last of the stairs.

"I see you made some alterations to your dress."

"The grandmothers did. Do you like it?"

"More than I should," he admitted. "And I think I'm much too handsome to be wearing this mask."

"It does give you an air of mystery," she countered.

When the door opened, she saw the most darkly beautiful carriage. She could easily see the lines of the pumpkin, but where it was once verdigris vines, they'd been morphed into black bats and wolves. Twin red torchères framed the entrance to the carriage and cast an eerie glow. She absolutely loved it, of course. Juniper was sure Betina did, too.

He leaned over and whispered in her ear once they were seated. "I don't think anyone wants mysterious airs."

She coughed into her hand.

Just then, doom from above swooped down to land on the open window space of the carriage.

"Oh no," Tomas grumbled.

Juniper gave the bird a pleading look and addressed him directly. "Please don't."

The bird cocked his head to the side, as if considering.

"Plus, you owe me."

Before today, she wouldn't have thought a bird could furrow its eyebrows, but this one did.

"You were a dirty bird earlier, weren't you?"

The bird tucked his head under his wing.

"Weren't you?"

The bird flew away.

"What. The. Hell."

"I just have a way with him."

"What did you mean he was being a dirty bird? This, I need to hear."

"He was listening outside the changing tent."

Tomas opened his mouth to speak, but then obviously thought better of it. He simply shook his head.

"Did you check your schedule? Do you think we can stay all of tomorrow?" she asked.

"Damn, I sure didn't. I knew I'd forgotten something." He patted his chest, and then his thighs, obviously looking for his phone. "Left it back at the cottage. I'll check when we get back tonight, okay?"

She nodded and looked back out the window. Dusk fell slowly on Ever After, and since their carriage was one of the first to ascend up the trail, twinkling lights popped to life marking their progress.

"I just saw a bat." Tomas pointed up to where a sliver of moon was framed by two dark clouds.

Juniper sighed happily. She bet the grandmothers had arranged it just for the wedding. "How lovely."

"Is it?" Tomas said in a tone that implied he knew better. "Don't bats eat bugs? The fireflies aren't going to be able to cross the veil with our messages if they're rotting in guano."

"I don't know why I hang out with you. You're literally the worst." She shook her head and snorted. She remembered that romance hadn't seemed so foreign to him when he was praising her body and telling her all kinds of pretty things with his lyrical, rolling tongue.

"Because you love me, of course."

"Of course," she answered quietly.

"Are you going to save me a dance?"

It was on the tip of her tongue to tell him that she'd save all of her dances for him, but she wasn't going to do that to herself.

"Definitely not," she teased.

He clutched his chest. "You wound me!"

"I think you'll survive."

"I will," he agreed. "But I won't like it."

The carriage finally rolled to a stop in front of the castle, and the entire courtyard had been lit with torches and the ground was covered in rose petals.

Tomas brushed the footman aside to offer her his own hand down from her perch, which she accepted, and they were guided to the back lawn for the wedding. After the ceremony, they would release the fireflies.

They were led to their seats, and Juniper was lost in her

own little world. She took in the sights, the sounds, the scents . . . burning leaves filled the air, they'd provide the smoke for the fireflies to ride through the veil, and the scent was obviously one of the bride's favorites. Everything had been crafted just so.

"If I ever get married, I'm going to have the grandmothers do my wedding. Everything about Betina's day is perfect."

"Hold on, I thought you were going to marry me?"

"Tomas, I could see you regretted saying yes to that the minute I suggested we do it for real."

"Well, let's not be hasty."

"*Corazon*," she purred the endearment, "if you want me to marry you, you have to ask me proper, and you have to mean it. You were right. I don't want anything fake or half-assed. As much as I love you, that's not enough for me."

Just then, the crowd that had gathered in their chairs grew silent and the bridesmaids and groomsmen walked down the aisle to where Grammy stood, looking quite dapper in all black, except for her red bow tie and her luminous moonlight-white hair.

Juniper craned her neck to see Betina in that red dress and she was not disappointed.

Betina was unearthly, and most important—more than the dress, more than the strategically placed clouds and bats—the love she felt for the man who waited for her at the end of the aisle was tattooed on her face.

It shone in her eyes like starlight.

Her excitement to join her life with the man she loved radiated from her with every step she took.

Everyone deserved that kind of joy when they committed to their person, however that looked. Whether it was a big wedding, a white wedding, a goth wedding, a handfasting, or simply vows to each other under a broad sky, this was the part that was the most important.

The part that Juniper had almost let herself sacrifice.

She believed in magic. She believed in fairy tales. She believed in love.

Juniper had decided she was going to follow through with her plan to completely consummate this burn between them tonight, but part of her had been hoping against hope that it would be the thing that made him see they were meant for each other.

Only that wasn't going to happen.

And she wasn't going to settle.

No matter how her heart broke. She'd put that bitch back together again, and she was determined not to succumb to the fear of pain. She wouldn't let it stop her from living.

The tears that rolled down her cheeks as Betina and Jackson recited their vows to each other were as much for herself, for the pain she had now, and the future she wanted, as it was for the beauty of the two souls who had just joined themselves together for this life, and the next.

Tomas silently offered her his pocket square, which she accepted gratefully and dabbed at the tears she'd promised herself she wouldn't shed.

Luckily, Jonquil had done her makeup with magic, too, so her eyeliner and mascara were firmly in place.

If only her willpower would be as bold.

Chapter 19

Tomas kept trying to steal surreptitious glances at Juniper from the corner of his eye throughout the ceremony.

Something had changed for her.

She'd decided something and he didn't know what.

He didn't like not being privy to her every thought. That was not the content he'd signed up for.

And what the hell did she mean she wasn't going to marry him? They'd decided. She'd asked. He'd said yes. There was no going back now.

Tomas realized that even though he'd been panicking, only slightly, he'd gotten used to the idea.

Dare he say, he liked it?

Now she was saying no? As if she was going to spend the rest of her life with anyone but him.

Only, that's how it had to be, wasn't it? She wasn't his, not in that way, and it wasn't fair to expect her to be. Not when he couldn't give her what she needed.

Tomas had to admit that he didn't care for this realization in the least. It made his guts sour, and something in his chest cold.

Was it his heart?

He cleared his throat to cover the snort that escaped from him. What a load of crap that was. He'd definitely been in Ever After too long. His heart? What kind of nonsense was that? The grandmothers had put some kind of hex on him, he was sure.

He realized he'd missed most of the ceremony when the bride and groom darted down the aisle past them and everyone was clapping.

Grammy, from her place at the podium, said, "Before the masque and reception, we're going to release the fireflies. Everyone to the parapets! Ushers will show you the way."

This was what Juniper had been waiting for. It was her favorite part about being here at Halloween. He was finally going to get to see this thing that meant so much to her.

A long line of people were led to a narrow, winding stone staircase, and they went up in pairs. As they stood in the line, he could feel Juniper's excitement.

"Did you remember to bring your message?" She held up a small, folded square of paper.

"I don't want to bother my ancestors. I figured I'd keep it to once a year." He grinned.

She seemed to consider for a moment. "That's fair. That's all I do."

The line began moving faster and they ascended the stairs. Tomas was grateful when they emerged on the parapets of the castle and the cool night breeze washed over him.

"Oh, wow!" Juniper gasped. "This view is even better than the B and B castle."

"Don't let Phillip hear you say that," a low sultry voice drawled.

Tomas looked over to see a tall, curvy woman with a fall of black hair streaked with purple dressed entirely in black silk. Her lips were painted purple to match her hair. Her eyes, they were somehow green flames.

That was not hyperbole. Her irises were literally flickering emerald flames.

"Those contacts are way cool," he said.

She threw back her head and laughed. "Aren't they just?" She winked at Juniper. "But really, you should actually tell Phillip the view is better here. It would please me much too much."

"I will tell him next time I see him," Juniper promised.

"I suppose you don't remember me?" the fierce woman said in a casual tone.

"I definitely remember you, Ms. Blackheart. You helped me open my Christmas account at the bank," Juniper replied.

"Nice to see you, and you as well, little Tomas." She clicked her teeth together, revealing her incisors were quite sharp. Then she turned back to Juniper. "And you may call me Ravenna. You're grown, after all." She eyed Juniper up and down. "Your grandmothers have had the talk with you, yes?"

Juniper gave her a secret smile. As if she were in on some great mystery no one else knew about. "Yes."

"Good." She turned back to Tomas and curled her lip. Then sighed, shook her head, and walked away.

"What was that?" Tomas asked.

Juniper gave him a look that almost seemed to be pity. "You wouldn't understand."

"Try me."

"I already did. You don't believe me." She held up her folded square of paper. "It's almost our turn."

Juniper dragged him forward toward a large brazier, and she chucked her piece of paper on the coals, and they followed the line to make room for the last of the guests who wanted to share their message.

Suddenly, he saw the grandmothers emerge from the mist.

Very dramatic, that. He had to hand it to them, they knew how to make an entrance.

"Tonight, when the veil between the worlds is at its thinnest, we entrust our messages of love, hope, and grief to the smoke, and to these sweet little creatures that have agreed to carry them to the other side." Petty moved toward a container that flashed to life as hundreds of fireflies blinked and winked.

He wasn't going to say it.

This was magic for her, and he wasn't going to ruin it.

He'd promised.

Tomas was going to pop like a tick.

"You might as well. I can feel you about to explode. Come on. Out with it," Juniper whispered in his ear.

Ah, sweet release! "You know that fireflies flash to get laid, right? All that blinking isn't about lighting the way to the dead. It's getting booty."

She snickered. "Well, what's more life-affirming than sex? I'd want to get laid, too, if I was taking a trip through the veil."

His hand slid to her hip. "Maybe we should, just to be sure. The veil is very thin tonight," he teased. "Just in case one of us crosses over."

Juniper snorted. "Oh really? I tell you what, if it looks like either one of us is going to eat it, I'll hop on and ride you like Seabiscuit."

"I'd throw myself off the edge over there if that's the reward."

She snorted again. "I have yet to see proof of that."

He eyed her. "I'll do it. I'd do anything . . ." He'd been about to say he'd do anything for her, but that wasn't true, was it?

Juniper rolled her eyes and turned her attention back to Petty and the grandmothers just to see them release the fireflies.

They swarmed out of the cage, blinking and flickering, but instead of diving toward the smoke as he'd been led to believe they would, they headed straight for him.

Just then, Ravenna stepped between him and the swarm. "No." She pointed toward the smoke.

They moved as a unit, making to push past her, when she said again, "No. That way." She pointed again.

The mass of bugs slowly turned toward the smoke, almost pausing to ask, *Are you sure?*, and she answered.

"Yes, I'm sure. He's like me. Dead inside, but still alive." She shooed them. "Go on."

Then they took to the skies, diving into the smoke until they became one with it, and their little blinks of luminescence were like lighthouses dotting a foggy sea.

Dead inside? He wasn't dead inside.

Tomas felt a lot of things. He felt more than what was healthy for anyone, he was sure. He wasn't dead inside, he reiterated to himself.

"Sorry. They can be determined." Ravenna shrugged. "They just had to learn you're not the land of the dead, the same way I'm not."

"I have feelings," he blurted.

"I'm sure you do," Ravenna agreed easily. "But you don't believe in love."

"I . . . why would I?"

"That's the question I've asked a million times, but I never get an answer." Ravenna turned and walked away, a single firefly having stayed with her, perched on her shoulder. "Little guy, you've chosen a lonely road," she mumbled.

He was suddenly afraid to meet Juniper's eyes, but he couldn't avoid them forever. He didn't want to.

Tomas looked up at her and he saw everything she wanted to say, everything she felt etched on her face. Only, she didn't say any of those things. Instead, she reached out and took his hand.

"What do they know? Nothing. They're just bugs."

Strains of orchestral music flooded the night and most of

the people had begun to filter back downstairs to the ballroom for the masque and the wedding reception.

"Dance with me," she said, and then Juniper was in his arms. "I know you're not dead inside."

"I can't be dead inside," he whispered against her hair. "If I were, I wouldn't feel this with you."

She smelled like everything good. Everything real. Everything that mattered.

The way she fit against him was like two puzzle pieces that clicked together. Symmetry. Balance. Perfection. Her skin was so soft and he wanted to touch all of it.

Taste all of it.

The way they moved together was a much older dance. It amazed him how something so primal could be so elegant. He wanted to tell her all of these things, but he wasn't the wordsmith. He didn't know how to make it beautiful like she did. So he tried to tell her with his body, with the press of her hand against his heart, the brush of his lips at her temple, and the way he didn't stop moving when the music did. He kept swaying with her beneath the arc of the dark sky to the music they made together. The music no one could hear except them.

It was in that moment he damned Ever After.

This castle that rose up into the clouds, with its fairy-tale affectation, made him want the dream. Want the mirage.

It made him wish that these moments would last forever.

Except they couldn't.

Nothing could.

This pull between them was simply biology having her wicked way, and he understood why people did it, now. He understood why they wanted to surrender to the cultural myth of love.

Everything he felt right now, it made him want so desperately to believe.

When the storm of pheromones had passed, when this fire had burned to a bitter ember, all that would be left would be ashes of something that was worth more than a few minutes in the fire.

But they'd already doused themselves in gasoline.

Her lips pressed against his neck, and he was drowning in visions of sweeping her off to some dark hallway and raising her skirts and taking her against the wall like in the first romance novel she'd read aloud to him over the tiny campfire in his mother's backyard.

"Do you remember *His Saxon Captive*?" she whispered.

Yes, this was why he couldn't take her against the wall like that, like in the story. Because of their history. Because of their future. Even though they both burned in the now.

"How could I forget?" he murmured.

"If I ran down one of those dark hallways, would you chase me?"

"Definitely not," he teased. "I don't want you to call me a bastard, even in play. And I mean, you'd have to, right? If we were sticking to the script."

"We could write our own script," she said softly.

He heard everything she didn't say in that promise. That being together, it could be whatever they wanted to make it. It didn't have to meet anyone else's standards or requirements. She was offering him everything. If only he'd be brave enough to take it.

"We could," he agreed hesitantly. "If only we could agree on an ending."

"Why does it have to end?"

"Because everything does."

She settled back against him, and he realized that they were the only ones left. Everyone else had made their way back down to the party. He supposed they should join them, but he didn't want to.

Tomas wanted to stay up here, dancing with her under the moon and stars. Up here, down there didn't matter so much.

What happened outside of Ever After didn't matter so much.

Juniper seemed to notice this too. "Looks like we're all alone up here."

There was no pressure here, no demands to label what was happening between him and Juniper. Only them, together.

"You're the only one I can see anyway," he confessed.

"Tomas," she began, but then closed her eyes and leaned against his chest again.

"What? What's wrong?"

"Don't say things you don't mean," she whispered. "You keep talking about biology and hormones and about how they're all transient, but then you say things like that. Don't do it. I'd rather just . . ." She exhaled heavily.

"You'd rather just what?" he asked, tilting her chin up with his thumb and forefinger so she'd look at him.

She blinked, her lashes fluttering like dark wings against the curve of her cheek. "I'd rather not forget that you don't love me the way I love you."

He'd never known that words could have the physical force of a bulldozer.

He knew they were powerful, and he definitely should have expected any words that Juniper chose to give him to pack a punch, but this was a wrecking ball into his guts.

"Juniper . . ." Juniper, what? What was he going to say that could make this okay? Nothing. He wouldn't lie to her. It wasn't that he didn't love her, he did. She knew that.

"Juniper, what?" She asked the very question he'd asked himself. "It's okay. I know how you feel. You've been clear. I'm not under any illusions. Except, I can't say that when you say pretty things to me. It makes it too easy to forget. So don't."

"Don't tell you that you're the only one I want to be here with? Don't tell you how beautiful you are? Don't tell you how much I want you?" Why had he said those things? That was exactly what she'd asked him not to do.

She pulled away from him. "Yes, jackass. That. Don't do it." Juniper sniffed and she dashed at her face with the back of her wrist.

"Then don't tell me that you love me, knowing damn well I have no defense."

"You don't need a defense. It's a gift."

"With strings."

"What have I asked you for, except not to make promises you can't keep?"

"It always comes down to something."

"That's where you're wrong. I don't expect anything from you. I know you don't want these feelings I have. Hell, I don't want them. They can only lead to pain."

"See?" he cried. At last, she was starting to understand.

"No, I don't. They only lead to sorrow because you don't want to have them with me. And that's okay. I get it. I'm not trying to change your mind. But the way I do things, the way I want to live, love is something that's meant to be given."

"And now, here we are in that place neither one of us wanted to be. Where we can't go forward, we can't go back." He was hungry to touch her again, to have her close, but it wasn't fair to either of them for him to reach for her.

"Yes, we can go forward. Just not the way either of us wanted to." She bit her lip. "But we can still have this culmination we've been fighting. We should at least give ourselves that."

"Juniper, do you really think that's fair to either of us?"

She flashed him a too bright smile. "It's unfair only if you suck in the sack."

He arched a brow. "A challenge, is it?"

"Always," she swore. Then she darted toward that dark hall. "Catch me if you can, conquering knight."

There was never any outcome in any universe that didn't end with him giving chase. He followed her into the darkness, both needing and fearing what was to come.

Chapter 20

It was going to happen.

She was going to have her passionate night with Tomas. She'd already confessed how she felt. There was nothing left to hide.

Nothing left to say.

Nothing left to do except experience him this way and then say goodbye.

Not forever, because he was Tomas. He was her best friend. But long enough to give herself some time to grieve, some time to convince her heart that it needed to exorcise these feelings, and some time to heal.

Yes, Juniper knew very well she was signing up to break her own heart.

Yet, it was all her heart wanted. It didn't care. It didn't matter. It was too bright, too full to be contained. So she had no choice but to let it spill out across them both until it was empty and tired.

She'd commit his every touch to memory. His every move. Then she'd fold it up like a love letter and keep it locked in her memory for cold, lonely nights when she let herself dream about "what if."

That meant they had to make this good.

She also hoped Ravenna would forgive her for doing filthy things in her castle. Just then, a door appeared, seemingly out of nowhere. When she pushed through to the inside, it was set up just like the scandalous hotel room had been.

"Uh, no."

The room rearranged itself to something a little more tasteful. The best part being the giant bed that was so overstuffed it looked almost like a bouncy house.

"Yes, thanks."

The fire in the grate crackled, as if answering her.

She wasn't going to question it. She was just going to roll with it. Because why not? Magic was real. So why shouldn't the castle be enchanted? It would be all kinds of wrong if it wasn't.

Although, it made her wonder if the items in said room were sentient? She didn't much like the idea that they'd be doing the dirty on a sentient being.

That was definitely a cold splash of water to the libido.

No, she wasn't going to think of that. Of course they weren't. Her grandmothers would have warned her, right? Or maybe they didn't think she'd be adventurous enough to do the dirty in the castle?

It wasn't long before Tomas was in the doorway, looking every inch a rogue in that suit and the Phantom mask.

Well, she'd always wanted to give the Phantom what for. She giggled.

"I know exactly what you're thinking, Juniper."

"Oh yeah? Prove it."

"I'll leave the mask on."

Damn, he really did know. She laughed again. "You are correct. But, no, I think the first time we're together like this, I don't want anything between us. No costumes. No mask. Nothing but this."

He reached up and slowly pulled the mask from his face.

It was then that it really hit her what was about to happen, and with whom. Not that she'd forgotten or was in any way unaware, it was just the reality of it was being driven home with a nail gun set to rapid fire.

He was Tomas. Just Tomas. Her best friend. She knew what he looked like when he woke up in the morning. She knew that he hated having his socks on at home. He didn't like green Jolly Ranchers, only cherry. She knew he could burp the ABCs.

(She could, too, if she tried hard enough, and drank enough root beer.)

There was no reason he should make her stomach flip-flop, or her body burn. He wasn't any kind of sex god. He was just Tomas.

Yet "Just Tomas" stood there in the doorway looking at her the way a wolf would a bunny.

Part of her was singing the Hallelujah chorus because she'd told him she was in love with him and he was here anyway. Logic, that sweet girl, reminded her that she knew his stance on those things, and yet she was here anyway, too.

"The first time, you say? Will there be more than one?" He closed the door behind him and slipped the latch into place.

"If you play your cards right."

"I shall play my very best." He held out a hand to her. "Come to me, *querida*."

She wet her lips and considered.

"Have I not chased you enough?" Tomas continued.

"Not nearly. Besides, you were supposed to take me against the wall, remember?"

"Perhaps I'll take you against the wall for round two."

"Are you so sure there will be round two?" she teased.

"More sure than I've ever been of anything else in my life." He took a step toward her. "If we're going to burn, it may as well be in the hottest fire."

She nodded and went to him, taking his hand. He turned her so that her back was to him and began undoing the military-grade hooks that held the bosom of her dress in place.

Juniper could feel his heat, and she was intently aware of each bit of her skin that he bared. His lips were on her throat and his arm around her waist. She leaned back into him and his other hand came up to cup her breast.

Cold fear clamped down on her with hungry jaws. After the heat had burned away, after that fire that he'd talked about had flickered to nothing, what would be left? This thing that had built between them and propelled them forward toward this inevitable moment . . . What if they never felt it again?

What if they did feel it again?

He knew her so well, he obviously sensed her distress because he stopped. "Have you changed your mind?"

It was still so surreal to her that it was Tomas who evoked these feelings in her. Tomas who made her body burn and her heart soar.

Yet, it shouldn't have surprised her.

After all, if she could write her own Happily Ever After, she would have chosen him every time.

She turned to face him.

"No, I haven't changed my mind. Just afraid of what's after."

He pressed his forehead against hers. "Me too."

"But things have already changed, and I'm tired of talking in circles. I want you."

He laughed softly then. "Oh, *querida*. Do you remember?"

She knew exactly what he was talking about. "How could I forget? Every day of freshman year, we kept grabbing each other in the hall, saying, 'I want you.' How stupid we thought it sounded. Like two people could never say that to each other and mean it."

"Or look each other in the face," he said, meeting her gaze squarely.

She reached between them then, her hand cupping his length.

"Yet, here we are. I want you to say it, too."

"It's obvious, though, isn't it?"

"I want to hear it."

"I want you, Juniper."

"That's right. Say my name!" she teased.

Which he took as the challenge it was meant to be. He took control then, winding his hand through her hair and angling her head back while he blazed a trail with his lips down her throat.

"It is you who will be saying my name."

"Thank everything you didn't say I'd be screaming your name in tongues. I've written that line so many times, it doesn't hold any appeal."

"*Corazoncita*, if you can remember your own name when I'm done with you tonight, I've failed."

She shivered with delight, and he continued his work. His hands were everywhere at once, it seemed. In her hair, on her breasts, her hips, and it wasn't long until her dress had been cast off to the floor.

He shed his jacket, his shirt, and then his mouth was on hers again.

In this kiss, there was no restraint. No holding back from her like the other times. His body was pressed flush against her and his hands roved her flesh at his pleasure.

She wanted to do the same to him, touching him in all the places that were new again. His shoulders, the expanse of his well-muscled back, that hard ridged line by his hips that led her straight to his hard cock. Juniper wanted to taste everything.

"You first," he murmured against her lips. "There's nothing special about my pleasure. It takes no talent. No real effort. But yours is a dance. Surrender to me. Let me make you fly."

She couldn't have written a better line if she'd tried.

And she had. Tried a lot.

He swept her up in his arms and she gasped. "Tomas!"

"This is how you want it, isn't it?"

It was. She'd always wanted someone who would literally sweep her off her feet.

"Don't you dare say not to drop you."

"I wasn't going to." She pressed her lips together after the lie. Juniper had definitely been about to say he should be careful.

But he lifted her with ease and grace, carrying her to the bed, where he laid her down gently.

The look in his eyes was one of adoration, and lust.

His dark hair had rebelled, and a lock hung down over his forehead, making him look like some kind of fallen angel.

Jesus, but he was beautiful.

And for right now, he belonged to her.

He took her hand and kissed the tips of her fingers, her knuckles, her palm. Then he moved to the inside of her wrist, and the bend of her elbow. Tomas took his time with each place where he touched his lips to her body, giving each one its due.

He was a supplicant, a devotee, a priest of all things Juniper. He made her feel like a goddess. His lips were a brand that marked her as his with every touch and she wanted him to mark her everywhere.

"Please, Tomas!"

"Please what? Tell me what you want."

"Everything."

His laugh was low and rumbled deep in his chest. "In time. I've only just begun."

His mouth was at her throat again, and he trailed hot kisses down into the valley of her breasts, his hands cupping her, thumbs stroking her tight nipples, and it seemed he'd be content to strum her so forever.

Time had lost meaning, moments bordered on eternal yet

were still somehow over much too soon. She was lost in a haze of him, and the sensation he wrought in her.

He moved down to her belly, but he didn't rush to the main event. He took his time, whispering words of praise as he worshipped her with his mouth. Tomas was careful to visit each hip, giving each their expected due before finally descending between her thighs.

Yet, that's not where he stayed. He kissed her inner thigh and then moved down to her knee, to the soft, delicate place just behind the knee . . .

She heard his sound of satisfaction as she huffed in frustration.

"I know what you want, baby, and I'm going to give it to you. It'll make it that much better."

"It's not fair how in control you are," she gasped.

"Practice." He brushed his lips against her skin again. "I want to remember every inch of you and how you ached for me."

This was a side of Tomas she didn't know. She thought she knew him inside and out, yet this was a different Tomas. He was so primal, so unapologetically masculine. He was decisive and in command, and she found she wanted him to be the one steering the ship.

The timbre of his voice when he'd commanded her to surrender to him, it still reverberated through her. She'd remember it forever.

Finally, he gave her what she wanted and settled between her thighs. His tongue was both heaven and hell, because it took her ever higher, but he had complete control over her culmination. Tomas kept her right on the edge, reading every body cue, every gasp of breath or shift of her hips.

Yes, he was indeed a master of his craft.

Not that she'd ever tell him that, of course.

"Please," she begged. "Please, Tomas."

He finally allowed her to hit that sweet peak, and when she did, that was when he settled his body between her thighs, his cock poised at her entrance.

"Look at me, *querida*. Open your eyes."

She was still flying, but she opened her eyes to look into the dark pools of his. He was so beautiful and the love she felt for him flooded her.

"Do you still want this?"

"Do you have a condom?" she managed to ask.

"Wrapped and ready."

"Yes."

He cupped her cheek, still looking into her eyes while he pressed into her.

With her previous lovers, she'd never enjoyed looking into their eyes while they had sex. She'd always wanted to be lost in sensation, but with Tomas, she only wanted to be lost in him.

When he was inside of her, she felt complete. That this was the most perfect experience of her life. He began to move, and everything she'd felt before this moment paled in comparison.

Tomas kissed her, his hands moving to her hips, and she locked her legs around him and clung to his body, drowning in him.

The shuddering waves of bliss that had carried her away only moments ago returned with all the force of a tsunami, and pinnacled again, coming apart in his arms.

He swore in Spanish; she wasn't sure what he said, but she was pleased with herself. She knew he was close to the culmination of pleasure he'd given her twice, and she wanted to make him lose control.

She wanted his surrender, too.

Juniper buried her face in his neck and she pulled him deeper, flexed her body around his with a tempered beat that only she could hear.

"You're going to end me," he ground out on a harsh whisper.

"Oh yes," she agreed, nipping at his ear.

He stiffened and tensed, rocking with her to that ancient rhythm of bliss, and his hips jerked as he spilled.

Tomas eased down on top of her, and she welcomed his weight, pressing her deeper into the bed. She played with the bit of his hair that curled under his ear, and stroked his back.

The moment felt too good, too perfect.

Reality intruded on her haven, reminding her that when he pulled away, this idyll they'd made, it would all turn to dust.

Maybe they'd share a moment like this again, maybe many moments, but they wouldn't last because Tomas wouldn't let them.

She had to accept that.

Juniper swore to herself that she *did* accept that. Only, it made it a little difficult to enjoy the now when she knew how much it was going to hurt.

The future came much sooner than what she was ready for. He pulled away.

"I need to clean up."

"Okay," she murmured, unsure of what to do now. Where to put her hands. Should she be getting dressed? Did they just leave this room like nothing had ever happened?

It wasn't long before he returned and began getting dressed.

She guessed that's what they were doing: leaving, and pretending it had never happened.

Juniper could do this.

She began to get dressed slowly, and she didn't question the new form her dress had taken. It was suddenly like one of those box-store Halloween costumes, made for easy on and easy off.

"Hey," he said.

She looked up at him.

"I hope you don't think I'm done with you. I promised you a ravishing against a wall. I intend to make good. Just maybe not on one of these walls because I'm sure the masque is over and we need to do the scurry of not quite shame back to our cottage."

She looked to see that dawn was indeed rising on the horizon. "Oh hell."

"Hopefully, everyone is still asleep."

On their way out of the castle, they passed that fat cardinal. He was sleeping in a basket of candy corn by the door.

He popped open one eye to look at Juniper, and she smiled at him and put a finger against her lips.

The cardinal ruffled his feathers, blinked at her, and then rolled over.

When they got back to the cottage, Tomas followed her into her room and didn't hesitate to strip his clothes off again and climb into her bed.

She settled in next to him and her last thought before drifting to sleep was that things were almost perfect.

She ignored the tiny voice in the back of her head that reminded her of all the reasons why this was going to crash and burn.

It probably would, but she wanted this too much to care.

Chapter 21

Tomas became aware of the world slowly.

He was warm, sleepy, and he'd been dreaming of things he had no business thinking about.

Namely, having amazing sex with Juniper.

Then he realized it hadn't been a dream. He was in her bed, and she was wrapped in his arms.

It was the oddest combination of feelings. Perfection, bliss, and the sharp trill of panic.

He stuffed it down. He didn't want to wake her. Mostly because he wanted to lie there buried in the dark curtain of her hair, hiding in the pre-waking haze still tinged with the afterglow of the night before.

Tomas wanted to wake up like this always.

The bitch of it was, he knew he could have it. If only he'd say the words.

He'd told her he loved her before, and they'd come to his lips so easily, so why wouldn't they once again? Why couldn't he say, right now, into the shell of her ear, "I love you."

Because he did love her. It just wasn't the fairy-tale kind of love. In fact, he'd say it was even better because what he felt for Juniper was solid and real. It was everlasting.

"I can hear you thinking," she mumbled, and burrowed deeper into the covers. "And you're freaking out. Stop it."

He tightened his arm around her waist. "No, I'm not." Tomas kissed her neck.

"Mmm. That's nice, but yes, you are."

"Okay. Maybe a little. Aren't you?"

"Nope."

"Show-off."

She giggled.

"Oh, what was that?" he teased. "A giggle?"

"No!" She grabbed his hands, attempting to lock them in place.

But he tickled her, albeit lightly, and she giggled again, squirming to get away from him.

"You just wait. I'm gonna . . ." She rolled over and then they both paused. "I'm actually going to go brush my teeth."

"Me too. My tongue feels like it's wearing a sweater."

"Yeah." She darted to the shared bathroom, and he followed close behind.

It wasn't until he realized that he'd become mesmerized by her breasts that it occurred to him they were brushing their teeth together, naked.

It hit him again how beautiful she was. Not just the pleasing shape of her body, but how she seemed to bring light with her wherever she went.

"What?" she asked as he stared.

"Are fireflies venomous?" They had to be, right, for him to be thinking thoughts like these. They definitely didn't belong to him.

"I don't think so? Why? What's wrong?"

"I'm seeing a glow."

"Are you having some kind of episode?" She put down her toothbrush and rinsed, then inspected him. "You seem okay." Then she narrowed her eyes. "Wait, are you going to fall over and then claim no memory of the weekend?"

At first, he laughed. "No, I'm actually seeing a glow." Then more quietly, "Around you."

It got under his skin that she'd think so little of him. Although, to be fair, he had been very clear about his feelings.

He just hadn't realized it would sound like that to her. That she'd think he'd be so dismissive of what had happened between them. Yet, as he replayed all of their conversations, as he listened to his own words, he understood why she'd think that. Or at least joke about it.

"Me?" She laughed. "Yeah, that must've been what happened. A firefly bit you and now every woman you want to have sex with is going to glow."

"Oh, good. Makes it easier." He nodded. "To be fair, we didn't know we wanted to have sex with each other. A glow would've helped."

He was glad things were still easy between them. Tomas could admit he'd thought that things would change for the worse. That they wouldn't be Tomas and Juniper anymore, at least not as he'd known them together.

He also knew Juniper would say that he'd endowed his dick with a lot of power, to think it could change who she was. Although, that wasn't it, either. Sex complicated things. It was why he'd not been with anyone in so long. And he'd been focused on work, and Juniper. He didn't have the time or space in his life for anything or anyone else.

She tucked herself against his chest and it felt good to hold her. Good to feel solid proof that she was still real.

"Thought I'd give you that last hug just in case something in your brain explodes."

He laughed and felt another wash of relief. "I think I'm good."

"Just checking." She pulled away to look up at him. "You know, if you want to go back to your own room now, that's okay. I'm not going to be upset with you."

He knew he should go back to his own room. That would be exactly the right solution. Too bad he didn't want the right solution.

"Hell no. I've got promises to keep."

"You did promise me against the wall."

Say it, idiota. *Say the words, and you can have this always. Just say it.*

Except he didn't. He wouldn't lie to her and he couldn't call these feelings something that they weren't.

Just then, his phone chirped. He knew it was the office.

Obviously, so did she. "Don't answer it. Just this once."

"I have to take it. It's Jocelyn's ringtone. She wouldn't call me if it wasn't important."

"Okay." Juniper seemed to wilt as she headed back to her room.

He grabbed his phone. "I'll just be a second. Promise."

Except as he swiped to answer, he saw that Juniper was sliding into an oversize sweatshirt and thick, fluffy socks.

"Hello?" he answered.

"It's me. So sorry to bother you on your long weekend, especially after your text last night about clearing your schedule Monday, but the Simmons case got moved to Monday morning."

"Fuck."

"Yeah, I know. I'm sorry," his assistant said.

"I'll be on my way in a few."

Relief washed over him, followed by guilt. If he had to go in to work, that was his escape hatch. Not that he'd been looking for one.

But the fact that one had presented itself so readily, well, he wasn't one to look a gift horse, so to speak.

"Let me guess. You have to go."

Something about her tone didn't sit right with him. Then he realized she'd said that he had to go. Not that they both did, which was factually correct, but he didn't like it.

He also noticed something else. The ring had come off her finger. She held it out to him.

"That's yours, fake marriage or no. I told you, it was always meant for you."

"Oh. Right." She put it on the nightstand.

"I'm so sorry, Juniper. But a case got moved up to tomorrow. It wasn't supposed to be until next week and I need to prepare. I need to get back to St. Louis today."

"I understand. I'm going to stay, though."

"How will you get back? Do you want me to come back and get you next weekend?" he offered.

"No. I'll figure it out." She hugged him again. "I'll see you back in the city. Have a safe trip. Text me when you get there."

"Juniper . . . this isn't what I wanted."

"I know you have to work. It's not like you can just miss court, or show up unprepared." She gave him a smile that didn't reach her eyes.

He knew he couldn't leave it like this. If he did, it would be a long time before anything was okay between them again.

"I'm not running away," he swore. Yet, he knew that he was. That's all it could be with the relief he felt. The convenient exit that wasn't his fault.

"Look, I'm disappointed I won't get my ravishing against the wall, but what can you do? It's just weird because we haven't talked it to death."

"I feel like if I leave before we do, that we're not going to be right for a long time. I don't want that. Just tell me it will be okay."

"It'll always be okay." She looked away from him for a moment and then took a deep breath. "We don't have to talk about it. Your expectations were clear when this started. It's not like I expected you to change them."

"What did you expect?" he blurted.

"Don't you need to pack and get back to St. Louis?"

"What I need is to know that when you get back to St. Louis, you'll still be my Juniper."

"Like I'm going to be someone else?"

"You know what I mean."

"It's not a big deal, right? You said it's just biology. So what's a little biology between friends? Go. Kick ass. Do your job. I'll stay here and finish my visit with my grandmothers and I'll see you when I get back. We'll pretend that this weekend never happened."

"Is that what you want?"

"I can't have what I want, Tomas."

He was momentarily at a loss for words, which wasn't something that normally happened to him. "What do you want?" he finally managed.

"I already told you, and it's not what you want. I'll get over it. I'll see you back in St. Louis." She gave him another of those smiles that didn't quite meet her eyes.

He didn't like knowing that he'd been the one who dimmed her smile.

It still felt wrong to leave, but he didn't know what else to do. "Give my love to the grandmothers?"

"Yeah. Next time they come visit me, you'll have to cook for them."

"I will," he swore. "Are you going to tell them the truth?"

"About our fake engagement?" This time her smile was genuine. "The stinkers already knew. I imagine our mothers did, too. I think they thought if we pretended enough, it would happen."

"Now I feel extra guilty for lying to them, but I shouldn't. All of their meddling." He shook his head.

"You just need to tell your boss."

"Yeah. I do need to tell my boss. If he's not cool with it, I have decided to open my own practice."

"Really? That's great."

"Yeah, I should have drawn that line in the sand a long time ago. I guess I wasn't ready."

"You're here now, that's what matters. You're a talented lawyer. You're good at what you do. You can succeed on your own. Although, you should probably steal Jocelyn when you go."

He grinned. "Obviously. She's probably half the reason I'm good at what I do. And you're the other half."

"Give yourself some of the credit. It wasn't either one of us who clawed our way through law school."

"But it was you who kept me fed."

"Okay, I'll accept those accolades. Now, get your ass in gear. *Vámanos*."

He liked it when she spoke Spanish. He liked it a lot.

"Oh really?" She nodded to his body's response to her.

"What can I say? I like hearing you use my native tongue."

"I could say I have plans for your tongue, but I don't. Because you're leaving."

"*Madre de Dios*, you kill me, woman."

He noticed how easy it was for them to quickly slide back into this blatant sexuality. Tomas didn't think it would be so easy to go back to the way they were, to pretend that this hadn't happened.

It occurred to him that he didn't want to pretend it hadn't happened. It had been the best sex of his life. He didn't want to forget it. Hell, he didn't think he'd be able to forget it if he tried.

If they did decide to change the parameters of their relationship, this right now would be part of it. He couldn't not go to work, even though he desperately wanted to stay. This would be something she'd have to understand.

What the hell was he thinking? They couldn't redefine the parameters of their relationship because she wanted something he couldn't give her. It was better to stop this now, while they'd only just taken a dip into the dangerous part of the water.

"Good," she replied. "You should think about me when you're back at home, all by yourself." Then she blushed. Hard. Her whole face went red.

He arched his brows. "Oh, should I?"

"That's not what I meant, but . . . hey, roll with it." She shrugged. "And now, I'm going to go die of embarrassment."

"Really? What if I told you I had thought of you?"

She squeaked, and he grinned.

But then he felt a particular ache in his chest. It would be a long time before they could go back to being "just friends."

If ever.

As evidenced by how everything so quickly turned back to carnality.

"Just miss me, okay?" she murmured.

"Of course I will."

She made it sound like it would be a long time before they'd see each other again, and while that was probably best, it wasn't tolerable.

"And you'll be home next week, right?" he added.

"I don't know. I might stay a bit. These weddings make me happy. Good for the muse, you know?" She hugged her knees to her. "Water my plants until I get back?"

He nodded silently. His phone buzzed again with a text from Jocelyn. Tomas glanced at it to see that she'd gathered all the documents he'd need and would be waiting for him at the office.

"I gotta go. But I'll call you."

He cringed. Tomas meant that he would actually call her, but he didn't like how it sounded right after their night together.

She must not have liked it, either, because she didn't say anything. She just nodded.

"I don't want to leave, you know," he added.

"Just go. Jesus. You could already be to the highway by now." She shooed him. "Go. I'll see you soon."

He went to his own room, quickly gathered his things, and dressed. After shoving everything into his bag, he went back to her to kiss her cheek.

"I will miss you. I will think about you. If you need me to come get you next weekend, or any time after that, call me."

She kissed his cheek, and he left her there, in that silly mushroom cottage, in that silly town, with the silly ideas about love that were going to do some not so silly, or easily dismissed, damage.

He thought about her the whole drive, which happened to be brightly sunny. No storm clouds in sight.

No weird little hotel in sight, either.

It was almost as if as soon as he'd left the borders of Ever After, the town had disappeared like that old movie *Brigadoon*, which Juniper made him watch on Valentine's Day.

He saw no signs leading to the place, and it occurred to him, as he neared civilization, that he'd never seen those highways on the GPS. Tomas could find no record of their existence.

But that was just stupid. He knew Ever After was real. He'd been there, after all.

When he took the exit toward his house, he had the uncomfortable sensation that he'd never see Juniper again. Almost as if he'd left her in some other dimension and he had no key to get back.

He reassured himself that it was only because she was with her grandmothers in that silly town where things made no sense to him.

The wrongness of it all settled like something rotten in the back of his mind while the memory of the ring falling off her finger played on a loop that he was determined not to watch.

Chapter 22

After she heard the sound of the engine and knew he'd pulled away, Juniper let the tears fall.

She didn't hate the tears. She wasn't angry at herself for crying, or for feeling something she knew was doomed. She wasn't even angry at Tomas.

Juniper hurt, but there was nowhere to put the blame.

Love wasn't something that deserved blame.

The sheets still smelled like him, and she wrapped herself up, laying her head on his pillow, and let it all out.

She cried for the enormity of the love she felt for him but that he didn't want. She cried for the time she'd wasted, waiting for other men to measure up. She cried because her heart hurt and she physically ached with the loss of him.

She cried because she knew when she went back to St. Louis, these feelings she had would be useless and she'd just have to wait until they grew to something else. Until they weren't a bramble of sharp thorns.

It might be a long time before she went back to St. Louis.

Juniper wasn't sure that distance would be the key, but she didn't have anything else.

The pillow she clung to slowly morphed into something more solid. It became a lap, covered in a pink gingham dress. The room suddenly smelled like sugar cookies, and it made Juniper cry harder.

Petty stroked her hair, Jonquil held her hand, and Bluebonnet patted her back.

"There, there, my little Junebug," Jonquil cooed.

"Sweet girl," Petty said.

"It's going to all be all right. We know these things," Bon-Bon promised.

"Did you have a fight?" Jonquil asked gently. "Tell your grammas all about it."

"My ring came off," she sniffed. "This morning. After."

"Ahh. I see," Jonquil said. "Well, darling. Do you know the answer to that?"

"No," she gulped.

"Put it back on," Jonquil chirped.

The grandmothers giggled.

"You don't understand. It was magic. It meant Tomas was my one," she sobbed.

"What Jonquil is trying to say," Bon-Bon began, still stroking her back gently, "is that this is where you choose. If you still want Tomas, if you have faith in not only him, yourself, but in love, you choose him. Choose the fate you want. Grab it with both hands."

"Doesn't he get a say in this?" she sniffed.

"Obviously. But he does love you, honey. If this were your story—" Petty said.

"And it is," Jonquil interjected.

"Hush hush, let me finish," Petty admonished. "Wouldn't he need some time? Wouldn't you both?"

Juniper realized that Petty was right, but in this case, she didn't know the outcome. Time could do many things, and she was sure in this case, it would make him forget what these last days had felt like. She knew he wanted to forget. He wanted to go back to the way things used to be.

"What did he say when he left?" Bon-Bon asked. "You didn't fight?"

"No," she managed through another sniff. "He said he'd call me. He said he'd miss me. I told him I might not go back to St. Louis for a while."

"You are, of course, welcome to stay as long as you like," Jonquil said. "But is that wise, given your situation?"

"I think it's the wisest. He still doesn't believe in love. I'm not going to change his mind, and I . . . I can't pretend nothing has changed. Even though I told him that's exactly what we'd do because I didn't want to have that same conversation again."

Petty nodded slowly. "The one where he says he loves you, but he's not in love with you, but he's doing everything like you're in a romantic relationship? Same thing happened to my cousin. They've been married a hundred years."

"Two hundred," Bon-Bon corrected.

"Oh, where does the time go?" Petty shook her head.

"How about we take you around Ever After today?" Jonquil patted her leg. "Show you the real, magical Ever After? Won't that be nice?"

"A soothing balm if there ever was one," Bon-Bon agreed. "With lots and lots of sweet treats. Caramel apples, cherry pie, and ice cream sodas."

"That's making my teeth hurt just thinking about it," Juniper said with another sniff. "But it sounds good."

"Magic will make your heart feel better, Junebug," Petty promised.

"It can do that? It can make it so it doesn't hurt?"

"No, but all magic comes from love. It's like a burn and magic is a salve. Slowly, being around these magical things, this place, it'll help you heal," Bon-Bon added.

"Maybe Bronx could come see us. I liked him. Maybe he'd let me pet him a little," Juniper said.

"I'm sure he would. I think he's helping Rosebud with cleanup today. We could find you a nice family of skunks to picnic with?" Jonquil offered. "Several families just had babies."

"I guess I could do that." The idea of holding baby skunks made her smile. "What else is magic?"

"We could show you the stores of magic at the bank. We could tell you about the fairy godmother academy," Bon-Bon suggested.

"I want to hear the story about how I came to be your granddaughter," she said.

"Must you?" Petty sighed.

"I must. Please?" She snuggled into Petty's lap. "It'll make me happy."

"Ugh. Fine," Petty agreed.

"Wait!" Bon-Bon said. "How many times have we said his name this week? Have to make sure we don't accidentally summon him."

"Like Rumplest—" A hand clamped over Juniper's mouth.

"Exactly that. Petty calls him Rumpled Foreskin," Jonquil whispered.

Juniper cackled around Bluebonnet's hand. "Oh, that's rich. He must be awful."

"He is. He and Petty once . . ." Bluebonnet coughed. "Well, anyway. I suppose that's a story for another time."

"Must it be? I feel I need both to truly understand what's going on," Juniper prodded.

"You would," Petty grumbled.

"I get it from you, of course," Juniper said.

Petty stroked her hair again. "Why, yes, I'm sure that you do."

The four of them laughed together, and Juniper's cackle was not out of place among the group.

"It's good to hear you laugh," Jonquil said.

"I know I won't be sad forever," Juniper admitted. "Plus, you're going to tell me stories of your hijinks to make it better."

"You're not going to let me out of that one, are you?" Petty said.

"Obviously not," Juniper teased.

"Once upon a time," Petty began.

"In a land far, far away?" Juniper added.

"No, shh, if you want the story. It was in the Cotswolds."

"Ohhhh." Juniper settled in, eyes wide and ready for the story.

Petty obviously waited to make sure even Jonquil and Bon-Bon were paying attention. Gramma Petty was a fantastic storyteller, although, she had certain requirements from her audience.

"There was a young woman named Eleanor. She wasn't particularly special, but she became the mistress of a wealthy man. Rumpled Butt got her to agree to a magical contract that would give her a child but was rather sneaky. Seeing as how she couldn't read, she simply signed the contract without understanding what was in the fine print," Petty said.

"Back then, we used to check in on all magical contracts," Bon-Bon said.

"We used to make Ravenna big mad," Jonquil added with a snicker. "So mad, once she turned into a dragon. But that's neither here nor there."

Juniper's eyes widened. "A dragon?"

"Pish posh." Petty waved it off. "It was fine. Eventually. Rosebud will forgive her one of these days. But that is a completely different story for another time."

"Yes, let's get back to Eleanor."

Juniper's heart was feeling much lighter since she'd cried, and since the grandmothers were all cuddling her and making a general fuss over her. She had to admit, it was the best medicine.

"So we decided that Eleanor, having not read the contract in full through no actual fault of her own, shouldn't have to become the slave of He-We-Do-Not-Name," Petty said.

"If you think it's a rough gig for women now, imagine back then. Utterly awful. So we intervened," Jonquil added.

"I am proud to say I was able to smite his contract and

shatter it," Petty said. "Of course, that's when there was a bit of magical runoff and it infected the baby, making her, and all her descendants, our family."

"That's really sweet." She sighed. "Too bad it didn't give me magic powers."

Bluebonnet tittered. "But of course it did."

"What do you mean?"

"Your stories, dear. They are a particular kind of magic."

"We all know books are magic, yada yada . . . ," Juniper replied.

"No, it's more than that, dear." Petty grinned. "The stories you tell make people believe in love. Not just romantic love. But all love. You tell tales with big villains, big darkness, and those monsters reflect the smaller more human darknesses. The fear of being unworthy, finding self-love, believing in yourself and that you deserve love. Those are all mountains to be scaled, dragons to be slain."

Juniper found herself tearing up again. "Really?"

"Why do you think Betina and Jackson wanted you to be part of their Happily Ever After? Why does Tomas read your books?" Jonquil prompted.

Juniper had toed the company line. She always said she wrote romance because she believed in love, but Petty's words struck home for her and it shored her up when she felt she was coming apart.

Which immediately turned her mind to Rumpled Butt. She needed the rest of the story because this was starting to sound like one of her other favorite tropes: enemies to lovers. To enemies again and maybe . . .

"So, Gramma Petty. What else happened with Rumpled Shit?"

"Ha. No. Your ears are much too young for that tale," Petty confessed.

"So you admit it!" Bon-Bon cried.

"I never denied it," Petty said.

"Come on. Give us the PG version," Juniper suggested.

"For a man who has earned the name Rumpled Ass Face, I don't think there is a PG version," Petty answered.

"Hmm, but you turned Phillip into a frog. Why not turn Ass Face into a frog? There's something we're missing here," Juniper prodded.

"They were betrothed," Jonquil whispered.

"So help me, if our granddaughter wasn't in the room with us, I would smite your face for uttering that abomination out loud," Petty said.

"It wasn't her fault. She accidentally drank some pomegranate juice that was supposed to be curing for a love spell," Jonquil continued on, unmindful of her sister's threats.

"But was it an accident?" Bon-Bon asked. "I feel like it was a trap. That was the only way You-Know-Who would ever get Petty to even speak to him."

"Yes, for six miserable, awful months, I was betrothed to him. I blocked his magic at every turn, even then. He thought he'd make me pay by wooing me, and then . . . then, I don't know what he had in mind. Something awful, I'm sure," Petty grumbled.

"Yet, where is the punishment?" Juniper grinned.

"If you even suggest what I think you're about to suggest . . ."

Juniper blinked several times and shrugged. "I didn't say it. You did."

"I did nothing of the sort!" Petty snorted. "My stomach is churning. I'm going to vomit."

"Don't be dramatic," Jonquil replied.

"Dramatic! You're not the one who kissed him!" Petty cried.

Jonquil and Bon-Bon both giggled and snorted.

"Let me guess," Juniper squeezed Petty closer. "It wasn't awful. If only those lips were attached to someone other than that reprobate!" She gave a dramatic gasp and then flung herself back on the bed.

Jonquil and Bon-Bon devolved from giggles to full-blown gales of laughter and Petty snorting like a pig.

"Now, who's the—" Jonquil began.

Bon-Bon cut her off. "Don't you dare."

"Sorry," Jonquil said.

"Yes, *this* one turned *that* one into a pig yesterday. Violence did ensue," Petty said, obviously glad to be able to turn their discussion away from her tryst with Ass Face.

Juniper knew it was probably a bad idea, but since that had never stopped her before, she decided she wanted to meet this Rumple person. Of course, he'd probably try to do something nefarious considering she was Petty's granddaughter, but maybe she'd be able to just get a look at him.

"I know exactly what you're thinking, Junebug. Absolutely not," Petty said.

"I just want to see what he looks like. Come on. In all the stories he's this little troll of a creature. Is he a troll?"

Jonquil fanned herself. "No, actually. He's rather delicious, as long as he doesn't talk."

Petty sighed heavily. "Fine. But if I conjure his picture and this beast crawls through it, I'm blaming you."

Juniper sat up to watch as Petty produced a wand and made it dance in a ballet. Glitter shot from the end of the wand, and it began to spout colors like a fireworks display. It wasn't long before the colors swirled together to make a picture of a man.

"Well, that's your problem, Gramma Petty," Juniper said with a grin.

"What?" she sighed.

"He's a ginger. He has no soul. Everyone knows that."

"He's an Irish devil straight from hell, you mean," Petty groused.

Bon-Bon and Jonquil were cackling again, but Juniper had an idea. It seemed like this guy was the only one capable of giving Gramma Petty tit for tat as the case happened to be. She might just have to do some meddling of her own.

Not today, though.

Today was for magic and for seeing the real Ever After.

"I think I'm ready to go get some chocolate chip cookies and hold baby skunks," Juniper said.

"Good, good. It's going to be a lovely day, you'll see."

Juniper got up from her nest in the bed and put on her sneakers. The grandmothers, being grandmothers, made the bed. She was grateful they hadn't tried to change the sheets. She wanted to still be able to smell him. To be close to him. Which was probably a mistake.

She gave the ring on the nightstand a backward glance as she walked out of the door, but in the end, decided not to put it on.

Maybe she would again one day, but today, it just felt like a sad, desperate wish for things to be anything other than what they were.

Chapter 23

Tomas had texted her when he'd gotten back to St. Louis, and he'd gotten a short reply, but he hadn't heard anything from her since.

To be fair, he hadn't texted her, either.

Or called, like he'd said he was going to, but he didn't know what to say.

The Simmons case had gone about like he expected. Another couple who had been good friends before they'd dated, but after they'd gotten married, something had happened. They stopped being the friends they were before they decided to have a romantic relationship. Everything important to both of them had been washed away.

He'd been sitting there, in the courtroom, and he'd become so very aware of a burning gaze on his shoulders, only it hadn't been directed at him. But at Margaret Simmons.

She'd cast the same intense, yet so incredibly sad, glance back at Jack.

They still had so many feelings for each other.

In the end, Tomas hadn't needed to prepare at all. They were both too willing to give the other anything they wanted. Yet, it seemed, after all was said and done, all they wanted was each other. The each other they'd been before they'd gotten married.

Tomas couldn't help but see the parallels in his own situation with Juniper.

However, this week without her sucked more than he'd known anything could suck. He needed her.

Part of him wanted to call her and tell her he was coming to get her because he couldn't be without her.

But she hadn't told him the same, had she? Juniper was in Ever After, just fine without him.

Of course, he couldn't know that for sure, since he hadn't spoken with her.

Before he called her, though, he did have something he had to do. He needed to speak to John Hernandez and Warren Williams about their offer of partner.

He was supposed to go in for a meeting with them so they could congratulate him on the Simmons case, but the meeting wasn't going to go the way any of them had thought it would.

It sucked, but he knew this was the right decision.

Lying had never sat well with Tomas and the ruse had gotten away from them and exploded into this epic thing that had consumed their entire lives. It was time to take their lives back and live on their own terms.

He couldn't help but remember what Juniper had said about fairy tales and Happily Ever After. How those things didn't look the same for any two people.

Maybe he was crafting his own fairy tale right now.

He snorted and then sighed, getting up from his desk to head to the conference room.

When he got there, he found that Williams and Hernandez were waiting for him, and both looking rather pleased with themselves.

"Such a great job you did with the Simmons case. You had them eating out of each other's hands," John began.

"I have to say, it wasn't me. Ultimately, they were both tired of hurting each other," Tomas said.

Warren nodded in understanding. "Yet, it takes a special attorney to see that and guide them toward a mutually beneficial goal. It was good work. Take the win."

Tomas nodded. "I will take the win."

"Then why don't you look more pleased with yourself?" John said, a knowing look on his face.

"A lot of the cases we handle are people who never really should have been together to start with, but sometimes, we get those that . . . well . . . at one time they really saw each other." Tomas shrugged. "Then they stop. That's sad."

"I suppose it is," John agreed. "We know you cut your vacation short to come back and handle this, and we appreciate your dedication to the job and to this firm."

"I don't know if you're going to feel that way in about five minutes," Tomas began.

"Oh? Something to confess?" Warren cocked a brow at him. "Could it be, that this fiancée has been fake all along?"

Relief washed over him. He was glad they knew. Although, he was torn between shame for lying, because that's not the kind of man he wanted to be, and irritation at the pressure they'd put on him to become this cookie-cutter version of their lives. The fact that they'd thought they knew better about what was best for him than he did.

He took a deep breath. "Yeah, it was fishy from the start. It was a ruse to get her grandmothers and our mothers off our backs that got away from us. I never actually intended to lie to either of you."

John drummed his fingers on the table. "We had hoped that maybe you'd go through with it."

"Why," Tomas asked quietly, "if you knew it was a lie? Isn't that worse than half the cases that cross our desks? Why would you want that for me? Why would you wish that on her? She's the one who believes in love. How cruel."

"That's not how we saw it. The two of you are perfect for each other. You always have been," Warren said.

"Her grandmothers encouraged it. They thought it would help you both to see what has been in front of your faces all along," John added.

Her grandmothers again! Was there nowhere free from their meddling?

"Well, much to their disappointment, we've come clean, and I've come to a decision about my employment here."

"Have you?" John perked. "What is it?"

"I've decided to terminate my position here." Hearing the words come out of his mouth wasn't as awful as he thought it would be. He'd been so afraid to cut the cord, afraid to go out on his own, but the time was right.

"We're very sorry to hear it. Anything we can do to change your mind?" Warren asked.

"You know, I thought I had an answer for that question. Of course, I wanted to make partner so badly. But even though it was well-intentioned, there have been too many tests. Too many times when I couldn't trust what was laid out before me as truth. That's not how I want to do business."

Warren looked at John. "She was right. You win."

John held out his hand, and Warren handed him a crisp one-hundred-dollar bill.

"I was sure you'd take partner, but Helen told me that you'd quit. John always bets on Helen."

"And you should know better. Your wife is always right."

"Don't let her hear you say that," Warren replied. "It'll go straight to her head."

"Well-deserved accolades, I say," John countered.

"Okay, then. I'll clean out my desk," Tomas said, surprised and a little disappointed they didn't try harder to keep him.

"Before you go," John said. "I'd like you to make me a promise."

"Seriously?" Tomas asked.

"It's a little thing. You see, Warren and I had another bet. We made it the day we hired you."

Could this fuckery get any more fucked? Yes, he was sure it could. But it didn't matter. He knew how he defined his success and nothing they said or had done could change it.

"You're talented. So please don't take this the wrong way, but I said you weren't meant to be a divorce attorney," Warren said.

Great. There was nothing like learning that his bosses had no confidence in him. "What did you think I'd be?"

"Prenup. It takes a certain sort," Warren said.

"I've handled prenups. They're not anything different from divorce. It's just planning for the inevitable."

"I'll tell you something else," Warren added. "I was completely expecting you to call from Ever After and say you'd decided to stay and open up shop."

"Have you actually lost your mind?" Tomas asked. It was like they hadn't listened to a thing he'd said. Ever.

Warren shrugged. "You win some, you lose some."

"You'll need to give a week or so to get your paperwork together. I trust you don't have any active cases on your desk now?" John asked.

"No, nothing active."

"How about you ride out your vacation days, and then we'll talk again," Warren said. "Finalize the paperwork."

That was a perk he hadn't been expecting but was happy to take. "Okay. Sounds good."

"You will, of course, still be attending the fundraiser next year?" John asked.

"Sure, if you'd still like me to come," he said.

"Tomas, even though things didn't work out, you're still part of the family here. We want you to do well. We want you to stay in touch," John said.

"That's just something that people say, isn't it?" Tomas volleyed.

"Hell yes, it is." Warren guffawed. "But we mean it. Of course we do. You've grown so much since you interned here during law school."

He knew Warren meant this as an endearment, but again, it was like the man still thought of him as a child, rather than the shark of a professional he'd become.

"We're sorry to see you go, but we want you to bloom wherever you decide to plant yourself," John added.

Tomas felt only slightly guilty for resenting their meddling, but what he needed absolutely everyone in his life to understand was that he was perfectly capable of making his own choices. He didn't want or need other people to test him, or to come up with impossible markers to be met as their definition of success when he already had his own.

This included his mother.

None of this should have gone this far.

Although, he supposed this was the first step toward righting these trespasses.

He held out his hand to shake Warren's and John's hand each in turn, but each man got up and hugged him with solid slaps on the back.

"Good luck," John said.

"Helen will call about dinner," Warren said after him.

He knew they meant well, but Tomas needed some space from expectation, from pressure, from people expecting more from him than he could give.

Tomas went back to his office and began packing up his desk. The main thing that caught his attention was the picture of Juniper. He brushed a thumb over her cheek. She wanted more from him, too, but she didn't expect it. She did see him for who he was.

She'd be proud of him for quitting. For taking a chance on himself.

He couldn't wait to tell her.

That would give him a reason to call her.

Not that he'd ever needed a reason before.

He looked at her picture again.

How he missed her. He missed the sound of her voice. He missed the touch of her hand. He missed her laughter. He missed knowing that after work, he could go over to her house and the door was always open for him.

He missed their schemes and plots, and he just missed *her*.

He thought about the copy of *Thunderbird* he hadn't read yet. Tomas opened his desk and pulled out the book, with its pristine uncracked spine. He opened it and saw her words.

For Tomas
Who Believed.

It hit him with all the force of a brick to the gut. That, apparently, he needed. He realized exactly why there were so many parallels between his situation with Juniper and the Simmons case.

He didn't believe.

He hadn't.

He'd stopped seeing her the way that Margaret and Jack had stopped seeing each other.

And it wasn't the sex that had done it. He'd failed long before that.

Of course she hadn't called him, or texted him. By not believing in love, he'd said he didn't believe in *her*.

Being a romance novelist wasn't only Juniper's job, it was an integral part of who she was. Love was almost a religion for her, and putting more love out into the world was what she lived and breathed for.

How could he have been so blind?

When he said he didn't believe in love, what she heard was that he didn't believe in her.

Fuck.

He scrubbed a hand over his face and he sat for a long moment with his epiphany. He didn't know what to do with it. How to fix what he'd broken.

It wasn't the sex that had changed them, he realized that now.

It was this.

And he didn't know how to reconcile it.

How could he say he believed in her, that he saw her, without seeing or acknowledging the basic tenets of this core part of her?

She'd still been willing to take the chance with him.

She'd still been willing to tell him that she loved him, and he knew that there was no ulterior motive, no hope on her part that he'd change his mind. Because she saw him, too. She saw him more clearly than he saw himself. She always had.

He didn't deserve her, of course, but that was something he'd always known.

Tomas had to talk to her.

He pulled out his phone and dialed her number, but she didn't answer. For the first time in years, she didn't immediately pick up the phone. Juniper would stop writing to answer a call from him.

His first panicked thought was that she was angry with him.

His second was that she'd been in some kind of accident.

The third was . . . it was a mix of the first two.

He eventually got her voice mail.

"Uh . . ." Then he clicked the button to end the call.

Yes, "uh" was exactly what he wanted to say to Juniper. That was exactly what she needed to hear. He shook his head.

He pulled out his phone again and decided to text her, but then he saw she'd texted him.

She hadn't answered his call, but she'd texted him. That meant she didn't want to talk to him, didn't it?

If he thought his world had been knocked on its ass before, this was the kicker. This one had launched everything he knew about the world off into space.

Never, in all of his life, had this happened to him. Even when they were kids. That time he got gum in her hair and cut off a braid trying to fix it, that time he'd threatened her Winter Royalty date with bodily harm so convincingly he'd canceled their date, and even that time when he was in law school and he forgot to pick her up from the bus station, she'd never not wanted to talk to him. No matter how mad she got at him, she always wanted to see him. Hear from him.

Maybe that wasn't what that meant.

He pressed to open the text and saw it there in black and white.

Not up to talking right now.

Tomas read the text several times as he attempted to process it. He began typing several responses before he settled on: *Is everything okay?*

It was a long time before she replied.

Juniper: *I just need a little space.*

You've never needed space from me before.

Juniper: *I've never been in love with you before.*

What was he supposed to say to that? He'd give her the space she needed, but he needed her to know that he understood his life sucked without her.

I miss you.

Juniper: *If you miss me come back to Ever After.*

He didn't understand. Why would she tell him to come back if she wanted space? Tomas decided the easiest way to figure that out was to simply ask her.

Thought you needed space?

Juniper: *You have to believe in Ever After to find it. There's zero chance in a million I'll see you until I come back to St. Louis.*

Damn. That was a blade straight to the heart, but he supposed he deserved it.

Ouch. He exhaled heavily and took a chance.

I believe in you, isn't that enough?

Juniper: *But you don't. Not really.*

How was he supposed to tell her that he understood if she didn't want to talk?

That's what I wanted to talk to you about.

Juniper: *Come to Ever After or wait until I get back.*

Juniper: *I'm working on a new book and eating cookies. Talk later.*

He needed to read *Thunderbird*. He'd been waiting all of this time for the end of Cordelia and Daniel's story, and maybe there would be a clue inside of how to fix this mess they were in.

Because he damn well wasn't going to wait for her to leave Ever After. In fact, he was afraid she might decide to stay and never come back to him.

He tried to remember the turns, and the highways that would lead him back to her. The way they seemed to have disappeared, it was almost like . . .

Magic.

Except magic wasn't real.

Much like love.

Was that what it was going to take to get her back? Would he have to find belief in something he knew to be false or risk losing his best friend?

But she was so much more than that, wasn't she?

Juniper was everything.

So why couldn't he just fucking believe?

Fuck it. He'd try.

He remembered that she'd written down the directions for him and left them on his desk at home.

Ever After was real, not some fevered dream. He'd been there. Juniper was still there. He'd find her.

Somehow, he'd find her.

Whatever it took.

Chapter 24

It had only been a week and she was doing exactly shit at working through her feelings for Tomas.

She thought about him every minute of every day.

The longer he went without calling or texting, the more it hurt and the more she wanted to root those feelings out of herself.

Juniper had thought she'd been prepared to deal with the fallout, but this week had proven her wrong a million times over.

When he finally did call, she hadn't been able to answer.

She'd stared at it, wondering what to say. Wondering what he wanted. Wondering what it would be like to hear his voice and then she'd decided she didn't want to. She wasn't ready.

So instead, she'd texted him, and that had gone over exactly as she'd imagined it would. Which was not at all. He wasn't about to let her get away with that.

Only it didn't get to be just up to him. She was allowed to draw boundaries and she was allowed to tell him she needed space.

Juniper knew she'd given him a challenge he could never conquer. He didn't have the tools.

But that didn't stop the tiny, sad flicker of hope that sputtered in her chest. If he could find his way to Ever After, if he could find his way back to her, he'd never need to say the words to her because he'd have proven them to her. She didn't want empty words, she wanted the emotion behind them.

Yet, he'd already told her he didn't have that to give.

So she'd set her unwinnable challenge.

This time, she couldn't believe enough for both of them.

The bitter part of her was tempted to say she didn't believe enough for herself, but she did. Even though he didn't, even though she'd led herself down this road knowing she'd be taking a sledgehammer to her own heart, her belief was immutable.

The truth was she wished she was able to put ideas about true love and Happily Ever After aside as childish things. It would make her life so much easier.

And so much smaller.

Sadder.

Darker.

Even as she admitted all of this to herself, the part of her that believed was waiting for him. For Tomas to show up in Ever After because he realized that everything he felt for her was a forever, Happily Ever After kind of love.

Her fingers were on the keyboard again, and she was writing a different kind of book this time. This one wasn't about the dark underworld, or the devils that lived and loved there. This one was about a girl who had loved a boy the whole of her life. And a boy who didn't believe in love who'd grown into a man that threw that love away with both hands.

She'd already made herself cry three times while writing it. That didn't usually happen until much further into the process. Although, it had been therapeutic. Juniper didn't think this one was going to be publishable, at least not under her romance novel name. But some things just had to happen regardless of where they ended up.

This book.

Making love with Tomas.

Some things were simply destined to be.

She looked at her phone again, and clicked on the picture of Tomas she used as his contact picture.

Juniper wished she didn't like looking at him so much. It would make this so much easier. Of course, when she really thought about it, lots of things would make this easier. Namely, not feeling this way about him.

Yet, she couldn't regret it.

No matter what Tomas believed, he was still the best man she knew. He would still be the model for all the heroes she brought to life on the page.

Oddly, that thought brought her comfort.

No, maybe she couldn't talk to him at the moment, but the day would come again when she would laugh with him and that easy camaraderie would return.

She'd written her pages for the day, so there was wedding work to be done. There was also lots of important work at the park that involved babysitting skunks so that sweet little mama could go get a moment's peace all on her own. Juniper was happy to help.

She made her way to the park, not bothering with a sweater. Even though it was early November, the weather was sunny, but temperate. With her water bottle in hand, and a picnic blanket, she spread out and waited for the skunks to take their daily outing to the park.

Juniper was thrilled when as soon as she sat down, the mama skunk, Shirley, and her litter of adorable, fat-bottomed babies came waddling toward her.

"I'm so glad to see you," Shirley cried, waddling faster. "I just need five minutes."

"Take as long as you like. I'm done with my work for the day."

Several of the little darlings climbed up on her lap, others began to play, and Shirley stood up on her hind legs, front paws braced on Juniper's arm.

"Please tell Bronx to watch his mouth around them. Cora told her brother she was going to wax his ass with a pineapple if he didn't get his motherfucking paws off her bowl of ticks."

Juniper tried her very best not to laugh. "Well, to be fair, Cora is a strong, independent woman. Who is admittedly very food motivated."

She looked down to see Cora, with her wide cartoonishly blue eyes half-lidded while she stretched and gave a lazy yawn.

"Tearing down the patriarchy is hard work, Mama," Cora said in a tiny voice.

"Must you do it with such foul language?" Shirley asked. "I know you heard it from that nasty-beaked bird."

"He mostly means well." Juniper grinned.

Shirley just sighed. "I think I will take you up on that. I'm going to the p-o-n-d."

"I can spell, Mama," Cora said, but curled into a more secure ball.

"What'd she say? What'd she say?" Keenan demanded.

"I'll tell you later." Cora yawned.

"Be good for Juniper," Shirley called as she trotted off for some obviously much needed alone time.

These little creatures brought Juniper such joy. Just sitting with them brought her to a happy Zen place.

Even when she saw Bronx approach, and try to sneak up on little Alistair to try to make him spray.

Alistair heard him coming and pretended to be surprised.

But then, Bronx made his way over to Juniper.

"How's tricks?" he asked her.

"Same as they were yesterday, my fine-feathered friend."

"Yeah? Well, youse knows . . . I mighta heard a ting."

"A ting?"

"Yeah, youse knows. A *ting*." He cocked his head to the side. "A good ting."

"Yeah? What did you hear?"

"Eh, you gotta give some sugar first, sweetheart. Scratch under my beak."

She was happy to scratch the bird under his beak, but she enjoyed being privy to all of the gossip.

"So what's the news?"

"Ever After has a dating app."

"A what?" That didn't sound like good news. In fact, it sounded like a fresh sort of hell dredged up from a nightmare.

"It's called Happily Ever After. Check it out."

"I'd rather clean a troll nest with my tongue."

"Such a way with words," Bronx said. "But uh, it matches up peoples who ain't even on there."

Now that, that was interesting. "Do you think the grandmothers intended for that to happen?"

"No way. This is Ravenna's baby."

"So we could all see Petty, Bluebonnet, and Jonquil's perfect matches."

"Precisely."

Juniper dug her phone out of her pocket, doing her best not to disturb the sleeping skunks in her lap and trying to ignore the weight of the ring she carried there as well.

She hadn't been able to bring herself to put it back on, but neither had she been able to leave it sitting on the nightstand. Neither option seemed quite right.

When her phone came to life, she saw the app had already installed itself. Juniper had to say that would cost Ravenna a star in the app store. Not cool.

Her finger hovered for a moment over the storybook icon.

Maybe she shouldn't open it. Some things were better off unknown. What if Tomas was her perfect match?

What if he wasn't?

Ravenna was the Evil Queen. So this app couldn't be for anything but nefarious purposes, right? The grandmothers had told her that she'd turned over a new leaf, but this dating app thing had to be an evil plot.

Didn't it?

"Open it!" Bronx cried. "I'm dyin' here."

"You?"

"Come on, let's see it. We can do me first. See if there are any pretty ladies who like a husky man."

She couldn't resist checking for Bronx because she definitely had more than just a little bit of her grandmothers' penchant for engineering Happily Ever Afters.

When she opened the app, the carousel with faces and names zoomed forward until it stopped on one fat, sassy, foul-mouthed cardinal.

"Bronx!" she cried, as the picture morphed into a face of a guy that would not be out of place on any construction crew. "Were you human?"

"Eh." He shrugged. "Once upon a time."

"What happened!"

"I don't remember. But enough with that." He waved with his wing. "What's the story? Is there a nice feathery broad waitin' for my dulcet song?"

"Yeah. She lives in New York. Her name is Vera. She's a waitress at Junior's."

"She ain't a bird?"

"Only in the UK sense of the word."

"How does that work?"

"I don't know." And really, Juniper didn't much care to think about it.

But then the stupid thing scrolled to her own face, and she slammed the phone down. She didn't want to see.

"Let's look up Rosebud next." He chortled. "Or Petty."

"I can't, not without seeing my own."

"Who cares? Just have a peek. Just one. Then we can make with the laughing at everyone else, yeah?"

"Fine." She was dying to see it anyway. Juniper took a deep breath and turned her phone back over.

She had two matches.

Two!

"You're a spicy meatball, ain't youse?" Bronx snickered. "Lemme see. Oh! Roderick. That guy. He's a lawyer, too. You got a type, huh?"

"I . . . do not have a type." Her squawk disturbed the snuggly babies in her lap and she stroked their little heads to reassure them while they went back to sleep.

"No? Well, ain't they both lawyers?"

"I didn't see the other one."

"Don't fib to me, girly."

"I'm not a fibber. I didn't. I was scared to." But even as she said the words, she looked again and there he was.

Tomas.

The one she thought of with every Happily Ever After she wrote. With every Happily Ever After she dreamed for herself. It was always him.

His picture moved up ahead of Roderick's.

"What does that mean?"

"Pretty sure it's because the future ain't a set thing, see? As our choices move us forward, whatever's in this app changes to match."

She never should have looked, because it had given her false hope. It was just because she wanted Tomas. The app could easily have picked up on that, couldn't it?

Her phone buzzed in her hand.

It was another text from Tomas.

I'm coming.

But he'd never find Ever After, or her, because he didn't believe.

Yet, she couldn't help but grab on to that tiny cord of hope. The app had moved him up in the rankings. He was going to try.

Her first instinct was to tell him not to, because even if he somehow managed to find his way here, it would do nothing to change this impasse; her wanting everything, the fairy tale, and him not believing.

So he missed her. So what?

So he loved her. So what? He refused to be in love with her and that was the crux of it all.

Her fingers moved of their own volition. *I'll be waiting.*

That's what she'd been doing this whole time already. Waiting. Waiting for him to realize that she was amazing. Waiting for him to realize he was in love with her. Waiting for him to stop being a stubborn fucko.

Basically, waiting for him to change his spots.

That was never a good recipe for a happy ending. People didn't change who they were. You had to take them or leave them in their current incarnation.

While her grandmothers had told her she had magic, she wasn't the one who was going to change him. No one could change him but himself.

It would be easy to believe it was because she wasn't enough, but Juniper knew she was. It was all up to him, now.

He was coming, but it didn't change anything, did it?

Except the app seemed to think it had. The app seemed to think it made their Happily Ever After much more likely.

She noticed then that the bird had wandered off and she got the feeling that he hadn't cared much about his own results at all. He'd just wanted her to look.

Just then, Shirley came trotting back looking very refreshed and ready to take her babies. Juniper surrendered each of them with a smooch on their little heads and Shirley took them to the bakery for some wildlife-approved treats.

Juniper looked at the app again and saw that Tomas had fallen behind Roderick again and that was when it hit her with a surety it was her doubt that moved the rankings.

Her grandmothers had told her time and again that she had to have faith.

She had to believe.

That had been a recurring theme these last weeks: staunch belief in the face of adversity.

This was not the time to give up. It was not the time to doubt.

It was time to hope harder.

It was time to believe in fairies, in magic, and most of all, in the power of love.

She pulled the ring out of her pocket and slipped it onto her finger, because that's where it belonged.

It stayed, but it wasn't tight, and she could remove it if she so chose.

Choice.

In this moment, she chose Tomas. Even if he couldn't find Ever After. He was her choice. He was her home.

And doubt had no place at the table.

She'd wait for him. No matter how long it took.

Chapter 25

Tomas looked at the map. Then to the handwritten directions. Then up to the place in the road where the first turnoff was supposed to be.

He remembered turning there, but the road they'd taken wasn't there.

Which was completely impossible.

His brain refused to process it.

She'd said he had to believe to find Ever After. He had to believe it was real.

Tomas knew that Ever After was real because he'd been there. There was no doubt the place existed and that's where she was. He'd do anything to get back to her.

A slight buzzing sound in his ear annoyed him and he swatted at the bug, but he couldn't see the little beast. He thought since it was November, they'd all fucked off back to hell where they belonged, but apparently not.

He wondered if something had caught a ride with him back from Ever After. Since the place had ridiculous weather and fireflies in October and November.

It had ridiculous weather.

Fireflies in October.

The place was impossible to find.

And it was full of fairy-tale kitsch.

He didn't like the direction his brain took. Tomas wanted

to jump off that train before it got anywhere near the station to which it was headed.

It was insane.

But so were roads that disappeared.

He scrubbed a hand over his face. It hadn't just "disappeared." He was remembering incorrectly. Maybe it was up the road a little farther. Or back.

Damn it, it had to be somewhere.

The buzzing sounded in his ear again and he rolled down the window.

"Listen, little bug. You need to get the hell out of my car, or I'm going to have to find something heavy and hit you with it." He didn't know why he was talking to the bug like it understood him, but he didn't want to kill a small creature just for being small.

And annoying.

Something hit his cheek.

The bug had smacked him in the head.

Tomas shook his head and swatted at the thing again, but yet again, it hit him in the face. This happened again and again, until finally, whether it was in self-defense or inspiration, he turned his head to the left.

That's when he caught sight of the wristwatch the grandmothers had given him. The one that had had no hands. Except now, there was a single hand and it pointed to the left. Almost like a compass. He moved his arm toward the left and the hand moved, consistently pointing in the same direction.

And he saw the faint outline of a road.

He was sure it had been on the right. Most highway exits were on the right.

Only maybe to get to Ever After, he had to take an unexpected way. He had to take a chance and just trust that the road was not only the correct one, but that he wouldn't end up in some farmer's field sinking in a bog of cow *caca*.

The bug buzzed near his ear again and he could almost swear he heard one of the grandmothers sing, "Hallelujah."

It was official. He'd lost his mind.

However, he knew for a fact that the road had not been there moments ago. If he ended up stranded in a bog of *caca*, well, he'd rather risk it if Juniper was on the other side of it.

Hell, he'd Shawshank that bog if it would get him back to her.

So he turned onto the place that looked like an impression of the road and the longer he drove, the dumber he felt. He was just about to turn back when he got dive-bombed in the ear once again by that buzzing little maniac.

Upon closer inspection, he realized it wasn't a mosquito like he'd thought. Not at all.

It was a firefly.

The poor little guy had to be cold, so Tomas turned on the heat to make sure he didn't freeze before he could get him back to Ever After.

The road became more defined, signs seemed to pop up out of nowhere. Strange little diners and gas stations he knew he hadn't seen on the way last time.

It wasn't long before he needed to stop for fuel. Well, he was at the halfway point on his gas tank and he had no idea when he'd see another filling station so he decided to stop.

He pulled the car into the pump and he noticed several animals emerged from the surrounding area to watch him.

He refused to be freaked out.

"Just don't shit on me, okay?" he asked them.

The chipmunks chittered, as if in answer.

He slid his credit card into the reader, and when he withdrew it, Tomas realized his hand was sticky with melted marshmallow.

The gas pumps weren't real, not in a normal human sense of the word.

The building itself had been crafted of graham crackers and . . .

And it was something straight out of the darkest telling of a fairy tale. Smoke stacks on the back of the graham cracker building huffed and puffed, and a kindly-looking old woman in an apron stepped outside and motioned for him to come inside.

Not a chance in hell.

The firefly started ramming into his face again and he realized the little bug was trying to steer him back to safety.

He could say he didn't believe, or he could acknowledge what he saw right in front of his face.

Tomas hopped back in his car and threw it into drive, tearing ass on down the road.

It made sense that if a place like Ever After existed, that these other kinds of places would, too.

He wondered how many of them he'd passed. How many times he'd unknowingly . . .

Tomas wouldn't think about that. He'd think about Juniper.

It wasn't long before he came to a T in the road and he could go either right or left. He sat there for a long moment, checking his handwritten directions, which didn't match his route in the least, and trying to remember again which highways led to Ever After.

The bug dive-bombed his left cheek, and when he turned his head, he saw a sign that said Ever After with an arrow pointing to the right. He checked his watch, and realized that it, too, was pointing him to the right.

This wasn't only a watch. It was a map of sorts. A map back to Juniper. Yet, that couldn't be real, could it? As he doubted, the watch hand faded out of existence right before his eyes.

Yes, this map back to Juniper was as real as a tour guide firefly. And he watched as the hand slowly but surely became solid and real.

"Okay, little guy. Thank you," he murmured, still trying to process all that happened.

If anyone had asked him as early as this morning if he'd be taking directions from a firefly, he'd have said they were crazy, but here he was and that wasn't the craziest part about it.

The firefly buzzed at his hand and then at the gear shift. He was pretty sure the thing wanted him to pull over.

So he went with it. He pulled over. "Now what?"

The firefly dive-bombed his chest, poking at his heart.

"No. We're not doing that," he replied.

Suddenly, the firefly wasn't a firefly anymore.

It was Jonquil, but she wasn't only Jonquil. She was Flying Jonquil. She had fairy wings that shimmered and glistened in the sun.

"Oh what the fuck?" he cried.

"Yes. What the fuck exactly." She smacked him right on the kisser with her wand. "This is so against the rules, but I just can't take it. This is driving me nuts."

"You?" he gasped.

"Yes, me." She pointed at herself with her wand, then looked down at herself and made sure to carefully point it away from herself. "I get going and there's just no telling what I'll do with that thing." She straightened her dress, but then rubbed her temples.

"How did you get in my car?"

"Catch up, Tomas. Magic is real. Wasn't the disappearing road your first clue? The wicked tourist-eating witch trap your second? Your watch, which was literally a gift-wrapped clue. And now here I am sitting in your car when I had previously been a firefly."

He cleared his throat. "Honestly, I thought it was some bad takeout."

She growled. "I can see this calls for tough love. How do you feel about Juniper?"

"I'm coming back to Ever After, aren't I?" He didn't like where this was going.

"Not. Good. Enough."

"What do you mean, not good enough? It's the grand gesture, right?" What else did they want from him?

"No."

He slumped in his seat. "I don't know what else to do."

"Yes, you do," she prompted.

He looked at her.

She looked at him.

Silence reigned.

"She may have decided she'll wait for you forever, but *I* have decided I won't let her. Get your shit together, Tomas. She deserves everything she's dreamed of."

Jonquil was right. Juniper deserved to have all her dreams come true. "I agree. Which is probably why I shouldn't be doing this. Is that what you're telling me?"

She smacked him with the wand again. "No, dumb-dumb. I'm waiting for you to have your epiphany. I can't have it for you."

"Hitting me obviously isn't working."

"Maybe I should smack you harder?" Jonquil narrowed her eyes.

He held up his hands in self-defense.

"Listen, I'm not usually so violent. I'm a fairy godmother, after all. But you have given me a migraine for the ages, young man."

"Fairy . . ." He trailed off, then shrugged. "Fine. Whatever. I'm just going to go with it. Is that better?"

"A little." She fluttered her wings. "Now, let's get to the next step."

Jonquil stared at him, theoretically waiting for him to surmise what the next step was to be, but he didn't have any clue.

"Get to Ever After?"

She huffed. "Yes, but how do we get to Ever After?"

"We . . . believe?"

"Thank the goddess!" she cried. "What do we believe in?"

He knew what he was supposed to say here; he'd known what he was *supposed* to say all along, and he wasn't going to lie.

"Okay, starting back at the beginning. And this is the last time. If you don't get it, you're not going to, and Juniper deserves someone who isn't afraid of how they feel. Isn't afraid that she won't live up to her promises."

He opened his mouth, but she smashed her wand against his lips once again.

"No. Not your turn for talking. Listening." She tapped his forehead. "Listening."

He nodded and decided he needed to be open to what she had to say. She was either a hallucination or she was actually a fairy godmother.

Tomas might have preferred the hallucination, because if she was who she said she was, what she said she was, it meant that all the things he'd been denying were real.

It meant that other people got Happily Ever After.

Just not him.

Almost as if she could see the path of his thoughts, she said, "No, no. Rewind to the part where you understand that magic is real."

Tomas took a deep breath. "Okay. Magic is real."

"Good. The source of all magic in the world is love. Love powers everything. And it's all kinds of love. It's familial love. It's self-love. It's even romantic love." Before he could speak, she continued on. "It's the way you turned on the heat for me so I wouldn't die before we got back to Ever After. It's your mother's ring on Juniper's finger. It's even in the way we convinced you both to pretend to be engaged. That's love. It's the strongest force in the known universes."

Universes? He wasn't going to even poke at that. His brain couldn't take it.

"It's the only thing that's going to bring you back to Juniper."

"I'm afraid, Gramma Jonquil," he confessed.

She finally put that cursed wand down and patted his hand. "Yes, it can be scary. But what are you afraid of, exactly? When has Juniper ever let you down?" She studied him for a long moment. "Or are you afraid that you're going to be the one to let her down?"

"No one ever stayed except for my mother and Juniper," he said quietly. "She's all I have and I'm not willing to risk her for biology."

"Yes, love is a biological imperative."

"Ha!" he cried, triumphant.

"I'm not finished. It's imperative because humans need love. They were made to give it, to receive it, to spread it around like sunshine and feed themselves and all other living things on earth." She patted his hand again. "So yes, it is biology, but not like you think. Relationships, even the most healthy, require effort. Establishing and maintaining healthy boundaries, good communication, growing together, changing together. Yes, change is inevitable, but stagnation is when things rot."

Tomas considered her words.

He couldn't imagine a future without Juniper, but the way he saw their future now had changed. He wanted what they'd had in the cottage that morning after they'd made love. Tomas wanted to see her face every morning, and he wanted to hold her when he went to sleep. He wanted to laugh with her every day, wanted to be the one she turned to when she needed . . . anything. He wanted those grandchildren playing together while they rocked on the porch to be theirs together.

And when this ride was over, when his last sunset turned to darkness, he wanted to have spent his time with her. He wanted to be holding her hand.

This longing, this need, it welled up in him from somewhere dark and secret, a place that had been hiding from him.

Or maybe he'd been hiding from it?

These feelings weren't new. He'd always known he and Juniper would be part of each other's forever.

Tomas was overwhelmed with emotion and turned to meet Jonquil's assessing gaze.

"Ah," she said kindly. "There we are. You are officially with the program."

"I can't believe I missed the program. I . . ." He thought back to the discussion they'd had that morning before he left. The way she'd distanced from him, yet still, had been ready to give him everything he didn't know he'd been dreaming of. Everything he hadn't dared to want.

"Yes, dear. We've all been watching you two fumble around, snatching defeat from the jaws of victory for years."

A new sign appeared.

Ever After, Drive Faster.

"Fate has spoken. Whatcha gonna do?" Jonquil grinned. "I trust you can find your way from here?"

"Yes, Gramma Jonquil. And thank you." He rubbed his face. "But maybe less hitting?"

"Not a chance. Your head has been like concrete. She's waiting for you."

He looked at his watch and realized it had only been an hour since he'd texted her. It should have been several.

Even time had stopped for this love.

How could he have ever doubted it?

Doubted her?

Because he had. When he'd said love wasn't real, he'd cast shadows on everything they had together. Everything she believed in. Everything she was. Yet still, she'd believed. She'd believed in him enough that she kept thanking him in her books.

Enough that she kept writing heroes and putting pieces of him in every one.

The breadth of those acts were finally being driven home, and he didn't know how he'd ever make it up to her.

He decided he was going to start by asking her to be his Happily Ever After.

Chapter 26

It was stupid of her to wait for him in the park.

It would be hours yet before he reached Ever After, if he reached it at all.

Yet, some awareness burned at the back of her neck and caused prickles of anticipation to run up and down her spine.

She also noticed the park began to clear out. The animals that normally frolicked and played were retreating to their dens. Ever After residents were leaving shops, looking at her and giggling, and then making their way home.

She didn't quite know what to do with it.

Even her grandmothers. They all exited Fairy Godmothers, Inc., pointed at her, giggled, then toddled off toward their cottage.

It was Zuri who made her way over to her and said with a grin, "He's coming."

"What?"

"Your Tomas. He's on the way. He'll be here soon."

"He just left St. Louis. He can't be here for hours yet, even if he finds the way."

"I wouldn't count on that. If the godmothers say he's almost here, then he's almost here."

"I . . . okay." She still wasn't ready to trust it.

"What are you doing? Go back to the cottage and wait there."

"What's going on?"

Zuri grinned. "What do you mean?"

"Come on. You see the way everyone is acting. It's nuts."

"The godmothers told me that you saw the cherry tree bloom. It's like that."

"I need a little bit more information."

"The town is about to be flooded with love. It'll be great for our stores, and great for the town, but things tend to pop and explode. Like the fireworks over the B and B. That's all love," Zuri explained. "And I'm sure that when your Tomas gets here, you'll want to celebrate in a private way."

"Oh, I think we're definitely going to have to talk first. No more private celebrating unless we can get on the same page."

"You're definitely on the same page. Jonquil said so."

"What does Jonquil know about it? You guys weren't discussing my love life, were you?" She cringed.

"Your love life, not your sex life." Zuri grinned wide. "Especially because I want to plan your wedding. It'll be so beautiful."

"I think everyone is getting a little ahead of themselves. You're all putting the fairy godmother before the carriage."

Zuri snickered. "Oh, I like that one. But no, we're definitely not. You know he wouldn't be able to find his way back here without a pure love."

"Friendship can be a pure love."

"It can. It is. But that's not what this is. Friendship doesn't drive a man to change his core beliefs and drive off into parts unknown just because he misses you."

"You don't know Tomas."

"Tomas doesn't know Tomas, but he's learning. You'll see." Zuri then rolled her eyes. "Ugh, I can't believe I just *you'll see*'d you. That was so irritating when Phillip and I were falling in love. Honestly, it doesn't get any better after you already admit you're stupid for each other. The godmothers just keep smiling with that smug nodding."

A laugh bubbled up and she surrendered to it. "I have an idea about that, actually. Have you seen that new app?"

"Oh! That thing has everyone in an uproar. Most especially the godmothers."

"Did Gramma Petty see who it paired her with?"

"She's refusing to look at it, and if anyone mentions it within her earshot, she's promised to turn them into dung beetles."

"I knew it! I think I have just the project for us. How would you like to matchmake my grandmothers?"

"I don't know that I would take my life in my hands like that, but I know someone who would love to. She is actually a fairy godmother in training. My sister, Zeva."

"You mean that literally, right? She's like, off somewhere, learning how to meddle?"

"Exactly that." Zuri grabbed her hand to pull her up off the ground. "Now, come on. Maybe we should brush your hair?"

"I brushed it this morning."

"You'll want to look your best for the grand gesture, don't you think?"

"I . . . I've never had to prepare. But I think he should want me the way I am."

"Of course he wants you the way you are, but magical memories are great in that you can pull them out, look at them like a picture book, then fold them up and put them away. Wouldn't you like to remember yourself like a classier Glamour Shots?"

She considered. "I suppose."

Juniper wasn't sure that all of this was going to play out the way that everyone seemed to anticipate. Yes, she believed in Tomas. She had faith in him, but it wasn't just like flipping a switch, was it?

Most importantly, she didn't want to set herself up for disappointment. She didn't want any weight of expectations to be hanging on the moment.

She just wanted to see him again.

To hear his voice.

To press against him and hold him tight.

Juniper allowed Zuri to drag her back to the cottage and to brush her hair and it was then that Petty popped in.

Literally.

One minute, it was only Zuri and Juniper, and the next, Petty had appeared with a pop and Juniper shrieked.

"Sorry, dear. Thought I'd help with the makeup. Jonquil wanted to, but she has a nasty headache."

"Oh no! Does Jonquil need me?"

"She's fine. She was just locking horns with the most stubborn man to ever walk the earth. Wait, I think I've said that before. Yes. So many stubborn charges, so little time. You're all like possessed goats, digging your cloven feetsies in at the most inopportune times."

"Makeup," Zuri reminded.

"Oh yes. I assume we'll need to go the magical route, because you're going to cry. I mean, I'm already crying, I'm so happy for you."

"Gramma?" she began hesitantly.

"Yes, dear?"

"I don't mean to sound ungrateful, but . . ."

"But you're going to say something completely ungrateful?" Petty gave her a soft smile. "Go ahead, dear. This is your story. You get to say how it goes."

Juniper released a deep breath. "Everyone is talking like this is some kind of a done deal. Can you stop? I don't know what he's going to say. You don't, either. Unless you do?" She quirked her brows.

"No, no. We just have the gist, but I understand wanting to go into it without any expectations. I'll stop with the portent talk. So eyeliner and mascara? Lippie, or no? I mean, you're so pale, so lipstick is usually a good choice, but you two have proven time and again that you're like rabbits."

"Gramma! No." Juniper held up her hand.

"Sorry. But those are the facts, my girl."

"Eyeliner and mascara," Zuri said for her.

Petty waved her arm and secured her makeup. Then both women smiled at her and hugged her.

Petty perked. "He's here."

"What?" Juniper shrieked. "No. I didn't . . . He didn't . . . He doesn't . . ."

"Oh, but, my child. He does," Petty said. "Sorry, last time. Okay, we're leaving." Petty grabbed Zuri and they disappeared.

Juniper wasn't ready for this.

She thought she was. She thought this was what she wanted, but what if he still didn't love her the way she wanted?

What if he did?

Juniper heard the door open, and she was so glad he didn't knock.

"Juniper? Are you here?"

She tried to reply but found she could only squeak, like a sad little mouse. She cleared her throat. "I'm upstairs." Ah. The bedrooms were upstairs. They needed neutral territory. "I'm coming down."

Her first sight of him twisted her heart. She had longed for the sight of him, and now that he was here, he took up all the space. Not just in the room, but in the world. Everything fell away but him.

His hair was tousled and hung over his brow. His slacks were rumpled and wrinkled, and his shirt, one corner of the collar was turned up. He looked like he'd been through something.

"I found you," he whispered. "I did it."

She swallowed hard, wanting nothing more than to run to him and fling herself into his arms. "You did."

"You didn't think I would."

"No, I didn't." She reached out for him, but then drew her arm back and pressed her fingers to her lips. "How?"

"Because I don't want to do this without you."

"I missed you, too," she said.

"No."

"No, you didn't miss me?" she teased.

"It's more than that. It started out missing you. I tried to find you, and I got lost. So fucking lost, Juniper."

She nodded. "So what happened? Did the grandmothers come get you?"

"Not in the way you'd think." He took a deep breath. "*Dios*, but you're beautiful."

"It's just makeup." She hugged her arms around herself.

"The same way Ever After is just a kitschy town?"

The hope that had been simmering in her chest welled. "You know? More importantly, you believe?"

"Well, I almost got eaten by an evil witch with a candy gas station. But yeah, I believe. It took a Jonquil-shaped firefly kicking my ass, but I made it. I got here."

"Did she show you the turns?"

"No." He looked away from her for a moment, down at his feet, then back up at her face. "At first, she helped a little. She dive-bombed my face to get me to look in the direction of the turns. Then she made me pull over and she beat me about the face and head with her wand until I listened."

"That's romantic," she said offhandedly.

"I think it is. I needed it to realize something I've known for my whole life."

"And what's that? You hate fireflies?"

"No, *mi amor*. That I've loved you since before I knew what love was."

Petty had been right; the tears spilled hot down her cheeks. "You don't have to say that, just because you missed me. I'll never leave you, Tomas. You'll always have me."

"It's not that at all." He took a step toward her. "While she was hitting me, I realized that it wasn't that I didn't believe. It was that I didn't believe it was for me. And in turn, I did you a great wrong. Because I didn't believe in you."

"Why now? Why do you believe?"

He took another step toward her. "Every hero you've ever written contains the best parts of me. You saw what I felt for you before you saw anything else. It's Daniel's sacrifice for Cordelia. It's in Anton's strength. Gabriel's honor. Benedict's passion. If I could sum up the width and breadth of what I feel for you, it would be written in your words in those books. They've been living what I've been afraid to. I'm so sorry it took me so long."

The tears came harder now and words failed her. But she didn't need them, because Tomas had a few more.

"I don't just love you, Juniper. I am in love with you. I want to spend the rest of my life by your side. The reason I could find Ever After is because my Ever After is you."

Juniper flung herself at him, and he caught her easily, pressing his lips to hers in a kiss that lit up the daytime sky.

Explosions rang out around them and Juniper realized they were the fireworks that Zuri had talked about.

All of Ever After was aware of what was going down between them, but she didn't care. All that mattered was that she had Tomas. Her perfect romance novel hero made flesh. Not a perfect man, but perfect for her.

"I love you," she said against his lips.

"Marry me for real, Juniper."

"What?" She pulled back to look into his eyes.

"I don't care when. I don't care where. I don't even care how. Just say you'll spend the rest of your life with me."

"Yes!" she cried, and kissed him again, but broke away yet again. "But I have conditions."

"Tamales and enchiladas whenever you want." He kissed her nose. "Although, no more *Ice Pirates* is a deal breaker," he teased, and pressed kisses to each cheek. "I have to warn you, though, now that you've already said yes and can't back out."

She laughed, and clung to him. "What now?"

"I quit the firm. I'm jobless." He laughed. "What a catch I am, huh?"

"I think I'm going to have to promote you from future husband to cabana boy." She took his face in her hands. "I am so proud of you."

"The partners thought I'd end up setting up shop here. Doing prenups." He studied her face.

"That's a fantastic idea. I'd love to live here. If you're sure?"

"Where else would I live with my romance novelist wife than here?"

She kissed him again. "What are we going to tell the mamas? When are we going to tell them?"

"Much, much later, *querida*. I have other things on my mind just now." He swept her up into his arms and carried her up the stairs.

"Don't forget, you owe me one against the wall."

"In the castle, no less. Maybe you can ask your grandmothers for an invisibility spell. Is that a thing?"

"You've taken to this much too quickly," she teased.

"I'm going to take something else much too— Wait, no. That's not what I'm going to do," Tomas teased back. "Actually, what I'm going to do is love you and get started on this Happily Ever Aftering."

For Juniper, writer of romances and engineer of Happily Ever Afters, she couldn't have written it any better herself.

They would live and love Happily Ever After.

If Petty didn't kill her first for hacking her account and swiping right on Rumpled Foreskin.

Chapter 27

"My head is killing me," Jonquil complained. "I need some oil of poppy." She massaged her temples and flopped in the old green velvet recliner, promptly putting her feet up and a pillow over her face.

"Yes, dear. He was a difficult one." Bluebonnet patted her shoulder and covered her up with a blanket.

"Those damn fireworks," she groused. "I mean, I'm glad, but they're so loud."

"I'd say we've earned this vacation," Petty said as she flopped onto the matching green velvet couch. "If your head ever stops hurting."

"You know, you didn't have to ram yourself into him all those times," Bluebonnet said unhelpfully as she starfished on the floor, making a carpet angel.

"He wasn't going to make it, otherwise. I had no choice," Jonquil said.

"You did good work, sister," Petty praised.

"I'd say we did a fantastic job as well," Estella said, pulling April inside the grandmothers' cottage behind her.

The godmothers didn't get up. April and Estella were family, April having spent much time in Ever After herself as a child.

"We made them kiss. Just like posing Barbie dolls in the sandbox," April said. "This could be addictive." She pulled out a stool at the kitchen table and sat down.

Bluebonnet perked. "Oh, did you have fun?"

"So much fun. Not just harassing our children and embarrassing them, because that's always fun. But it was so satisfying seeing them find their way to each other," Estella said as she packed in next to April.

They reminded Petty of kids. Of course, her charges were always children to her, even if they were in their sixties.

"I have an idea," Petty said.

"Oh no," Jonquil countered, and pulled the pillow tighter around her ears.

"Here we go," Bluebonnet mumbled.

"What? I have great ideas," Petty replied, crossing her arms. She did. Her ideas were the best. It was because of her ideas that they had reached peak fairy godmother.

"Yes, dear. But I don't think we've had enough sugar for another of your ideas so soon," Bluebonnet answered. "Let me get the ice cream." She started to try to get up off the floor.

"Oh no, no." Estella waved at them to sit down. "I will make you something delicious."

"One mustn't argue with Mama Estella, or so I've been told," Jonquil agreed, and pulled the blanket more securely around herself.

April began moving through the kitchen, getting things out for Estella, and they were an unstoppable unit of sugar and joy.

"What are we having?" Bon-Bon asked from her position on the floor.

"A caramel chocolate flan. More sugar in it than should ever be consumed by a human being," April promised.

"Such good girls you are." Petty allowed herself to relax. Her feet needed a good massage by goblins. They did such good work, and she was so tired. She knew her sisters had to be exhausted.

"What were you thinking, Gramma Petty?" April asked.

"That you kids could take over for us while we're on vacation."

"That's actually not a bad idea," Jonquil agreed. "It would give you both something to do. That is, if you enjoyed it that much."

"Oh, we did." Estella gathered the items she needed from the pantry and refrigerator. "Hell, I'm going to have to make two. If Tomas discovers I've made the flan, he'll need one as well."

"I'm team double flan," April agreed. "And we'd love to help you matchmake, Grammas."

"In case you weren't sure, I most definitely did not mean me," Petty added.

"Why would we think you meant you?" April asked.

"Some wiseacre swiped right on one of my matches on the new HEA dating app. I had to go throw up." When she found whoever had done that to her, she was going to turn them into . . . into something awful. She hadn't decided what yet. She couldn't think of anything gross enough.

Bon-Bon giggled. "It's not that—"

Petty fixed her with a hard look.

"Okay, it was that bad. But it was funny." Bon-Bon held up her hand. "And before you try to tell me you're going to turn me into a dung beetle for laughing, I've already been a pig. You owe me."

Petty was too tired to argue. "Fine. Honestly, I really just want to go to the beach and roast myself like a rotisserie chicken by the water. No matchmaking. Definitely no men."

"What if we took our own vacations?" Bon-Bon suggested, her expression one of supreme distaste.

"Whyever would we do that?" Jonquil asked.

"Because your sister wants to catch her a man," Petty said.

"Eww. Gross. Why?" Jonquil said. "I mean . . ." She coughed. "We've been really busy."

"Drake Gregorian, of course," Bon-Bon reminded them.

"Oh, too right," Jonquil agreed. "I mean, I don't need one, but I see why you like that one."

April and Estella shared a knowing look.

Petty pointed her wand at them. "Don't even think it. Whatever that is, just stop."

"Us?" Estella asked. "We weren't doing anything at all."

"You point your skills toward those who are deserving. Or I'll have to take drastic steps," Petty warned.

"Well, to be honest, I don't think you could match us with worse than we've done on our own," April said.

Jonquil suddenly seemed to be feeling better. "Oh, does that mean we can set you up after vacation?"

"Sure. Why not?" April and Estella both agreed.

"It'll be good to get started while the kids are honeymooning, don't you think?" Estella said.

"I am also on board for this plan, too," Bon-Bon said.

"So, Petty and I will go to Key West, and you, Bon-Bon, can go to Captiva," Jonquil said.

Petty pushed her spectacles up on her nose. "I meant what I said earlier. I am not putting on my party body. This is it."

"Me either," Jonquil said.

"Rest, relaxation, and those little drinks with umbrellas in them," Petty swore.

"There's a wrinkle in the plan," Bon-Bon interrupted.

"What is it?" Petty demanded.

"Roderick's fairy godmother. She's been in town for some time, and I'm worried she's going to make a mess while we're gone," Bon-Bon said.

"Well, what are we going to do? Boot her out of Ever After until we get back? Or just never go anywhere?" Jonquil asked.

"That's not a bad idea." Petty tapped her forefinger on her chin. "Although, uninviting fairies from places never ends well."

"Grammas, I think you are all three overtired, because

you're missing the most obvious way to keep her occupied," April said.

"What's that, dear?" Petty asked.

"You have a suitor who you do not enjoy. You have a fairy godmother who is meddling in your affairs. If they were inclined to meddle with each other, they'd have to leave you two alone, now wouldn't they?"

"You. Are. Diabolical," Petty cried. "Oh, I'm so proud."

Jonquil patted her chest. "So much pride."

"Indeed," Bon-Bon said.

"And while we're at it, I could nudge Roderick and Gwen along." Petty was feeling very satisfied with herself indeed.

"All in all, it's been a good run, sisters," Bon-Bon began. "Of course, this is usually when something catastrophic happens and everything goes to shit. But I'm not going to be a Stormy Sue and wait for the shoe."

"We're allowed to take a vacation. It's been quite some time since we've been anywhere. As evidenced by the bats in the bell tower we were discussing before we embarked on this last mission."

"Bats in the bell tower?" April cackled.

Estella shook her head.

"Oh, look, she's got the cackle down," Jonquil said.

"She should. She's our granddaughter, too," Bon-Bon said.

"Yes, I am," April reminded them. "So you three go off and have some fun and relaxation. Estella and I can handle the store."

With that, the three meddling, mostly-sweet fairy godmothers made their plans.

Little did they know that fate and Rumpelstiltskin (otherwise known as Ass Face) had other ideas.

Don't miss the rest of the Ever After adventures
FAIRY GODMOTHERS, INC.
and
MEN ARE FROGS,
available now from
Saranna DeWylde
and
Zebra Books